SUPERIMPOSED

OMAR ALBADRI

VERSION 1.1

COPYRIGHT

This is a work of fiction. Names, characters, places, and incidents either are the product of the author's imagination or are used fictitiously.

Any resemblance to actual persons, living or dead, events, or locales is entirely coincidental.

Names: AlBadri, Omar, author.
Title: Superimposed, a novel/ by Omar AlBadri
Description: First edition. | San Francisco: Just Prepared Inc, [2023]
Identifiers: ISBN 9798987062609 (paperback)|ISBN 9798987062623 (ebook)
Subjects: | GFASD: Science Fiction | Suspense Fiction

ISBN: 9798987062609
Ebook ISBN: 9798987062623

DEDICATION

For my parents, my sister, my wife, and everyone who entered my life. This one is for you...

"We all make mistakes. But Social Media can frame those mistakes and display them infinitely."

-Darshan Soni

CHAPTER 1 - HMC

Ben sits alone.

He absentmindedly stares at his coffee cup, trying to ignore a splitting headache. He rubs his temples with his fingers. He takes a long sip and glances around the shop. The usual morning people are around. All are wearing masks and lifting them to get a drink of their coffee or a sip of their tea. The cafe is simple and generic. Boring brown tables and dull green paint, with informative signs handing on the boring gray walls. Verbiage like "Try the new Mint Caramel Ice Mocha!" or "Ask about our Cake of the Day!" The standard "Masks are Required!" sits apart from the other signs.

Ben takes a deep breath and forces another sip of coffee down his throat. He wonders who was the first to suggest coffee after a heavy night of drinking. The best way he knew to cure a hangover was to drink a beer or a spiked seltzer, but considering it was 9:00 a.m. Monday morning, and he has a meeting in half an hour; drinking alcohol is not the best idea.

Maybe I should get something to eat? Ben thinks as his stomach churns uneasily. He decides against it. He sighs a little more audibly and starts to fidget with his mask. *It's 9:07 and I am hungover in the world's most generic coffee shop—I really need to get my life together,* he thinks reflectively.

Ben pulls out his phone and begins watching YouTube. He puts on a news show where they are comically mocking the 1,250th day of the pandemic. *Has it been that long?* Ben wonders. He tries to recall what life was like pre-pandemic but only has fuzzy memories. He remembers waiting in lines less and seeing people's faces more. The news show goes on to explain the history of the pandemic and how both vaccine attempts had failed, and now a third one is on the way.

Ben coughs hard. In the middle of his third cough, he starts to retch. He places his hand over his mask to stifle his heaving. The few people in the shop stare in his direction, some getting up and moving away. Ben composes himself and takes another sip of his coffee to wash down the bile. He can taste the alcohol he had consumed last night.

No more drinking during the week, more exercise, and I need to find a goddamn hobby! He hammers the table lightly. Ben has tried his hand at hobbies before. At thirty-eight, he has found that nothing excites him anymore. He thought about comic book collecting, but he found it tedious and expensive. He tried to write a novel but did not have the patience or the skill. He even tried to start a side business but quickly realized he had no sound business ideas. His life during the pandemic has become just one long monotonous day. He wakes up, works, drinks, plays video games, watches YouTube, and sleeps. He thinks about what he did before the pandemic and tries to think about how he filled his hours and days—eating out, dating, happy hours with co-workers, bar hopping, and messing around at the office. Once that is taken away, he realizes how little growth he has had in the past few years. Most of his peers are married or in long-term relationships. They have kids, partners, and school to worry about. He has video games, Instagram, and vodka.

Ben thinks about his former friend Raj. Raj has just bought a new apartment in a great neighborhood that needs much work. Every day, Raj posts pictures and videos of all the work he and his wife had done that day. From painting the walls to installing new fixtures to redoing the kitchen. Ben got so sick and tired of seeing their stupid smiling faces that he quickly unfollowed him on Instagram.

After a few days, Ben regrets his decision as he realizes that browsing social media is one of the few things that occupy his time. He considers re-following Raj's account, but since it is private, he does not want the confrontation of Raj asking why he unfollowed him in the first place. So he follows Raj's wife instead. Indra is one of the few people in the world he can tolerate, and she's one of the few who seems to like him. A few minutes after following her, he gets a DM from her:

Ben! How have you been? It's been a long time. I hope all is well!

Ben replies:

All is well. Just trying to get through these trying times.

Indra responds:

Glad to hear we miss you. Stay safe out there!

Ben silently curses himself. Now Raj's wife will mention to her husband that she has talked to Ben. Raj will see that Ben is no longer following him and question why. Ben just deactivates all his social media accounts to avoid dealing with that situation.

Ben looks at the face of his phone. It says it's 9:11 a.m. He stretches and lets out a loud yawn. He has about nineteen minutes until his first meeting and feels a bit better now. The weak coffee has soothed his head enough that he can start being productive.

"Benny?" A voice calls out near him.

Ben freezes mid-stretch. He turns his head towards the voice and sees what he thinks is an old acquaintance. (The mask on the person's face causes Ben to pause).

"Jeremy?" Ben says tentatively, finishing his stretch.

"What's up, man! Long time no see." Jeremy leans against the chair opposite Ben. Ben stiffens for a second, thinking that Jeremy is about to sit, but he stays standing. "I thought that was you. I just grabbed a latte and was like, 'Wait, is that Benji? I got to go say hi.'"

"It's me," Ben informs him.

"Yeah, no shit; how have you been?"

"You know." Ben shrugs and points towards his mask.

"Yeah, man, we've all been like that. So what's new with you?" Jeremy asks. Ben runs his hands through his hair and lets out a deep breath.

"Just trying to … you know … get through these trying times."

"I hear you; I've been trying to get through this shit too." Jeremy pulls out the chair he has been leaning on and sits. Ben and Jeremy sit quietly for a moment. Ben starts playing with his coffee cup as Jeremy slurps his coffee loudly. Ben and Jeremy have always had a tumultuous relationship. Ben is suspicious about why Jeremy appears friendly now. *Perhaps,* he thinks *the lockdown changed us all.*

Ben and Jeremy were on opposite ends of the societal spectrum. Ben is 5'9, acceptable-looking, introverted, and book-smart. Jeremy is 6'2, handsome, outgoing, and street-smart. Both achieved different kinds of successes in their past

—Ben through hard work and dedication to his craft, Jeremy through hustle and networking. After things had shut down, Ben prospered while Jeremy had hit hard times.

Ben recalls the time he first met Jeremy over ten years ago.

Ben was twenty-six or twenty-seven when they first met. Ben had been working for FrontSpark and living in San Francisco for a few years. He had gotten promoted that day, and his only friend at the company, Raj, had suggested they go out for a few drinks to celebrate. Raj had been working at FrontSpark for over a year and was the only person Ben could consider a friend.

"Sure!" Ben said a little too enthusiastically when Raj suggested going out. It turned out that Raj, despite his relatively serious work demeanor, had a pretty active nightlife. He took Ben to a rooftop bar that Ben had no idea existed. Raj skipped the impressively long line to tip the bouncer forty dollars to get them in immediately. They found a spot at the end of the bar and ordered drinks.

"How did you find this place?" Ben asked, looking around in disbelief. Raj just smiled and winked at Ben. They had just ordered more drinks when Raj noticed someone he knew. Raj waved him over. The tall man nodded at Raj and escorted himself and his companion towards them.

"You got to meet this guy," Raj told Ben as the tall man moved towards them. "Jeremy, meet my friend Ben. Ben, Jeremy." Ben looked at the guy. He was good-looking, with long straight brown hair escaping from his beanie. He stood three or four inches taller than Ben. Standing beside him in a skin-tight purple dress was a pretty blonde clutching her purse. When Raj introduced them, Jeremy turned his head ever so slightly in Ben's direction and gave him the faintest nod before reverting his attention to the pretty blonde he was with. After a while, the girl left (not without first giving Jeremy her number), and Jeremy turned his attention to Ben and Raj.

"Jeremy, what's good tonight?" Raj asked, leaning up against the bar.

"What you fellows drinking?" Jeremy asked, ignoring Raj's question.

"Vodka," Ben said.

"I think I'll join you fellows for a shot or two," Jeremy said, nodding at Raj. Raj turned around to face the bartender to order more drinks. Jeremy turned his head towards Ben.

"So Benjamin, what's your story?" Jeremy asked.

Ben raised his eyebrows at Jeremy, "It's Ben, not Benjamin. Just Ben."

Jeremy looked at him and started chuckling. "Sorry, 'Ben,' what's your story?"

"Well," Ben started. "I moved here about three years ago from southern California. I just finished college and interviewed at this start-up where I have been working ever since, and I got promoted today."

"Uh-huh, uh-huh." Jeremy looked around, distracted.

"Raj decided to take me out to celebrate," Ben continued. "It's been a long hard journey with this company, but I think we are in a good place now. It's always a risk to join a start-up, but I think that risk will pay off. Raj says I work too much and need to have more of a social life, so here I am. What's your—" Ben trailed off as he saw Jeremy had stopped paying attention and was now looking at a brunette waiting by the bar.

"S'cuse me, fellows," Jeremy mumbled and started walking towards the brunette. Raj finally got the bartender's attention and ordered three shots.

"Where's Jeremy?" Raj asked, looking around. He passed Ben his shot.

Ben motioned his head towards Jeremy and the brunette. Raj slaps Ben hard on the back, nearly spilling his drink.

"Oh … dude. Jeremy is the man!" Raj laughed.

"Apparently," Ben said, taking a sip of his drink. A few minutes later, Jeremy walked over to the both of them with the brunette in his arm.

"Fellows, this is Tiffany, Tiffany, fellows. What do you say we do one more shot and get the fuck out of here and party?"

"Yes!" Raj said as he turned and started frantically waving at the bartender again.

#

"What are you up to these days?" Ben asks, picking at his coffee cup. Jeremy leans back in his chair and yawns.

"The same old, just trying to live in this stupid, crazy world."

"Yeah?" Ben asks.

"Yeah, Ben-Ten, been driving a little Uber, doing some Postmates, and trying to get my NikNak channel up and running."

"NikNak?" Ben asks.

Jeremy looks strangely at him and shakes his head in mock disbelief. "Ben, the big tech nerd, doesn't know about the hottest new thing on the internet." Jeremy shakes his head again and laughs. "Man, you are getting old."

Ben ignores the comment and asks, "Do you mean the app where those young girls dance and lip-synch in skimpy outfits? I've heard of that."

"Ben-mo, it's much, much more than that. It's a movement and idea that will define a generation. You know how it got started, right?"

Ben shakes his head.

"The legend goes that two ex-YouTube employees got tired of all the restrictions on that platform. So they created a new decentralized platform where anything goes, and I mean anything." Jeremy winks at Ben and takes another sip of his coffee. "Last week, some guy posted a video of another guy shooting him in the leg."

"What?" Ben questions, shocked.

"I know it's crazy and stupid, but it did get over a million views and half a million Niks," Jeremy states. "Before you ask, Niks are 'Likes,'" Jeremy clarifies.

"I figured that," Ben says defensively. He leans back in his chair and crosses his arms over his chest.

"So I think to myself, what the hell, let's jump on this train while it's hot. I started my NikNak channel and posted some Naks." Jeremy pauses. "Naks are videos," he explains.

"I get it," Ben shoots back. Jeremy always found a way to get under his skin.

"Anyhow, I figure who gots a crazier life than me, so why not let everyone see how I'm living." Jeremy pulls out his phone and starts tapping on the screen. He begins showing Ben various videos of him partying, jumping his bike off the pier into the ocean (nearly hitting a fisherman), and finally, a close-up of him and some pretty girls snorting coke off a table.

"Wait," Ben asks in disbelief. "You can post stuff like that?"

"Yeah, as I said, anything goes on this platform. It's freedom of speech in short-form video." Jeremy pulls his phone back and starts typing on it.

"You have to see this." He holds the phone in front of Ben's face. A very young-looking blonde girl wearing red underwear and a red bra is on the screen. She is dancing and bouncing around her room. As the song gets louder and louder, the girl whips off her bra and starts dancing around the room half-naked. She has tape covering her nipples. She then turns and twerks for the camera in her red thong underwear. On the screen in bright green letters were the words: "Join my private channel for $15 in crypto a month!"

Ben recoils. Jeremy takes back his phone.

"Hot, huh?" Jeremy asks as he raises his eyebrow.

"Who the fuck was that?" Ben asks, feeling a little uncomfortable.

"That is Kitty Josephine. She is the hottest thing right now on NikNak," Jeremy explains. "You should see her private channel," he says with a wink. Jeremy puts his phone away and takes another sip of his latte.

Ben decides that he has had enough. "Well, Jeremy, it was nice catching up with you, but I got to—" Ben starts as he looks at his phone.

"Oh shit," Jeremy interrupts as he looks at his Apple Watch and jumps to his feet. "Bro, it's been great, but I got to go. I am late. Great seeing you; download NikNak and follow me @JerBear69. See ya." In one quick motion, Jeremy is gone.

Ben sighs as Jeremy leaves. He never really liked that guy. There is something about him that rubs him the wrong way.

Ben continues recalling what had also happened that night when he first met Jeremy.

After they had taken their shots, Jeremy pulled Raj aside to talk with him. After Jeremy left (with the pretty brunette in tow), Raj sat next to him.

"Dude," Raj said excitedly. "Jeremy asked if we wanted to join him later at Lithium." Lithium was the hot new nightclub in town. Ben had heard from some of his coworkers how amazing that place was.

"But there is a catch," Raj said.

"What's the catch?" Ben asked.

Raj explained that if they wanted to come and sit at Jeremy's table, it would cost them $200 each. Ben thought this over and asked what Raj thought.

"C'mon, we are celebrating your promotion and my first anniversary at FrontSpark; let's live a little. $200 is not life-changing money, but this night could be!"

Ben laughed at Raj's optimism and told him that he was in. After a quick stop at the ATM, Raj and Ben stood in front of Lithium, where a huge line had already amassed. After waiting twenty minutes, Jeremy met them out front, pocketed their money, and guided them into the club. He led them to the back, to a small table where eight other guys were standing around. He shook their hands and told them to have fun. A few minutes later, two bottles of vodka appeared. The group quickly finished it and then awkwardly looked at each other. Ben promptly put two and two together.

Jeremy had bought the table for $1000 and invited ten guys, each paying $200. Jeremy pocketed the $1000 and left them on their own. That was only half of it. One time Ben brought his now ex-girlfriend Jinni to Lithium, and Jeremy spent the whole night hitting on her.

#

Back at the coffee shop, Ben shakes his head and laughs. He throws away his cup and leaves.

CHAPTER 2 - WYWH

The next day Ben logs in to Slack to check up on his team. It is a slow day at FrontSpark. After his morning stand-up, Ben goes into his kitchen to make breakfast. It was just an average day in Ben's life until it wasn't.

Ben did not love or hate his job. He had spent the last fifteen years at the same company. He never thought he would stay for this long, but he is comfortable at FrontSpark and dreads the interviewing process. So he stays.

When Ben joined FrontSpark, it was a small company with only 15 other employees. Now it is much bigger as they just crossed the 300-person threshold. The pandemic has been good for business.

His team is twenty—a mix of Front End, Back End, Mobile, and Security engineers. Ben's role is twofold. When a company contracts FrontSpark to help it go public, Ben makes sure that he guides his engineering team to help support the contracting company's roadmap for its IPO. His second role is to review their infrastructure and codebase to ensure they have no security vulnerabilities. Being hacked right after going public is a big no-no. The work is sometimes satisfying, and the pay is decent.

Ben's phone buzzes and chirps that a text has come through. He picks it up and opens the Messaging app. It is Jeremy. Ben frowns as he opens up the message. He and Jeremy usually do not communicate.

Jeremy: *Yo! Did you see what happened? Damn, I'm so sorry.*

Ben: *???*

Jeremy: *You didn't see? It's the number one trending Nak right now!*

Ben: *See what?*

Jeremy: *Bro!*

Ben: *What!*

"..." the ellipsis appears, signifying that Jeremy is typing a response. Ben feels a knot grow in his stomach.

Jeremy: *Jinni dead! She killed herself, and someone posted it on NikNak.*

Ben: *What!*

Jeremy: *Download NikNak. It's the first video on the public feed!*

Ben sits motionless in his living room. He goes to the app store and starts downloading NikNak. But first, he needs to call Jinni's sister Yumi, and make sure this isn't some sort of hoax. After a few rings, someone picks up.

"Yeo-bo-se-yo?" A quiet sad voice answers.

"Soh-Yun ... it's Ben." Jinni had introduced Ben to her mom many years ago. She did not speak much English and was always warm to him. Jinni once told him that her mom liked him very much.

"Ben?" Jinni's mom says in a cracking voice.

"Yes," Ben replies. He can hear Jinni's mom crying; He realizes what Jeremy had messaged is true. The call goes silent. Ben starts tapping his fingers on the kitchen table.

"I'm just calling to offer my condolences," he says, breaking the silence.

"Ben, is that you?" Jinni's mom asks again in broken English.

"Yes ... Yes, it's me."

"Ben," she says.

"I am so sorry," Ben replies, his voice beginning to crack. There is a long pause; Jinni's mother quietly sobs.

"Ben ... thank you ... you were always a good boy ... a very good boy," Jinni's mom says sadly.

"Are you ok?" Ben asks.

"Yes," she replies quietly. Ben can hear her continue to cry.

"Ben?" Another voice speaks.

"Yes ... Yumi, is that you?"

"Yes," Yumi says softly.

"What the hell is going on? Are you two ok?"

"Jinni killed herself," Yumi says flatly. "She jumped off a building and killed herself."

Ben lets out a deep breath and leans back in his chair. His vision starts to blur as the tears begin to well up in his eyes.

"I ... I ... I don't know what to say," Ben stammers.

"I know."

"I mean ... Jesus. What happened?"

"She just wasn't happy; she couldn't deal with life anymore." Yumi sniffles. After a few more minutes of awkward conversations and uncomfortable silences, Yumi tells Ben that the funeral will be held this Thursday at 6 p.m.

"Will you come?" Yumi asks.

"Yes," he says after hesitating for a few seconds.

"Good ... I think Jinni would have wanted you there."

Ben sits quietly and motionless in his kitchen. His mind wanders back to the last time he, Jinni, and Yumi were together.

Yumi had just turned twenty-one, and Jinni had asked him if he wanted to join them for Yumi's twenty-first birthday celebration. At this point in their relationship, Jinni and Ben constantly argued. She had moved in almost two years ago, and while things were good at first, the last six months had been strenuous for them. Ben agreed, and Jinni called Yumi and made plans for her to show up at their place.

"Ben," Jinni called from the doorway of their bedroom.

"Yeah?" Ben was lying in bed, reading and replying to emails on his phone.

"I know things have not been that great between us lately, but can we put aside our differences for one night and try to enjoy ourselves?" Jinni asked.

Ben felt his anger rise. He wanted to scream at her: *Put aside our differences, our differences? You're the one who has been acting out, and you're the one destroying this relationship. There are no differences! It's been all you. You!*

Ben swallowed and said, "Sure."

Yumi came over around 8 p.m., and Jinni brought out some shots. Yumi tried to get Jinni to pose for selfies, but Jinni politely declined. Ben took a video of Yumi doing her first "legal" shot. After a quick toast to a happy birthday, they were off to dinner. At dinner, Ben asked Yumi about college and how her classes were going.

"It's been good." Yumi took a sip of her drink. "I am about a semester away from graduating and then summer break, and after that, I will take the LSATs in the fall."

"Little sis, the big-time lawyer," Jinni commented sarcastically. Ben took a long swallow of his drink.

"School is important to some of us," Yumi said as she took a bite of her food. She shot Jinni a look. "Some of us take our lives seriously."

Both sisters stared at each other. Ben had been involved in this fight a few times. Yumi was considered the good kid, and Jinni the bad one. Yumi got straight As in school. Jinni never went to college. Ben thought Jinni was slightly envious of her sister. One night while drinking, they talked about their career aspirations. Ben spoke about wanting to be a CTO one day. When he asked Jinni the same question, she grew quiet. Ben did not press. A few weeks later, when they were drunk again, she told Ben about her desire to become a lawyer when she was younger. She wanted to help people defend themselves against cops, big firms, etc. She said she would even do it for free.

"There is so much injustice in this world," she had told him.

"Let's not talk about school tonight, it's a celebration, and we should all be celebrating," Ben said, trying to defuse the situation. He motioned to the waiter for another round of drinks. Ben grabbed Jinni's hand. Jinni pulled her hand away.

"You're right, Ben. It is time for celebration," Jinni said coldly as she downed her drink.

After dinner, they went bar hopping, Yumi proudly showing off her ID to the bouncers. Many wished her a happy birthday and gave her free drink tickets. Towards the night's end, they headed towards Michaels, an upscale bar with a dance floor. As soon as they got in, Yumi rushed to the dance floor. Ben smiled as he watched Yumi run off to dance. Jinni grabbed him.

"Let her have her fun. Let's go grab a drink," she said in his ear over the loud music.

Ben nodded and took her hand. He guided her to the much quieter lounge area. Ben ordered two drinks, his usual vodka and soda, and a margarita for Jinni. Ben leaned on the bar and turned towards his girlfriend.

"You ok?" he asked.

"Yeah."

"You seemed a little upset at dinner."

Jinni looked at him and said, "I'm fine."

Ben smiled and said, "You know what FINE stands for, right? Fucked up, Insecure, Neurotic, and Emotional." Ben laughed. Jinni did not.

"Oh, then I am good," Jinni replied, turning her gaze away from Ben's.

"Honey, it's an old Aerosmith song. I was trying to get you to laugh," Ben explained to Jinni. Given the difference in their ages, they often did not get the other cultural references. Ben paid for the drinks. He could sense the tension.

"Can we sit down and talk? There is something I need to tell you," Jinni asked.

Ben motioned towards some recently opened chairs and grabbed both their drinks as they went to sit down. After she sat and Ben was about to sit, he felt a hand grab him. It was Yumi, glistening with sweat, her hair a little more out of place than the night's start.

"Is this for me? Thanks, Ben." She took Jinni's margarita out of Ben's hand and downed the whole glass. Ben looked at Jinni and shrugged. "C'mon, I love this song. Let's dance." She grabbed Ben by the hand and dragged him to the crowded dance floor. Ben took one last look at Jinni. She did not look pleased.

Ben had not danced in a long time. At the time, he was thirty-five, and his dancing days were long behind him. He decided the best course of action was to limit his motion and move as close to the beat as he could. Yumi, on the other hand, had no issues. She twirled, strutted, shook, and moved around Ben like he was guiding her through ballroom dancing. Ben tried to catch a glance of Jinni but could not see her through the crowd. Yumi moved closer to him.

"How are things with you and Jinni?" Yumi shouted over the loud music. Ben shrugged and made the "you know how it goes" face, hoping to drop the conversation. Yumi twirled and swayed around him, finally backing up and grinding on him a little. Ben let out an embarrassed laugh, backed away, and continued to look for Jinni. "Don't worry about her; she'll be fine," Yumi said as she pulled Ben closer. Ben relaxed and started mimicking Yumi's movements. They started moving in unison, and Ben started to enjoy himself.

"There you go, Ben!" Yumi said, laughing. Ben smiled and relaxed. He grabbed her hand, twirled her, and then caught her with the drape of his arm as she came out of the spin.

"Wow!" Yumi proclaimed, and Ben's smile widened. Ben used to dance with his mom when he was younger. She had taught him that move. After a few more songs, Ben started to tire and told Yumi he was returning to Jinni. Yumi hugged him, took a selfie of them, and thanked him for the dance. Ben stared back at where Jinni was sitting, but he couldn't see her.

As he was walking away, Yumi grabbed his arm. She whispered in his ear. "Be careful; Jinni has a way of making things harder than they should be." She kissed Ben on the cheek and disappeared back on the dance floor before he could ask what she meant.

Ben, troubled over the words Yumi had told him, returned to where Jinni had been sitting. When he arrived, he saw that another couple occupied the seats. Ben looked around. He went to the bar and the line for the bathroom. He walked around the place a few times, but Jinni was nowhere to be found.

#

Ben squeezes into his black suit. It barely fits. He thinks back to his proclamation where he said he would use this downtime in the lockdown to get into the best shape of his life. After a few weeks of exercising, he was back in sweatpants drinking vodka and eating chips while watching YouTube on the couch.

Ben realizes this is the first time he has been anywhere but the coffee shop, the grocery store, or his apartment in many months. He takes one final look at himself in the hallway mirror, adjusts his hair, grabs his keys and mask, and heads out the door.

The funeral is being held at a Korean Church about thirty minutes from his place. Ben crosses the Bay Bridge and heads into Oakland. When he arrives, he parks his car in the near-empty lot and proceeds to the entrance. The walkway, he notices, is covered in white flowers. He moves up the steps towards the door. At the entrance is a young man holding a book and a pen. When Ben gets to the top of the stairs, the young man slowly shoves a book towards him and asks him to sign in. Ben grabs the pen and signs his name. The young man nods once, pulls the ledger back towards him, and holds out his hand. Ben stands motionless, not understanding the gesture.

The young man asks, "Donation?"

Ben can feel his cheeks burning as he pretends to look in his jacket for an envelope that does not exist. He brings out his wallet. Inside are his credit cards but no cash. Ben scratches the back of his head.

"I didn't know I needed to bring a donation," he says meekly.

The young man nods again and pulls his hand back to his chest. "That's ok—please go on inside." He motions his other arm towards the double doors to his left. Ben, embarrassed, pushes the safety handles and walks into the church.

The church is more expansive than he had anticipated. It looks more like a university lecture hall than a place of worship. Ben looks around. At the front are Jinni's mom and sister. Their friends surround them. Ben guesses that about twenty or so people have shown up. Ben sits on a bench in the back. *I should go down and say something,* he thinks. Jinni's best friend Jayne is to his right and down a few rows. She catches his eye, covers her mask in mock surprise, and starts walking towards him.

Ben and Jayne's relationship has always been cordial but never that friendly. Despite being nearly the same age, they both had very different outlooks on life. Ben has always considered himself a mature adult, while Jayne clung to the past, holding on to her youth like a child who refused to go to bed. She dresses in the latest youthful styles and applies makeup learned directly from watching how-to videos on Instagram. She constantly sings the latest pop songs by the newest hit artists. She is thirty-six years old, acting like her best years are still ahead of her instead of behind.

Trailing behind her, looking exceedingly uncomfortable, is a younger black male with his hands in his suit pockets. He moves cautiously behind her like a soldier crossing a minefield. In typical Jayne fashion, she has brought a date to the funeral.

Jayne sits next to him and turns towards him. "This is so tragic," she proclaims. She starts awkwardly playing with her gloved fingers. "I just spoke with Jinni a few weeks ago, and we had made plans to go to the Taylor Swift relief concert." Jayne sighs. "Well," she continues. "I guess I could always find someone else to go with," she says, darting her eyes at her bored date. He is casually staring around the church. "Or just sell them online," she says, resigned. "How are you holding up, Ben?"

Ben continues looking forward, not meeting Jayne's gaze. He never understood Jinni and Jayne's friendship. Their nights out usually consisted of getting black-out drunk or coked-up high and trying to find Jayne a hook-up. Jinni knew many people but had very few friends. Ben looks around and realizes that Jayne is the only one of Jinni's friends who has bothered to show up. Jinni tended to rub people the wrong way. Jayne is too self-centered to even notice. Maybe that's why they worked. He wonders if Jinni ever talked to Jayne about her past. He doubted it, as Jayne usually wanted to speak rather than listen. Jayne probably came to the funeral to post Instagram Stories about her terrible loss.

He knew this funeral might become a horror show for him. Between talking with Jinni's "friend" and then her mom and sister, Ben felt a strong urge to run.

"I'm ok," he finally replies, his voice muffled through his mask.

Jayne moves closer and starts patting Ben's knee like a guidance counselor. "I understand," she says softly. They sit there quietly for a minute. From the corner of Ben's eye, he watches her un-introduced (boyfriend? date?) male friend, who is still standing, swaying impatiently.

"Wait, you said concert; concerts are back?" Ben asks.

Jayne looks at him with wide eyes and chuckles as she shakes her head incredulously. "Yes, they have concerts now. Where have you been? Taylor is having it at Golden Gate Park, outside on the knoll. It's fascinating. They set up these elevated booths where eight people can sit, paired up, correctly socially distanced from one another."

Ben considers asking a follow-up question but decides against it. He does not want to go down the rabbit hole that often happens when talking with Jayne.

"This is so tragic," Jayne repeats, slumping back on the bench. "Oh," she exclaims as she sits up. "This is Toby. Toby, Ben." She motions her arm to the man standing beside her. Ben reaches over his hand with a closed fist and gives Toby the customary fist bump.

"Hey," Toby says.

"Hey," Ben says.

"Toby and I have been dating for how long, sweetie?" Jayne asks Toby, wide-eyed and loving.

"Dunno, a couple of weeks or so," Toby replies.

"Oh silly," Jayne responds, swatting at him like a common fly. "It's definitely been over two months."

"Sure," Toby replies, uninterested.

Ben reaches up and starts rubbing the bridge of his nose with the tips of his thumb and forefingers.

"I should go down and pay my respects," Ben announces as he stands up.

"Yes, I think that is an excellent idea." Jayne nods approvingly. "Toby and I have been here with the family as soon as the church opened." Jayne looks up at Ben. "Toby and I decided that the family needed all the support they could get today." She twists her back and cracks her neck, symbolizing the extreme effort and hard work she had put in. "Toby, be a dear and bring me some punch; if they have anything stronger, bring that as well." Toby lets a breath out of his mouth and moves towards the concession table. Ben quietly slinks away. As he exits the bench row, he hears Jayne again proclaim, "This is so tragic."

Ben is walking towards the front of the church when he starts having an anxiety attack. Tiny beads of sweat start making their way down his forehead. He stops for a second and grabs the back of a bench for support. He removes his mask and takes a few deep breaths before putting it back on and proceeding forward.

Ben has not seen Jinni's mom since well before their break up over three years ago. She sits on the front-most bench, and a crowd of people surrounds her. Ben stands at the back of the small crowd, hands in his pockets, swaying in slow motion. He looks around at the large, nearly empty church. He looks up at the LCD screens, which he assumes held ceremonious messages prior, but now were black and lifeless. His eyes shoot to his left, where a dark cherry wood casket looks lonely at the very front. Ben has avoided looking towards it since he arrived. He knows what its contents contain, and as soon as it enters his peripheral, he quickly averts his eyes. *Jesus,* he thinks. *How old was Jinni? Twenty-seven? Twenty-eight?* He brings out his phone and looks at the date. She would have been twenty-eight in a couple of months.

Ben shuffles forward a little more as the crowd in front of him slowly disperses. Through the narrow openings, he manages to lock eyes with Yumi. Yumi gives him a small smile, finishes shaking the hand of one older gentleman, and starts parting the crowd to walk towards him. She moves slowly, locking eyes with funeral patrons and thanking them for coming. As she gets closer and closer to Ben, her velocity increases. She is now moving past people slipping by them as they try and talk to her. When she arrives, Ben clumsily sticks out his hand, and she proceeds to softly swat it away and move in for a tight embrace.

"Thank you for coming," she says softly in his ear.

Ben stiffens; it has been many years since someone has hugged him. She grabs him by the arm and takes him outside the church. She leads him outside through a side entrance and asks him to prevent the door from closing. She reaches into her pocket, pulls out a vape pen, puts it in her mouth, and inhales deeply.

"God, I hate this shit," she finally says after taking a few hits from her vape. She slumps on the wall next to Ben. Ben has his shoe in the doorway to prevent it from locking, leaning up against the second door a few feet away from her. They stand in silence, Yumi occasionally sucking on her vape, blowing large crystalized smoke clouds. After a while, she speaks.

"This has been a crazy and sad week. I cannot wait for this day to end. Between the funeral arrangements, people calling non-stop, and my mom crying, it has been horrible." She sighs. "You know, Ben, my sister and I were never close … She left us when I was only eight years old, and I didn't see her again for another six years. She left Korea when she was twelve. We had major financial and legal issues at the time, and my dad struggled to support us. So he decided to send her to live with his brother in California. I was too young to go." She takes another puff and turns towards him. "By the time I saw her again, she was eighteen and living in Los Angeles. Sometimes she would text me her modeling pictures, and I was in awe of her. I thought she had the coolest life ever, living in L.A., modeling; she was going to be a star, that was what I thought."

Ben looks at Yumi. She is staring off at the horizon as she smokes.

Yumi slumps down on the concrete slab, sitting in a frog-like position with her feet firmly on the ground and her back against the wall. "Six years later, my family and I moved to

Oakland because one of my dad's friends had offered him a job. Jinni lived about five hours away. My mom and dad both asked her to move in with us, but she refused. After about a month of living here, we all went to visit her. She was living with some guy who had to be at least in his early forties even though she was barely eighteen." She takes another deep drag from her vape. "Even though I thought the guy was kinda old, the house she lived in was beautiful. It sat on top of the hill overlooking the city and the ocean. It was the most amazing house I have ever seen. The only thing I couldn't figure out was why Jinni always seemed so unhappy. She lived in a mansion!"

Ben stands quietly, listening to Yumi. He had not heard this story before, as Jinni had been very private about her life. He would ask about her experiences moving here at twelve from a foreign country, and she would respond with one-line anecdotes saying, "You know ... it was hard," or "I did not have a choice," or "There was trouble back at home," or "It was fine." Ben soon stopped asking her about it. He recalls that one day she was showing him her old modeling photos. It was mostly of her in suggestive poses, leaning up against expensive cars. When he asked her about the pictures, she gave him some vague response about how some ex-boyfriend had paid her to be at this car show so he could show off his cars. Ben can now guess who this "some ex-boyfriend" was.

Yumi stirs, breaking Ben's thoughts. She stands, and Ben can see the tears rising in her eyes. She turns and looks at him. "Ben, I know you work in tech. Do you have any contacts at NikNak?" she asks.

Ben, slightly startled by the ask, looks at her inquisitively. "No, I don't … I just found out about the app a few days ago. Why?"

Tears start to stream down her face. Her body starts shaking, and her face contorts to anger. "Somebody posted a video of Jinni's suicide."

"I know," Ben replies.

"Yeah." Yumi wipes her eyes. "Some asshole was making a video of some bitch doing some dance when Jinni jumped from the top of a building. They filmed her death and posted the video on NikNak." Yumi wipes her nose with the back of her hand. "I've been trying to contact someone at NikNak to get the video taken down, but I kept getting a generic email response saying they will get back to me soon." Ben stands silent. "I can't get it taken down," Yumi continues. "No one is responding to my emails. I know you work in that field, so I was hoping you could help."

Ben looks at her. "I'm sorry, I don't know anyone who works there."

"Fuck this world, Ben. Fuck it. It's all about views and popularity and being edgy; no one gives a fuck anymore." She moves past Ben and re-enters the church. Ben considers bolting to the parking lot and leaving. He thinks before going back in, *This is tragic.*

As Ben walks back into the church, he thinks about Jinni. They had broken up a few months before the pandemic, and the lockdown had hit. He had tried to contact her a few times to ask her how she was doing, but she rarely returned any of his messages. He heard from a mutual friend that she had gone to live with Jayne for a while before moving out to her own place. She entirely stopped contact with him after the pandemic was in full force. Ben often wondered how she was doing alone, dealing with the lockdown.

Ben goes up to Jinni's mother. He offers her his sorrows and condolences. He tells her if there is anything he could do, anything at all, to ask him. Jinni's mom takes his hand and says his name softly. He nods and walks away. He sits on a bench a few rows from the front and waits for the memorial service to start.

Ben didn't understand any of the sermon as it was entirely in Korean. His eyes constantly move towards the coffin to the preacher's right. The casket is covered in flowers with a "We will miss you!" message spelled out above it. Jinni's high school graduation photo is on top of the coffin. She looked as stunning as ever with her bright crooked smile. Her makeup and hair are perfect. Jinni once told him she was voted the most popular girl in her senior class. Judging by her picture, Ben could see why.

People gather in a line behind the coffin when the sermon is over. Ben follows. He watches as they approach the casket and bow three times, appearing to say a prayer beneath their masks. Ben waits in line for his turn. A second anxiety attack washes over him as he gets nearer and nearer to the front. He feels the beads of sweat starting to form on his forehead. He begins to breathe heavily, so he loosens his tie and unbuttons the top button of his dress shirt. Ben stands in front of the line and pauses. *I can't do this*, he thinks. He feels a small hand on his shoulder. Behind him is Jayne, urging him forward like an annoyed parent. Ben takes a deep breath, blinks the dizziness from his eyes, and walks up to the coffin.

He stands there for what feels like an hour but couldn't have been more than a few seconds. *Bow once, say a small prayer, bow again, and then bow a third time,* are the thoughts running through his head. He starts to bow and feels his equilibrium give. He needs to take a step forward with his right foot to maintain his balance. He rises quickly and snaps his head back like a figure skater trying to regain their balance after a long spin. He wipes his forehead with the back of his hand, conscious of the many eyes pointed in his direction. He bows for the second time, this time much shorter, forgetting to say a prayer.

Once more, he thinks. *Once more, and I am out of here.*

He begins bowing for the third and final time. As he starts his descent, he hears a sound coming from the phone in his jacket pocket.

"DOOOOOOT, DOOOOOOOT!"

Ben freezes halfway into his bow.

"DOOOOOOT, DOOOOOOT!"

The sound is getting louder. He can hear the crowd murmur behind him.

"DOOOOOOT, DOOOOOOOOT!"

Ben fumbles with his jacket. He reaches into his inside pocket and tries to pull his phone out to stop the sound.

"DOOOOOOT, DOOOOOOT!" The phone screams.

Ben fumbles with sweaty hands, trying to pull the oversized phone out of his inner jacket pocket that is a size too small for it.

"DOOOOOOT, DOOOOOOT!" The phone continues angrily.

Ben fumbles, face red with embarrassment, hands sweaty with anxiety. He yanks hard at his phone. He hears his pocket rip as the phone finally comes free, but it is coming out too fast. He hears the crowd's gasps as his phone flies from his sweaty fingers. Ben watches in horror as the phone flies directly towards Jinni's coffin. It lands on her high school graduation photo, cracking the glass right where her smile is. The phone then hits the coffin beneath the picture and falls to the ground, landing with a loud thud. The phone has shattered the picture's glass in an almost demonic way. It distorts the glass, so it looks like Jinni is broken instead of showing her proud smiling face. Still stuck in his half-bow position, Ben barges towards his phone.

"DOOOOOT, DOOOOOT!" The phone continues. Anyone who owned a phone in modern times would have recognized that sound. It is an Amber Alert; Ben has never bothered to shut it off. Ben picks up his phone and stops the blaring. The phone feels hot in his hands. He looks down at the screen. On it are the words:

> *Amber Alert!*
> *Girl missing. If seen, please call…*

CHAPTER 3 - IDC

Ben slams his empty glass on the kitchen counter and immediately refills it. He remakes his vodka and soda and watches the carbonation of the soda settle to a halt. He closes his eyes and gulps down the liquid until the ice hits him in the teeth. After the funeral debacle, he feels he must kill all the brain cells that retain that day's memory. Ben usually did not drink this early (it is Friday at 2 p.m.), but after calling in sick this morning, he strongly felt the need to de-stress. After finishing his latest drink, he leans on the granite counter with both hands.

His mind wanders to his time with Jinni.

They had lived together for almost two years. The first six months sometimes called the "Honeymoon Phase," were some of the best times of his life. Jinni was considerably younger than him, Ben was thirty-three, Jinni at twenty-two, and her youth sparked a lost ember in his life. Ben dreaded the aging process. Every morning he checked his pubic hair for the inevitable white hair. He had begun applying facial cream to smooth his emerging wrinkles and bought a special dying shampoo to rid himself of his graying temples.

Jinni had found him attractive and encouraged him to stop coloring his hair and let the gray come out. On their second date, she told him that she usually dated older men and found that the guys her age were too immature and uninteresting. Ben had not been going out much when he met Jinni. His good friend Raj was recently engaged and had told Ben they were too old to be hitting the nightclubs, the bars, and day drinking. With Jinni, he now had someone to enjoy his time with. This time he was not a young, relatively broke engineer who had just moved into one of the most expensive cities in the world. This time he was making good money (Ben had just gotten promoted a few months before meeting Jinni) at a decently sized company (FrontSpark had almost 250 employees at that point). While once before, the city had seemed very expensive, now it was much more manageable. They enjoyed all the city had to offer.

Ben had never done cocaine before Jinni, but on their third date, she whipped out a little clear baggie and smiled at him. He protested at first, but she grabbed his hand and guided him to the bathroom. In the closed stall, she pulled down her dress, tapped some white powder on her breast, and pulled Ben down to her chest. She told him to hold one of his nostrils closed with his finger and snort away.

Ben was conflicted about the feeling of coke in his system. He felt as if he was walking a few centimeters off the ground. He realized a lot of his neurotic behavior and nervousness were gone. Jinni and Ben drank and snorted throughout the night. They made love for the first time that night. The drugs and alcohol flowing through their systems compelled them. Ben had some performance issues at first, but Jinni smiled and told him she knew exactly how to take care of that. Their lovemaking was always intense. Jinni knew precisely how to titillate, tease, and control him. It was the best sex he had ever had. Once after a particularly intense session, Ben asked her how she learned to do the things she did. She just shrugged and told him that she just did. By their fifth date, they were already discussing her moving in.

When they first met, Jinni had just lost her job as a restaurant host or something (he was never unequivocal on what she did). She had moved to the city a year ago to be closer to her mom and sister after her dad passed. On their fifth date, she told Ben that she would have to move far away as she could not afford her share of the rent (she lived with three other girls) and did not want to move in with her mom and sister. Ben made the love-sick suggestion of having her stay with him for a few months, just until she got back on her feet. She ended up living with him for almost two years.

#

His smartphone rings, breaking his thoughts.

"Ben, I heard you're out sick," Ulysses starts as soon as Ben says hello. Ben silently groans. The last thing he wants to do is engage in a conversation with his boss and the company's CEO.

"Ben, are you there?" Ulysses asks impatiently.

Ben fakes a cough and tries to make his voice groggy. "Yes, Ulysses, I am here."

"Good." Ulysses clears his throat. "I just spoke with John Symens in HR, and he said you were too sick to work today?"

"Yes," Ben replies.

Ulysses sighs audibly. "With everything going on, I understand being sick, but next week is important for us here at FrontSpark." Ulysses pauses for a moment and then continues. "You know we have that meeting with that new start-up. Alice Conner in marketing tells me they will be the next big thing." Ben can hear Ulysses take a loud slurp of his tea. "We have the preliminaries all set up for them and need your expert analysis to finalize the contract. This could be huge for us, Ben. Huge." Ulysses exaggerates the word huge. Ben leans back on his couch and covers his eyes. He had entirely forgotten about his Monday morning meeting, even though it's been on his calendar for a couple of weeks.

"Are you still there?"

"Yes, I am still here," Ben replies irritably.

"So I take it you're ready? Do you have your presentation all set to go? I need your 'A' game for this."

"Ulysses, it might be the cough medicine, but could you tell me who we are meeting again?" Ben asks.

"Whom. Not who," Ulysses corrects.

Ben shifts on his couch, holding back the urge to shout. "Ulysses, 'whom' are we meeting with?"

"It's some new start-up that burst on the scene a few years ago, I never heard of them, but my daughter swears they are great. They are some new social video-sharing app. Now, where is that email—" Ben could hear Ulysses type some stuff on his keyboard. "Shit, what was their name—Tic Tac or something."

"NikNak?" Ben asks. *There is no way this can be a coincidence*, he thinks.

"Yes … Yes … NikNak. All I know is that they might be the next big thing, the next billion-dollar baby, and I want their business. So I expect to see you in the meeting bright, early and prepared. We will be joined by their CEO, COO, and CTO. This is the final meeting before we sign off on the contracts. They want to meet the head of the major departments— Technology, Finance, and Legal." Ulysses pauses. "Are you still there?" Ulysses asks for the third time.

"Yes!" Ben replies for the third time.

"Good—have a good weekend, get better, and see you virtually on Monday." Ulysses hangs up. Ben sighs and lays down on his couch.

His mind returns to Jinni.

Someone had once told him: "No one can hide their true self for more than six months." Ben does not remember who had said that to him. Was it his cousin Kairo, the proverbial playboy with a disdain for relationships? Was it Raj, the serial lover who would fall in and out of love in the span of six hours? A girl he had dated who had dumped him when she got tired of his constant need to fix things? He could not recall, but that proverb always stuck in his head.

Six months into his relationship with Jinni, cracks began to show. He would constantly catch her staring out into space for an extended period. Her face contorted into a combination of pain, guilt, and shame. He saw her doing this a few times in the early days of their relationship, but more and more towards the latter days. He occasionally would ask her what she was thinking about, and she would immediately snap out of it and respond with a witty comeback like "Just thinking about you, babe," or "Just thinking about how great we are together," accompanied by her ever endearing crooked smile.

Jinni was extremely private about her life. She would often sidestep or evade Ben's questions about her, especially about her early days. Ben always had a nagging feeling that she was hiding something but was too happy with the relationship to push the topic. Still, he began to notice things.

The first thing Ben noticed was that her drinking was problematic. When they went out, she usually went as hard as him, matching him drink for drink, even though he was almost double her weight. (Jinni was 5'3 and weighed, at most, a hundred pounds). The nights usually ended with him carrying her to their apartment and laying her on the bed. He noticed her excessive drug use. She would often go out with Jayne and show up early the next day with slivers of white powder covering her nostrils. He was concerned, but the fantastic sex and the fact that his ego was boosted by having this beautiful young woman with him caused him to push those concerns aside.

He swept them under the rug.

#

Ben looks at his empty glass and decides whether to get another drink or finish his presentation. Ben considers reusing an old PowerPoint he had used for the last company they pitched to. He immediately rejects that as he knows Ulysses would "flip the fuck out" if he tried that. Ulysses required and demanded a new presentation curated directly for each client.

Ben has limited experience with the NikNak app. He tangentially had been aware of it, as many of the Facebook and Instagram accounts he followed regularly featured content shared from NikNak. Ben messages his team, hoping to catch a few before they get off for the weekend. He asks his team what their impression of the app is. Some respond that it is terrific; others say it is weird and disconcerting.

Ben sighs as his team, as usual, gives him nothing. His job title is Director of Engineering, but his responsibilities are, in reality, hand-holding his team and getting them to stop arguing. His team's role is to support these up-and-coming startups until they can manage their own needs. It is tedious and exhausting work. It is not life-changing for any of them.

Ben grabs his phone and opens the NikNak app. The app is what Ben thought it would be. A bunch of young high school girls and boys half-naked, displaying their bodies, lip-synching to popular songs, and dancing, lots and lots of dancing. It contains thirst traps, skits, and funny animal videos. It is somewhat interesting, but Ben doesn't understand the mass appeal. Ben takes a deep breath. Ulysses's voice rings: "I want their business!" He has spent maybe ten minutes on the app, and already it is showing him some questionable content.

An hour later, Ben puts down his phone and walks to the bathroom. He washes his face with cold water and puts his hands on the basin. He feels every day of his thirty-eight years. It is not that he does not understand today's youth (well, maybe he doesn't); the depravity they sank to for views disturbed him. In the last hour, he had seen fatal car crashes where bodies were flung from the windshield, various teen strip teases, and videos ("Naks") asking him to subscribe to specific channels. Naks containing content like "Barely Legal, daily sexting, and little surprises for all fans of my channel. Hottest vids and pics. Join my private channel now!" Most of these videos are of an almost nude teenage-looking girl or boy smiling blankly at the camera.

He had come across a channel called "GrueZome DeathZ," which depicted various industrial accidents by shipping crates, fatal car accidents, people impaled by rebar, and crushed by different large objects. One Nak is an old video of an army officer shooting someone point-blank in the back of the head. Ben is saddened and disgusted by what he has seen.

Ben returns to the couch and taps the screen to bring up the next Nak. Many of the Naks he has seen are prefaced with pitches by content creators selling cheap-looking jewelry or sugary "energy" drinks that they push like snake oil salesmen.

"Buy Y-Fuel," a content creator named "KillyBilly" gushes brightly. "The only energy drink you need to get through your day!" He takes a long drink and begins talking, "In today's Nak, we try to negotiate with sex workers on the streets of New York. Can we get the best price? Tommy, Johnny, and I find out!"

The video then cuts to the car's interior, where three young men in masks drive slowly down a seedy street. They roll down their vehicle's window and speak with a young woman in a short white dress and a white satin mask. Her eyes are cold and desperate. One of the men begins talking to her, recording while his friend drives the car. The girl seemed unsure and hesitant.

She asks them, "Are you filming?" to which the guys in the car laugh.

"No, we aren't—so how much?" one of the guys asks.

She looks into the car and asks, "For who?"

The same guy answers, "All three of us," as they break into another round of laughter. She takes a step back from the car and starts to walk away. The driver moves the vehicle to keep pace with her. "C'mon, darling," the guy in the passenger seat says. "We will be nice … I promise." This is followed by even more laughter from the vehicle. The girl in the white dress stops and turns towards them.

"Three hundred," she announces. "Twenty minutes each." The guy in the passenger seat leans towards the window.

"Three hundred? Come on, baby; we can do better than that. How about one-fifty?" The girl gives them a look of contempt and starts walking away again.

"Ok, ok," says the guy in the passenger seat. "How about an even two hundred?" The guy in the passenger seat starts flapping two hundred dollar bills towards the window. The girl stops and peers towards the car.

"Sorry, three hundred is the lowest I can go," she says as she turns and starts walking away. The guy in the passenger seat turns toward the camera and winks. He then looks out the window, still waving the bills at her.

"C'mon, babe, times are tough; how much business are you getting these days?" he asks the girl. "You seriously going to turn down an easy two-hundy? Shit, Tommy here will bust in like ten seconds." The camera moves towards the driver, who Ben guesses is Tommy. This is followed by more hyena-like laughter from the car. The girl crosses her arms and soothes herself. The guy in the passenger seat (who Ben guesses is KillyBilly) continues to wave the two hundred dollar bills in her direction. The screen goes black, and KillyBilly reappears on camera. "Guys, if we get one hundred thousand Niks, I will show part two of this video." And with that, the video ends, and the adjudication appears.

Nak by:

Ben reviews the comments; some encourage the content creators, while others complain about the exploitation.

Ben taps the screen to bring up the next video.

"What's up, guys, KM-Asher here. In today's Nak, I show you how to defend yourself using Krav-Maga. Watch what happens here." The video cuts to a bar or nightclub. A shaky handheld video of a group of mid-thirties patrons all standing at a bar. KM-Asher talks to some women, and a larger man bumps into him. KM-Asher turns around and says some unintelligible words to the larger man. The bigger guy has a mean look on his face. His mouth is in a snarl, spitting profanity directly at KM-Asher. Suddenly, the more prominent man lifts a giant arm and attempts to shove or strangle KM-Asher. In a smooth motion, KM-Asher grabs the man's wrist with his left hand, twists, and then breaks the man's arm with a vicious upward-moving movement with his other hand. The last image is of the bigger man on the floor screaming in pain, holding a dangling arm. The video cuts back to KM-Asher. "Now let me explain what happened here—"

Ben closes the app and goes into the kitchen to make another drink.

#

Ben wakes up with a splitting headache. After his in-depth debacle with NikNak, he badly needs hydration and coffee to overcome his mental and physical anguish. He throws on his hoodie, sweatpants, and mask and braves the world outside.

By "braves" he means taking the elevator down to the first floor, turning right, and walking twenty steps to the coffee shop below his building. He walks up to the counter and orders his usual. He waits the few minutes it takes to concoct such a drink, nursing his headache by rubbing his temples. When the barista shouts "Ben! Ben?" to an empty store, he walks up to the counter to get his beverage. After getting his drink, he sits at his usual table and fishes into his pocket for a two-pack of aspirin. He takes the pills and washes them down with the scalding hot coffee, carefully moving his mask to drink. He leans back in his chair and lets out a hard breath.

CHAPTER 4 - ICYMI

Ben sits on his couch, staring at his phone. It is Saturday night, and he still has no idea what he will present on Monday. NikNak is just a video-sharing app very similar to the now-defunct Vine. The only difference Ben could find is that videos are longer, the interface is better, and there is less content moderation.

He goes to the kitchen to make himself a drink. The cold vodka and soda hit his throat nicely. He stirs the glass in his hand and takes another sip. He wipes his mouth with the back of his hand and lets out an enormous belch. He downs his drink and makes himself another.

After a few drinks, Ben sits back down on his couch. Laying next to him is his phone. He starts reaching for it but stops and decides he needs a break. He leans back and closes his eyes. His mind starts to wander.

He recalls the first day he met Jinni.

They met at a party. His cousin, Kairo Abyad, had invited Ben to a potential client's table at a downtown nightclub. His cousin had flown in that afternoon and stayed with Ben for the night. Ben was nervous, but Kairo had told him to "man the fuck up." His cousin Kairo had prepped him before their night out.

"Ben," Kairo started. "Whatever you do, do not embarrass me."

"When have I ever embarrassed you?" Ben asked defensively.

"Previous actions don't guarantee future results," Kairo explained as he took another sip of their pre-game drinks. "His name is Bobby Chitz. He just sold his company for half a billion dollars, and I want his business."

Ben stared at his cousin. Kairo was an investment banker, the crown jewel of the family. Like Ben, Kairo came from a middle-class family in Los Angeles. His father was a mechanical engineer, and his mother was a pharmacist. Kairo was fiercely competitive, even at a young age. Ben, who was older, always had to let him win when they played video games, or Kairo would continuously challenge him. Kairo got straight A's in high school, went to UCLA on a full scholarship, got his CFA at twenty-four, and immediately joined one of the top venture capital companies in Southern California. Ben may have brains, but Kairo had more brains and more drive. Kairo would wake up at 5 a.m. to work out. He was always in great shape, his hair and facial hair immaculately groomed. Ben let out a sigh. He had been looking forward to this night for many days. At thirty-three, the invites were drying up.

"OK, I promise I will be on my best behavior. Sir!" Ben stood up, kicked his heels together, and offered Kairo a military salute. Kairo shook his head in disgust, but he could not hide the smile on his face.

"Whatever, just don't throw up on him." Kairo checked his phone. "C'mon, let's go!" With that, they headed out the door towards their Uber.

They arrived at a table in the middle of the club. Kairo waved at an older, well-dressed man, who motioned towards the bouncer to let them in. Kairo opened his arms widely and did the cool half-hug half-handshake thing that Ben could never pull off. Kairo motioned for Ben to come closer. Ben extended his hand to the man.

"Bobby, nice to meet you!" he shouted. The music was loud, and they had to yell loudly to converse. Bobby nodded hello, shook Ben's hand, and turned away to look at the dance floor.

"That's not Bobby," Kairo hissed at him as he pulled him aside. Kairo waved down the hostess and ordered a drink for Ben and him.

"So where is the guy you're trying to swoon?" Ben shouted. Kairo turned and looked at him like he was the stupidest person in the world.

"That's him," Kairo said, motioning his head ever so slightly towards the real Bobby.

"What? Really? What is he like, twenty-three or something?" Ben looked at Bobby, shocked. Kairo shook his head no.

"He's twenty-five and worth half a billion dollars. So shut the fuck up about it and play nicely." Ben took a step back and raised his hands in defeat. Kairo gave him one more of his looks and turned back towards the hostess.

Ben tried to enjoy himself that night but felt out of place. The crowd was younger, better dressed, more prosperous, and social. Everyone was taking selfies and videos around him. Ben felt awkward, like he didn't belong there. He felt a hand clasp him on his shoulder. Ben turned, expecting Kairo to continue berating him, but it was the real Bobby.

"Are you having a good time?" Bobby asked him while looking at the dance floor, his hand still on Ben's shoulder.

"Yes ... Yes, I am," Ben stammered. "Thank you for the invite."

"No problem," Bobby said as he clasped Ben on his shoulder a few more times. "Kairo tells me you're also in tech; any company that I would know?"

Ben shuffled his feet. "It's a smaller company; I am sure you haven't heard of it."

"Try me," Bobby replied.

"It's called FrontSpark," Ben said, looking for any hint of recognition.

Bobby, still not looking at Ben, rubbed his chin. "Isn't that the company that Ulysses runs? What do you guys do again?"

"We provide engineering, financial, and legal to companies before they go public," Ben explained. He nervously took a sip of his drink. The way Bobby talked to him, never looking at him, made him nervous.

"Sounds interesting," Bobby replied casually.

"I heard you have had some success lately," Ben said.

Suddenly, Bobby turned and faced Ben, grinning ear to ear, showing off his impossibly white teeth. He laughed. "You could say that."

Ben looked back towards the crowd at the table where Kairo was eyeing him intensely. Ben ignored him and turned back towards Bobby. "Tell me, Bobby, what did your company do?"

Bobby turned back towards the dance floor and leaned closer to Ben. "I created a video compression algorithm that will allow companies to stream videos using eighty percent less bandwidth and storage with minimal loss of quality. It will revolutionize short-video." Bobby paused. "Give it a few years, and this will change the world. Just you watch." He turned towards Ben and gave him a wink. "Now, c'mon," he said as he clasped Ben on the back and led him back to the table. "We are out of here in about thirty minutes. We are going back to my place to party some more." He turned towards Ben again. "Oh, and," Bobby said, looking Ben in the eyes, "it would be nice if you didn't come alone." He gave Ben a nod and walked back to the couch behind the table.

Ben was never good under pressure. Bobby had made it clear: "Do not come back to my place empty-handed." He approached a few ladies and only got laughed at and told no. Ben desperately looked for Kairo, but he was nowhere to be found. Bobby had left the table, and Ben stood alone, unsure of what to do.

"Where the fuck have you been?" Kairo said, coming up behind him. "C'mon, we are getting out of here." Ben noticed two girls standing beside Kairo. "Meet Kary and Michelle." He motioned towards the ladies standing next to him.

"I have to use the bathroom," said one of the girls. Kairo nodded towards the facilities and told them they would wait for them.

"Bobby has a no girls, no entry policy. It has to be one-for-one," Kairo explained. "Thank god Kary had a friend, or else you wouldn't have been able to get in."

"Which one's Kary?" Ben asked.

"The blonde one," Kairo replied.

"They're both blondes!" Ben pointed out.

Kairo laughed. "Well, Kary is the one I am going to fuck tonight. You can have whichever is the other one." Kairo gestured towards the restrooms. "Here they come. Let's go!"

Driving up to the mansion was everything that Ben expected. Overly imposing, creamy white, with a gate and a security guard out front. The security guard stuck his head in the car and looked around. Satisfied, he nodded at the guard box and waved them in. They arrived at the front of the house, where another guard opened the doors and ushered them in.

The house was bathed in ambient amber light. It was tastefully decorated and smelled like lilacs despite the many people inside. Ben looked around and found the kitchen; Kary or Michelle followed him as he poured himself a drink.

"I'll have a rum and coke," Kary or Michelle stated. Ben sighed and looked around for the mixer and booze. After she had her drink, she grabbed his arm, and they walked around the mansion. "Isn't this place amazing?" she asked.

"Uh-huh," Ben grunted. He was suddenly tired and was thinking of calling it a night. Kary or Michelle guided him to the living room, where he sat on the edge of an oversized crowded couch. He found out she was an Instagram model—"with 18,762 followers," she happily proclaimed. She asked how he knew the person who owned this house. Ben made up a story about how they were old war buddies. She nodded in wide-eyed fascination. Ben was bored; he looked at his phone and debated calling an Uber.

Ben heard a laugh; Kary or Michele was in the middle of some story about her time in the Maldives. "It was so boring!" she said. "All we did was party at tables all night and then drink at mansions during the day." Ben turned towards the laugh and saw a beautiful girl standing on the other side of the couch. Ben's eyes met hers. She gave him a crooked smile. He would never know whether the alcohol, the boredom, or the loneliness compelled him to approach her. He just knew he needed to talk to her. Kary or Michelle was standing in front of him, blocking his path. Ben gently reached out his arms, moved her aside, and walked towards the girl.

She was standing with her purse tucked under her left arm. She nodded politely at some young drunk guy attempting to tell her a story. Their eyes met again. Ben was not the most forthright guy in the world. His last girlfriend had to kiss him first because Ben was not the guy who made the first move. Something about her completely changed his usual demeanor. He walked up to her. They all stood there for a second. The young drunk guy looked annoyed. The girl widened her beautiful crooked smile, and Ben introduced himself.

"Hello, I'm Ben," he said as he stuck out his hand.

"You have really pretty eyes." Was the first thing she said to him. "I'm Jinni." She smiled as she took his hand.

"Join me for a drink?" Ben asked.

She looked down at his hands and said, "But you already have one." Her crooked smile widened. Ben looked down at his untouched drink and then at the young drunk guy standing next to them. The young drunk guy's expression had changed from annoyance to anger.

"Here you go, bud." Ben handed the guy his drink. "Don't worry; I didn't touch it." He winked and then proceeded to guide Jinni to the kitchen.

#

Ben snaps awake from his stupor. His drink is still in his hand, although the ice has fully melted. He looks down at his phone on the couch. The screen lock had turned on, and he could see his blackened reflection on the screen. He puts his drink down and reaches over to grab his phone. As he touches the phone, he pulls his hand away in shock.

The phone is hot, very hot.

"Ow!" he screams in the empty room. *What the fuck was that?* he thinks. He shakes his hand, trying to cool it. He pokes at the phone again, this time more gingerly. The phone feels like a cast iron pan that has been sitting on the stove for a while.

"Goddamn lithium-ion batteries," he says out loud to an empty room. He carefully puts the phone down on the coffee table and goes to refresh his drink.

A few drinks later, Ben unlocks his phone (after poking at it first) and opens the NikNak app. He searches for one thing. It does not take him long. He finds the Nak; he takes a deep breath, takes a deep swig of his drink, and presses play.

Immediately a young girl appears. She is wearing a stylish blue floral bumper. She has on large hoop earrings that shine in the sun. Her hair is tied back into a ponytail. She is walking backward, lip-synching, and dancing to a song Ben doesn't recognize. She jumps, turns away from the camera, and then looks over her shoulder, her lips not missing a beat.

52

Ben sits mesmerized by the music, the choreography, and the composition of the Nak. A few quick edits have her walking down different streets, city blocks, and suburbs. Her lips never miss a vocal from the song she is lip-synching to. Finally, the video cuts to an area that seems familiar to Ben. He sits straight up.

The girl keeps singing and dancing, moving effortlessly to the song's beat. Suddenly her hair blows away from her body as a fast-moving object falls behind her. The singing girl freezes in her tracks as the music continues to play. The camera person asks, "What the fuck was that?" Ben watches the video become shaky as the person filming rushes towards the singing girl. Ben's heart starts racing. *Don't show her face, don't show her face, please do not show her face*, his mind screams. He knows what is coming next.

The camera person reaches the singing girl who is looking at the ground. The camera starts to pan in front of her. Ben can make out black Jimmy Choo sneakers, a leg with blood streaking, and a protruding bone. The camera pans up further. Ben can make out a sensible yet dirty black skirt, a black shirt, and a gold jacket. He knows those clothes. He had bought Jinni that gold jacket.

"No … Please no!" he whimpers at his phone. Everything is telling him to look away, to shut down his phone. The camera pans further upward to reveal Jinni's cold dead face. Her makeup is done as always. Her eyes are open but rolled back. Her colored streaks blow gently in the wind. Beneath her head, blood begins to pool. Both girls scream. Someone shouts to call 911. The video stops. The adjudication appears:

Ben sits frozen on the sofa. He starts to shake and trembles so hard that the phone falls from his hand onto the floor. He rubs his eyes to try and remove the images he has just seen. *That video is fake,* he thinks. He knew kids these days were saviors of technology. "It's a joke." He shakes his head and laughs. "A fuckin' sick joke. You got me, @koryBrewer; you got me good!" He continues to laugh uncomfortably as he reaches for his phone. "Ow!" he shouts as he touches it. A static shock strikes his hand hard. He puts his fingers in his mouth and sucks on them. He slowly reaches back for the phone, prodding it first with his finger before quickly pulling it away. This time there is no shock, but the phone is again hot. Ben looks at the phone and can hear a brief hum. *I need to get a new one. This one is about to blow*, he thinks. *I'll watch the video again and look for edits or superimpositions. It has to be a fake.*

But first, he needs another drink.

A few drinks later, he has significantly calmed down. He rubs his temples and presses play.

CHAPTER 5 - WTF

Ben watches the Nak a few more times, carefully observing the background, looking for any visual tricks that could prove the Nak is fake. He watches and replays, watches and replays. He takes a look at the comments:

@sicarioplays: *Don't do drugs kids lol*

@leftfootrightfoot: *SPLAT RIP!*

@heather86: *poor girl she must have been in a really bad place to take her life*

And so on.

Ben puts the phone down. He notices it is getting too hot to hold. He rubs his eyes and massages his hands. He blinks his eyes back into focus. He sees a shadow forming around his vision, a telltale sign that a blackout is near. He slowly sways to his feet. He goes to the kitchen to pour himself another drink. *Last drink*, he thinks. *This is the last drink for tonight.*

Three drinks later, he stumbles back to his couch and stares at his phone. He gently touches it and finds that it has cooled down. He unlocks it and watches the Nak a few more times. After another three drinks, the black shadow becomes a full circle with a pinhole dot in the middle. Ben is lying on his stomach, halfway off the couch, with his phone in his left hand on the floor. To focus, he has to shut one of his eyes.

"Fuck you, Jinni. Why you go and do something like that?" he slurs, his voice muffled by the couch cushions. He thinks he knows the answer, but he pushes that thought away. Ben presses play again. He tries to lift his phone, but it fumbles in his hand. He quickly readjusts his hands and grips the top left corner of the screen with his thumb to steady it. He blinks hard…

Everything is too bright. Ben notices he is now standing. Swaying, to be more exact, like a flag in a soft wind. He sees that he is outside, in broad daylight, standing on a sidewalk.

"What da fuck," he mumbles as he rubs his eyes. Ben blinks his eyes open and looks around through blurred vision. He is outside on a sunny street. Music and singing are coming directly in front of him. He puts out his hands for balance as he feels he will tumble to the floor at any second. Ben shuts one eye and forces the other to focus. He looks towards where the music is coming from. He is on a long sidewalk with tall buildings to his left. The sun is bearing down on him, setting to his left. He holds his hand over his open eye to block out the light to help him see more clearly. His left hand is still extended as he feels his balance can go at any time. He recognizes this street, but his eyes will not focus enough to read the street signs.

He peers up the sidewalk and sees two girls. One walks backward, singing, dancing, and posing for another girl. The other girl is holding a phone in front of her, laughing and encouraging the other girl with hand movements.

"What da fuck," Ben repeats as his balance gives. He catches himself at the last moment falling to one knee in an absurd praying pose. Ben violently shakes his head and rubs his eyes. His stomach gurgles, and he has to swallow hard to keep in its contents. He places a hand on the warm sidewalk and slowly and carefully pushes himself back to his feet. The sudden adrenaline rush clears his head, and now he can see a little more clearly. Ben does a quick survey of where he is. Cars drive by him on his right, and many tall buildings are to his left. Directly in front of him are the two girls. *Where the fuck am I?* he thinks, trying to recall where he had seen this street before. He brings his hand to his head and slaps himself hard on the side of it. A moment of panic starts to rise inside him.

Did I drink myself into a blackout stupor and decide to take a walk? he looks down at his hand for his phone, but it is not there. Ben takes another survey of his location. A sense of deja-vu engulfs him. *I know this place,* he thinks as his mind scrambles to recall how and where. He scratches the back of his head, blinking his eyes a few times to try and clear them up. The two girls are edging closer to him.

"Haay … Haay!" Ben shouts. Both girls stop in their tracks and turn to face him. The one filming lowers the camera to the ground. "Haay!" Ben slurs again. "Where am I?" he says as he stumbles towards them. The girl who had been dancing quickly moves to her friend's side and places an arm on her shoulder. Ben can make out the look of fear and concern in their eyes. He stops, his hand frozen in front of him. He looks down and realizes he is still in his pajamas, his eyes are probably bloodshot, and he hasn't shaved or showered in three days. Ben chuckles. *To them,* he thinks, *I probably look like a psycho homeless lunatic.* "Whoa, whoa," he says as he holds up his hands to show he is safe. "I just wanna know where da hell I—"

Ben feels the rush of the wind against his face. His hair blows back, and something flashes in front of him. He flinches backward instinctively and gets his feet caught under him; he is on his way to falling to his backside. Ben hears the sound of something hitting concrete. He can best describe the sound as a watermelon being hit with a sledgehammer. He tries to remember the name of that comic that would smash watermelons on TV when he was a kid. *What was his name?* Ben wonders as he stumbles backward. *Galileo? Gardner?* He finally loses his balance and lands hard on his backside. He hears the screams.

One of the girls screams. Then the second one screams. Then they both scream in unison. Ben cocks his head to try and get an angle in front of him; his knees are blocking his vision. He can see the two teenage girls about ten yards ahead of him. Both have their hands to their mouths, one holding her phone to the object on the ground and the other holding her friend's shoulder.

Ben tries to focus on the object on the ground, but his vision won't allow it. The object appears to be in the shape of a small woman. Ben takes a deep breath and tries to blink his eyes into focus. *Focus, damn you!* Ben screams at himself as he tries to will his eyesight. It is a body. It is contorted and twisted in a way that is not natural. He sees the two girls standing over the body of a small woman with black hair. Her face faces Ben; her eyes rolled up in her head.

It is Jinni. She is on the ground, dead right in front of him.

"Makena! Stop filming and call 9-1…" is the last thing Ben hears. As the bright lights disappear around him, his final thought is *Gallagher, the guy who smashes watermelons; his name is Gallagher!*

CHAPTER 6 - YLYL

Ben stumbles off the couch and falls on his side. He scrambles backward on his hands and feet, desperately trying to get away from his phone. After a few feet, the back of his head hits the wall.

"Ouch," he cries, grabbing the back of his head. He pulls his hand away and looks at it. He does not see any blood. He gazes down at his shirt; it has tiny drops of red liquid splattered all over it. Ben pushes himself off the floor and stumbles towards the bathroom, holding the wall for balance. He turns on the bathroom light. He walks to the sink and lays his hands on the porcelain basin, supporting his weight. He lifts his head and looks at himself in the mirror. His eyes are bloodshot, and bags of darkness have formed under them.

"You look like shit," Ben tells the person in the mirror. He turns on the water and washes his face. He slowly reaches behind his head and gently touches it. "Ow," he says softly. He looks at his hand again to confirm there is no blood. He tries looking at the back of his head in the mirror but realizes it is impossible. He inspects his shirt. It is a baby blue shirt that he has had forever. He could not remember when or where he had bought it, only that he had slept in it most nights.

"What a shitty dream," he whispers, drying his face with a towel. On his shirt are small specks of red. He touches one of the stains. It smears deeper into his shirt.

"That looks like blood," he says out loud. He grabs a towel, runs it under the sink, and tries to wipe the red dots from his shirt. Doing that only smears it more.

"Well, it's official," he announces sarcastically. "All the drinking is causing me to hallucinate!"

He faces the mirror and looks himself up and down. There is another black, white, and red smudge near his shoulder. He claws at it and brings it up towards the light to inspect it. It is a piece of colored hair attached to a small amount of flesh-covered bone. The water is still running, and Ben stares at the clockwise swirl it makes. He drops the hair-like substance into the sink and watches it drain. He takes off his shirt and places it into the hamper. He turns off the light and goes to bed.

He did not sleep well that night.

The following day, Ben gets up and makes breakfast; he sits at his small dining table. He sings.

"It was all a dream—" he repeats for the third time this morning. "I used to read 'Word Up!' magazine—" he adds. Ben cannot remember the rest of the lyrics, so he stops. He sits in his chair, his breakfast in front of him. He grabs his fork and rhythmically taps it on the plate.

"It was all a dream," he repeats quietly.

If it is a dream, why was there blood on your shirt? his mind asks.

"Maybe the blood was there already; I could have hurt myself when I banged my head against the wall." He nods, satisfied at his undebatable logic.

Oh, so this is magic blood? his brain questions sarcastically. *It magically bounced off the wall and landed on the front of your shirt? What about the piece of skull, was that magic too? Come on!* Ben slams his fork down on the table.

"It was a dream; I blacked out and had a nightmare!" Ben screams into the empty room. He stands, hands clenched into tight fists. He waits for his mind to reply.

None came.

Satisfied with his victory, he picks up his plate, empties the contents in the trash, and places it in the sink. He is no longer hungry.

Ben goes about his day. He works on his presentation and tries to keep himself occupied. He does not touch or look at his phone. Ben walks into the kitchen when his work is done and makes himself a drink. He goes to sit on his couch. He stares at his phone sitting on top of the coffee table. After a few minutes, Ben sighs and picks it up. The battery reads 8%. He curses himself for not charging it. Ben plugs it into the charging cord next to his couch and starts rapping his fingers on the screen.

Did that really happen? he wonders. *Or was I just drunk dreaming?* Ben continues to tap his fingers on the phone screen. He walks to his bathroom. He will consider it all a stupid dream if the shirt has no blood on it. He opens his hamper. *And if it does?* his mind questions. *Then what?* Ben reaches into the hamper and pulls out his shirt. Grabbing it by the edges, he opens and exposes its surface. There are tiny droplets of blood all over the shirt. Ben scratches at the stains, hoping they are nothing more than dirt marks. After several unsuccessful attempts, he places the shirt back in the hamper. He takes a deep breath and expels it.

"It had to be a dream; it had to...." he tells himself as he goes into the kitchen to make another drink.

CHAPTER 7 - IMYSM

Ben has had only three girlfriends in his life. The first one, Pam, was when he was a freshman in college. Ben was under the legal drinking age when one of his college friends invited him to a rave. Ben had never been to one and was excited. He had heard about these drug-fueled underground parties. They were all the rage back in his day.

Ben took his first ecstasy pill that night. He was sweating and dizzy, so he walked outside to get some fresh air. The fresh air made the drug hit harder. He was leaning against the outdoor rail when she approached him and asked him if he was okay.

"I am fuckin' fantastic!" Ben told her. She laughed, brought out a napkin from her purse, and wiped his forehead. They dated for almost a year.

Pam was adopted by some upper-middle-class family and clung to him desperately. Her fear of rejection was so intense that she was always overly agreeable with him, which made Ben quickly grow weary. The breakup process was long, drawn out, and painful. It wasn't that he did not like her; he did; it was just that she always wanted to be by him. She would lie on his bed and watch him when he was studying. This was severely affecting his grades. So much so he was in danger of flunking a few of his classes. He calmly, carefully tried to break it off, only for her to break down into tears, begging him to reconsider. After many unsuccessful attempts, Ben angrily got through to her. He shouted at her, called her names, and told her to fuck off. She is now married with two kids.

Ben met his second girlfriend, Beth, about four years later. She was a coddled daughter from a wealthy family who believed in putting as little effort as possible in life. She liked to lay on the couch, smoke weed, and drink a lot. She cared little about the world and her well-being. She also cared little about Ben; for her, he was convenient. When bored or horny, she would call Ben over and ask him to "hang out." After hanging out, getting drunk, smoking weed, and making love many times, Ben asked her if he was her boyfriend. Her response was, "Yeah, sure." Ben didn't know but found out later that she had many other "Bens" lying around. When he confronted her about this, her response was, "I didn't think it was a big deal." He broke it off with her and soon after moved to San Francisco.

Ben did not have a girlfriend for another eight years. He moved up north and started focusing on his work. Jinni was Ben's third and last girlfriend. She seemed to have it all. She was intelligent, funny, beautiful, and had a youthful exuberance that appealed to him.

Ben sat nervously on the bar stool, waiting for Jinni. It had been three weeks since they had met at the party. They had both texted each other a few times until Ben got the nerve to ask her out for a drink. Jinni agreed. The bartenders kept pestering him to order, but he politely declined, explaining he was waiting for someone. Ben checked his phone and realized that she was late. After waiting a few more minutes, he conceded and ordered. When his drink arrived, he took a few sips and heard her voice behind him.

"Couldn't wait, huh," Jinni said, laughing. Ben slowly turned around and saw her. He smiled, slightly embarrassed, and motioned for her to sit.

"So what are you drinking there?" she asked, sitting on the stool next to him.

"It's a … vodka and soda," he explained.

"Oh fancy," she mocked. She turned to the bartender and asked for the same. "Cheers to us!" She clinked her glass to his and took a large swig of her drink. They sat for a moment in silence. Ben unsuccessfully tried to come up with a topic to talk about. He was nervous and tongue-tied. His leg shimmied up and down as it did when he got nervous. He caught Jinni looking at him, smiling. He moved his eyes away from her and back to his drink.

"You're not nervous, are you?" Jinni asked playfully.

"No, not at all." Ben tried to sound calm and collected.

"You seem nervous." She put a hand on his leg to stop it from shimming. "There, that's better." He turned towards her. She was smiling her large bright crooked smile at him. At that moment, he knew he was starting to fall for her.

That night they talked and drank for hours. She told him a bit about her life. She was thinking of quitting her job and trying something else. "I thought about being a paralegal," she said sadly, but now she worked in a place she hated. She had moved here from L.A. about a year ago to be closer to her mom and sister after her dad died. Ben offered his condolences.

Ben and Jinni were having a great night. After the initial awkwardness, they got into an enjoyable rhythm of talking, laughing, and drinking. After a few hours, Jinni looked at her phone and claimed she had to go as she had to work in the morning. Ben stood up and stuck out his hand. Jinni looked at him and smiled. She grabbed him by the shoulder and sat him back down. She then slowly moved in and kissed him.

"Call me," she said before leaving a happy and excited Ben.

#

Ben sits on his couch, drink in hand, laptop on his lap, reminiscing about Jinni. He has gone over his presentation three times and emailed Ulysses a copy. He downs his drink, puts his laptop back on his desk, shuts off the living room light, and goes to bed. He has a big day tomorrow.

66

CHAPTER 8 - OMG

Ben wakes up early the following day to prepare for his meeting with NikNak. Ulysses calls Ben twice to ensure he is ready.

"Ben, I'm just checking if we are all set," he asks for the second time.

"Yes, Ulysses," Ben answers irritably. "We were set thirty minutes ago when you called then."

"Fair enough; I cannot stress enough how important this meeting is. This deal could take this company to new heights and open new doors for us." Ulysses reaches over and adjusts something off-camera. "Is all your research set? I knew I should have met with you last Friday to review your material." Ulysses rubs his forehead in a worrying gesture.

"I was sick that day," Ben points out. "Plus, I had plenty of time on Saturday and Sunday to review the app. This is not the first time I have done this." Ben reminds him as he scratches obscenities on his notepad.

"Fine … fine." Ulysses closes his eyes. "Same as last time, I will start. Dave will go over legal and compliance. You cover engineering and security. Mark will be there if they have any accounting questions. I will take any final questions and do the closing. I feel good about this one, Ben. I feel like Captain Ahab about to harpoon Moby Dick!" Ulysses mimes throwing a spear.

"Didn't Ahab drown at the end?" Ben asks.

"Whatever." Ulysses throws up his hands in apathy. "Anyways, I got to go; Dave is calling." Ulysses quickly cuts Ben off. Ben pushes back his laptop, leans back in his chair, and lets out a loud yawn. *If he is Ahab, does that make me Ishmael?* he wonders. Ben pulls his laptop towards him and types his final notes.

Ulysses, Ben thinks while reviewing his presentation, *what a fucking stupid name.* He remembers their first conversation in his interview over fifteen years ago.

Ulysses looked at Ben's resume and back at Ben. "This company is going somewhere, Ben," his soon-to-be employer explained. "Will you join us on the journey?"

"Um … Sure."

"Sure?" Ulysses raised an eyebrow.

"I mean … Yes, I will," Ben nodded confidently.

Ulysses peered over his resume and looked directly at Ben. Ben looked around the large office. He was sitting on a costly couch in front of a large, dark wooden desk. This corner office was on the sixth floor, and windows surrounded Ben on the front and right. He looked out at the sky; it was a beautiful clear day. He was still groggy from the 6 a.m. flight he had taken that morning. The company had flown him from LAX to San Francisco for the final onsite. Ben had been up since four in the morning. It was now past 4 p.m.

"You don't seem sure … Are you sure, Ben?"

"I'm sure," Ben replied, faking confidence as best he could. This would be his second job, and the salary would be much higher than his current one. He currently works as a junior software engineer for a small IT consulting firm. He liked it there, and the money he made had paid for his college. Ben stared out the window. He could not believe he was in San Francisco, the world's tech capital. When Ben was in college studying Computer Science, he had always dreamed of moving to San Francisco and joining the next big start-up, the next Facebook, Instagram, or Google. Instead, he had joined FrontSpark.

"Here at FrontSpark, we have a mission; our mission is to help businesses be successful, and we want to start that mission internally by helping our employees be successful. Success is a choice." Ulysses walked around his desk and sat on its edge directly in front of Ben. "So I have to ask you, do you want to be successful?" Ben watched Ulysses. Ben thought that Ulysses could not have been more than ten years older than him. But Ben was the one interviewing, and Ulysses was the CEO of his own company. Ben was in awe, if not a little intimidated.

Ben moved uncomfortably in his chair and said, "I think so."

"You think or are you going to choose to be successful?" Ulysses asked with a slight tinge of irritation in his voice.

"I … choose to be successful," Ben eked out.

"Good … Good … Good," Ulysses said, walking back around his desk towards his chair. "The team here likes you; I read all their feedback, and they recommend we hire you. What do you think about that?"

Ben raised his eyebrows. His interviews had been brutal, with lots of coding and system design problems. Behavioral and situational interviews had stumped him. They asked him odd questions like: "What would you do if you had a conflict with your manager?" or "When did you take a risk, make a mistake, or fail? How did you respond, and how did you grow from that experience?" Ben did not know how to respond to some of those questions. In his last job, his current manager, Ron, was a nice guy with whom Ben never had any conflict with. He also had not taken many risks in his career. He primarily built websites for small businesses.

"I think that's great," Ben finally responded.

"You start this upcoming Monday," Ulysses said as he sat down and proceeded to sign off on some form.

Ben looked at the calendar app on his phone. It was Tuesday.

"But ... but ..." Ben stammered. "I need time to pack my things and find a place to live out here."

"You start this Monday. Any issues?" Ulysses looked at Ben.

"No," Ben said, resigned. "No issues at all."

#

At 8 a.m. on the dot—Ulysses hates when anyone is late—Ben logs into the meeting and waits for the other recipients. Ulysses, Dave Harold, and Mark Fischer are already on the Zoom call, making small talk and laughing. Ben tunes them out and reviews his notes again. Maybe he should have met with Ulysses before this meeting. He has a lot to say.

A few minutes later, Ben sees on his screen:

Pavlov and Demetri joined the meeting.

Jason Whire joined the meeting.

There is a brief moment of polite hellos and quick introductions. Ben is looking at his screen and sees Dave Harold, their head of legal, dressed as always in his three-

70

piece suit, even though he is working from home. Ulysses in his usual polo shirt, Mark Fischer in his v-neck t-shirt and a motorcycle jacket. On the NikNak side is Jason Whire, their COO, dressed in a white button-down. Sitting somewhat awkwardly together are two young Anglo-Slavic-looking men in t-shirts. They both look about twenty-five, maybe a few years younger or older. The one who introduced himself as Demetri has long black hair, a thin-shaped mouth, and small eyes. The other, Pavlov, has short-cropped blonde hair on the side and long-styled locks slicked back on the top. They both look tired.

Ulysses clears his throat. "Gentlemen, welcome." He holds out his hands in a welcoming gesture. "I am Ulysses Cawford, President and CEO of FrontSpark. For those unaware of what we do, let me give a quick introduction." Ulysses places his hands beneath the table, cracking his knuckles. Ben has to keep himself from smiling, as this is a common thing Ulysses does before starting a meeting.

"I started FrontSpark with a mission: A mission to help others achieve their dreams." Ulysses shares his screen and starts his presentation. Ben tunes out for a few minutes as he has heard this speech numerous times.

"What is FrontSpark?" Ulysses asks. "Well, to put it simply, we are your partners, your consul, your navigator, your technical guide to help you achieve your goals."

Pavlov coughs.

"Now, I am sure the biggest question you have on your minds is: Why FrontSpark? Well, to put it quite simply: Do you want to navigate these murky waters alone, or would you rather have an experienced partner who can guide, advise and provide all the tools, partnerships, and know-how to take your company to the next level? From what Jason has told me…." Ulysses nods at Jason; Jason nods back. "You would like to take your company public? He feels that you have the users, the revenue, and the technical know-how to do that. What you lack is the experience and possibly the connections to ensure success. That is where we come in." Ulysses pauses and lets his words sink in.

"FrontSpark can provide you with legal counsel, access to brokers, and full access to our talented engineering team to help you scale. We also provide a full security review, so you don't get hacked or DDOS'd before or after you go public. It is a long road ahead going from a private company to a publicly traded one, and FrontSpark is just the partner you need."

Pavlov leans over and whispers something to Demetri, who nods and chuckles.

"Now, gentlemen," Ulysses continues, not breaking stride. "Please fully introduce yourselves and tell us how FrontSpark can help you." He nods to the camera, presumably at Demetri and Pavlov.

Jason speaks first and says, "Ulysses, thank you for the introduction, my name is Jason Whire, and I am the Chief Operating Officer at NikNak." Jason pauses for a second as if his name means something. "Demetri and Pavlov approached me over a year ago and asked me to join their company to help take their product to the next level. Under my guidance and their leadership, we now rank in the top fifty actively visited sites according to Alexa.com; we have become a top five app on both the Apple and Google Play app stores.

Organically we have achieved over 200 million unique monthly active users and over 300 million registered users worldwide. Daily our users spend 128 minutes on the app. The app has been downloaded almost half a billion times."

Ben perks up. He knew NikNak was big but did not expect those numbers.

"When Demetri and Pavlov hired me, my first question to them was: What do you want to achieve with this?" Jason pauses. "Their answer was simple. They want the world's most profitable, popular, free-thinking, user-generated content and social media app on the planet. I then asked: How do they plan on achieving this? Their reply was: Help us go public, and we will figure it out along the way." Jason throws back his head and lets out a big laugh.

Ben checks Ulysses' feed and observes him smiling and nodding his head. *He must be loving this,* Ben thinks.

"Ulysses and I met a while back—whose party did we meet at, Ulysses?" Jason asks.

"I believe it was at Bobby's house ... his holiday party," Ulysses clarifies.

"Yes ... Yes, that's right," Jason continues. "Anyways, I was impressed with Ulysses. His introduction to Bobby Chitz, whose video compression technology was the key turning point to making NikNak ultra-successful. NikNak is one of the proprietors of said license, and it has proven to be the golden ticket that allows NikNak to compete with the big boys."

"H.V.300," Pavlov says aloud.

"Excuse me, Pavlov?" Jason pauses.

"H.V.300 is the name of the video compression technology." Ben notices Pavlov had a thick Slavic accent. It reminds him of a bouncer at a club he used to visit or a bad guy in a movie.

"Yes ... Yes, H.V.300, thank you, Pavlov," Jason continues. "Ulysses and I have kept in touch over the years. When I landed this position, I contacted Ulysses to see if we could arrange a meet and greet that could potentially lead to a lucrative partnership for all involved. Demetri?"

"Thank you, Jason," Demetri breaks in. "Hello all, my name is Demetri Sokolov. I am the President and CEO of NikNak."

Ben notices that while Pavlov has a thick accent, Demetri has none. Ben leans forward.

"For those unaware of the history of NikNak, it started when Pavlov and I were working for YouTube. I was the Product Owner for the Content Creation team, and Pavlov was the Lead Engineer of that team. Daily, we had to field complaints from content creators on an ever-changing restrictive ecosystem that the higher-ups were imposing on us. We got questions like: 'Why was my video removed?', or 'Why can I not post this content?' Generally, we responded that it broke our User Guidelines or Terms of Service, but increasingly this felt unsatisfactory to us. Our breaking point was when one user sent us a sad email complaining that her channel of over one million subscribers had suddenly been permanently banned because she breached the T.O.S.

"When I reviewed her content, I found one video where she was trying on lingerie and providing ratings for those items, which the company had deemed inappropriate. She went from making thousands a month to being completely cut off financially and creatively. I went to Pavlov and complained. We both moved to this country at a young age. We thought the United States of America was the land of the free, where people could express themselves freely and not be beholden to government or organizational regulations. When the pandemic hit, Pavlov and I spent a few hours on the phone that day. We talked about the company we worked for and how we felt we could do a better job. The next day, Pavlov and I quit and started our own company. We decided from day one that all content would be deregulated and allow any freedom of expression within reason. That day was over three years ago. We named the company after one of our favorite American childhood songs, NikNak."

Ben sang the familiar lyrics of the song in his head:

> *"This old man he played one,*
> *He played nick nack on my drum,*
> *With a nick nack paddy whack,*
> *Give a dog a bone,*
> *This old man came rolling home."*

"Today," Demetri continues, "Pavlov and I have built one of the fastest-growing apps in the world. We have a decentralized, deregulated ecosystem that allows our content creators to express themselves fully without fear of retribution or de-platforming. We have a subscription-based service that is not beholden to advertisers. We are currently profitable and looking to take the business to the next level by going public. That's where you and your team come in—"

Ben briefly thinks of Jinni's suicide video, and her eyes rolled into the back of her head.

"Decentralized and deregulated?" Ben interrupts. "How?"

Demetri stares at his screen. "Sorry, who asked that question?"

"Demetri, that is Ben White. He is our Director of Engineering here at FrontSpark," Ulysses chimes in. "Ben, maybe hold the question until the end?"

"No, that is fine," Demetri interjects, visibly annoyed. "Ben, what was your question?"

"I was asking how is your site decentralized and deregulated?" Ben asks again.

"Sure, Ben, I was getting to that." Demetri looks over at Pavlov and rolls his eyes. "As I said, Pavlov and I built this site with one core philosophy: freedom of expression. Most sites like YouTube have a problem; they host your content on their servers when you upload. This makes them liable for the content you produce. As a content creator, you are beholden to their terms and agreements. You are also beholden to their advertisers. If you are too controversial or extreme, YouTube will demonetize or age-restrict you. If you violate that, they have the right to remove your content or, in extreme cases, ban your channel outright." Demetri pauses, letting his words set in.

"So I asked Pavlov what happens if we remove the hosting and advertising aspect of the platform. What happens if we become the framework and provide the tools and access, but the content hosting is decentralized across all our users? Does that problem go away?" Demetri looks at his partner.

"The problem goes away," Pavlov replies sternly.

"Thank you, Pavlov." Demetri nods at his partner. "For those who don't know, sitting to my right is Pavlov Josef, probably one of the most talented engineers and system architects I have ever had the pleasure to work with. He is our Chief Technical Officer and is the true genius behind NikNak."

"Question," Ben speaks up. Even over a virtual call, he can feel Ulysses' eyes boring holes into him. "If you don't host content on your servers, where is the content hosted?"

Pavlov reaches into his pocket and pulls out his phone. "This," he replies in his thick Slavic accent. "This is where the content is hosted."

Pavlov went on to explain the complex infrastructure of NikNak. Pavlov explains that everyone who downloads the app would reserve a certain amount of space to host their content and other individuals' content based on its popularity, location and need. With the H.V.300 compression algorithm, the content could be hyper-compressed, allowing high-quality video to be stored without needing dedicated storage servers.

"In conclusion," continues Pavlov, "we have created the market's first decentralized video-sharing platform." He looks at Demetri and gives him a nod. Demetri smiles and nods back.

"Thank you, Pavlov," Ulysses begins. "Demetri, you mentioned profitability. Do you want to tell us about your income streams?"

"Of course, Ulysses, I was just getting to that," Demetri replies. "Most accounts have a private and public channel. If a user posts to the public channel, the content will be available to all registered and unregistered users on the platform. Some of our content creators focus exclusively on the public channel, where they secure lucrative brand deals and such. Where things get interesting is our use of private channels. The content creator can assign a subscription model or pay-to-play to their private channel and videos, which we call Naks. We act as the payment broker and take a small percentage of each fee."

Pavlov begins talking and says, "Each of our private channels is encrypted, and the act of subscribing causes a key exchange for accessing that channel—"

"Question," Ben interrupts. "Who holds the encryption keys?"

"The channel owner," Pavlov clarifies. "They download and store it on their devices."

"Then you don't have access to the private channels?" Ben asks, shocked.

Ulysses is staring daggers at Ben.

"You are correct," Pavlov states nonchalantly. "That was the plan all along. We want to give the users full control over their content. Even Demetri and I cannot see what is in these private channels unless the channel admin grants us access."

"But ... aren't you concerned that your content creators might be doing something..." Ben searches for the right word. "Illicit?"

Pavlov and Demetri look at each other.

"No, Ben," Demetri answers. "What users do in their private channel is like what you do in your home. None of anyone's business. That is the NikNak philosophy."

Ben lets out a deep breath and starts rubbing the back of his neck. He fully understands what these two have created. It is perilous. He starts to Slack Ulysses.

Ben: *Are you sure you want to get into bed with these guys?*

Ulysses: *Why not? They could be the next big thing, and we are on the ground floor.*

Ben: *What they are doing could be dangerous.*

Ulysses: *Calm down, and stop messaging me! I am trying to listen.*

"... and we currently have over ten million subscribers paying on average five-and-a-half dollars per month in subscriptions," Demetri says; Ben returns his attention to the conversation. "We are growing at ten million new users and about half a million paid subscribers per month."

Ben's mind flashes to Jinni lying dead on the sidewalk.

"Demetri, thank you for that amazing presentation and overview," Ulysses says when Demetri is done. "Let me go over some of the ways FrontSpark can help you—" Ulysses goes into his usual spiel. Ben zones out. His chest is pounding, and beads of sweat are forming on his forehead. Ulysses is talking about FrontSpark, but all Ben hears is "Blah blah blah."

"... so we can offer you access to private investors and our legal team," Ulysses says, nodding at Dave. "Access to an in-house marketing team, and until you get your hiring in order, we can provide access to a talented engineering and security team to help you with any scaling problems. Ben heads up our Engineering and Security team." Ulysses gives Ben a dark look.

"We don't need any fucking engineering team." Pavlov hisses quietly. Ulysses' face goes white.

"Ulysses, Mark, David, and Ben … Thank you all," Jason says, nodding to each individual. "We can all agree that this is a mutually beneficial arrangement for all parties involved—"

"Question!" Ben interrupts.

Ulysses closes his eyes and clenches his hand into fists. He begins to type on his keyboard.

"Sure, what is it?" Demetri asks.

A message comes to Ben's screen.

Ulysses: *Stop asking FUCKING QUESTIONS!*

Ben ignores that and continues, "A friend of mine showed me a video of what appears to be an underage girl dancing in her underwear; her name is—" Ben looks at his notes. "Her name is Kitty Josephine."

Pavlov mutters something to Demetri, who nods and laughs. Ben could not hear what they were saying; he could only make out the word: Kitty. Pavlov smiles and covers his mouth.

"Ben, we are aware of this user. She has over twenty thousand paid subscribers. She has become very successful on our platform. What is your question?" Demetri asks.

"Also, one of my friends committed suicide last week, and someone happened to film her death," Ben states. "Do you not worry about the backlash this sort of content will bring?"

"First, sorry for your loss," replies Demetri. "Second, I don't think you understand what we do here. We only provide the platform. The content creators own their content." Demetri leans forward, emphasizing his point. "We are protected by Title 47, Section 230. Your lawyer here," he says, motioning towards Dave, "can explain if you don't understand what that is."

"That won't be necessary," Ulysses butts in. "Dave here has done a full legal review. Dave?"

"We in the legal department find no issues with the Terms of Use or Service that NikNak provides." Dave removes his glasses and starts wiping them with his shirt, signifying that he is done talking.

The conversation goes quiet for a second before Jason speaks. "I need to have a private chat with my colleagues. We will drop off and join in about five minutes." With that, all their screens go blank.

"What the fuck was that!" Ulysses hisses at Ben.

"What? You asked me to vet them, so I did," Ben replies defensively.

"Vet them from a technical standpoint, not a legal one. Dave." Dave looks up at his screen. "Explain to Ben what the fuck Section 230 is."

"Sure," Dave places his glasses back on his head. "Section 230 says that: No provider or user of an interactive computer service shall be treated as the publisher or speaker of any information provided by another information content provider." Dave takes his glasses off his head, glares at them, and continues to wipe them with his shirt. "In layman's terms, companies such as NikNak are protected against a range of laws that might otherwise be used to hold them legally responsible for what others say and do." With a satisfying nod, Dave stares at his glasses again and places them back on his face.

"Given the sheer size of user content created websites and applications," Dave continues. "It would be deemed infeasible for online intermediaries to prevent objectionable content from being uploaded to their site." Dave scratches the side of his head. "So Demetri is correct in saying they are protected by Section 230 from a legal standpoint. From a moral standpoint, that's a different story, but we in Legal don't do moral standpoints." Dave breaks into loud laughter. Ben leans back into his chair, defeated.

Ulysses chimes in, "Are we good here, Ben?"

"Yes," Ben replies softly.

"Five minutes are almost up, and they will be back online soon; please shut your fucking mouth so we can close the deal, ok, buddy?"

"Ok."

"Great—here they come." Ulysses sits up straighter and adjusts his shirt. "Gentlemen, welcome back ... so can we proceed forward?"

Ben spends the rest of the call thinking about Jinni. He never got the chance to do his presentation.

Ben messages Ulysses after the meeting to let him know he still is not feeling well and will take the rest of the day off.

Fine, Ulysses replies.

Ben felt fine; he was just annoyed at how the meeting went. He also knew Ulysses would be okay with him taking the day off, inspired by the malcontent with his performance. They had closed a massive deal for the company, and Ulysses was on cloud nine. Ben could have asked if he could fuck

Ulysses's sister, and the response would have been the same: *Fine*.

Ben sits on the couch, bored. He discovers he is exhausted and decides to lie down. He turns on his side, reaches into his pockets, and retrieves his phone. He holds it for a minute, caressing the angular lines of the device. He feels sleepy. He unlocks his phone and opens up the NikNak app. On the landing page are various videos. He scrolls through the feed, seeing various previews of different things. Some are pretty young girls asking viewers to subscribe to their private channels, others appear to be funny short skits, and others still seem to be serious discussions about one cinematic universe or another.

Ben taps through the feed, occasionally stopping to watch a few of the Naks. Some are quite clever. A few even make him laugh. Many are funny skits on various races, religions, and topical content. There are these weird question-and-response videos where a question is asked, and some other users attempt to answer the question without stating the question. Ben is impressed by some of the inventive responses.

Every so often, a Nak will appear, an enticement to join a private channel. Primarily these are young women and a few men, speaking in sultry voices, sparsely clothed, asking the patron to sign up for their private channels. Ben can not guess the ages of these creators. He thinks some are over eighteen, but others look much younger. Ben continues to go through the feed; it is almost 4 p.m. when he looks up again.

"I can see why this app is so popular," he mutters to an empty room, rubbing his eyes. He considers getting up from the comfortable couch and making a late lunch, but he does not move.

"C'mon, Ben, old buddy, old pal, you know what you want to look at," he says quietly. He scrolls to the search bar and types in some words. When the search results return, he finds the Nak he is looking for; he takes a deep breath; he clicks on it.

The familiar pan down from the sky shot, and the song that Ben could not place emerges. It is quite a catchy song; he admits as he hums along. After a few seconds, the dancing girl appears. The camera zooms in and out on her. She lip-synchs to the song perfectly, dancing to the beats. At one point, she grabs her knees and proceeds to rock her hips up and down in a rhythmic motion. Ben notices something behind them.

"What!" Ben screams. He snaps straight up on the couch. He pauses the Nak. He sees the playback slider on the bottom of the screen and uses his finger to go back a few seconds. Holding that position, he arrives at the frame that has stunned him. Deep in the background of the video is a middle-aged man wearing a baby blue t-shirt and pajama bottoms. He is looking dumbly around with a drunken red face. Ben squints at the blurry image in the background. He knows who that person is. One can always recognize themselves. Ben blinks in confusion.

A brief vibration starts at the tip of his finger. Ben looks down at his hand and realizes he is still holding the playback slider, locking it into its current position. The vibration gets stronger and stronger. *Ok ... Ok,* Ben thinks as he closes his eyes.

The bright light hits him first. He squints, turns his head, and lifts his hand to block the sunlight. After a few seconds, his eyes adjust to the light. Ben takes stock of where he is. Directly in front of him are the two girls he had seen before. This time he is behind the camera girl. The other girl is dancing and singing ahead of them. Ben freezes in place. He moves to the left and stares beyond the two. He spots what he is looking for.

About twenty to thirty yards in front of him is "him." Comically, the other "Ben" is stuttering, lost in what is happening to him. Ben wants to laugh, but seeing himself look so lost and helpless, he quickly stifles that. Ben looks up at the tall building to his right. The setting sun is directly in his eyes, so he moves his hand to block it. As the sunspots disappear, he can make out a broken silhouette of a thin female standing ten stories above him on the roof's edge.

Ben freezes.

He wants to shout at her and call out her name, but he just stands there. He looks at the girls and then back up. Jinni turns around, so her back is now showing. She lifts her arms like a diver about to perform a complicated dive. Her gold jacket gleams in the sunlight. She leans her shoulder back and proceeds to let gravity do its work. He can hear a "Haay … Haay!" from a familiar voice.

Ben watches her fall. He looks at his feet and tries to will them to move. His feet stay planted. His eyes follow her, watching her accelerate in the air and following her graceful arc until she hits the ground.

Ben flinches as he hears the sound of her hitting the ground. Again it reminds him of a watermelon being smashed open. He watches the ensuing carnage, the girls screaming. He looks behind the chaos and sees himself lying on the sidewalk with a befuddled, confused look.

"I feel you, buddy," Ben mutters quietly. He can hear the girls screaming and one shouting, "Makena! Stop filming and call 9-1..." Ben closes his eyes and holds his breath.

When he opens them again, he is back in the living room, sitting on the couch in the same position as before. His chest aches, and he finds it hard to breathe. He puts his hand over his heart to slow it down. After a few minutes, his heart slows down. He looks down at his phone.

Nak by:
@koryBrewer
11,420,876 views
1,232,234 Niks
NikNak©

Ben scrolls down to the comments. After reviewing a few, he finds the one he is looking for.

@dababysneezes: *Y'all see the idiot in the background omegaLUL!*

"I did see him, @dababysneezes," Ben says softly. "I did."

#

Ben is having a nightmare. In his dream, he is standing on a sidewalk, looking up. On top of the building is Jinni's silhouette. Every time he tries to call out to her, nothing comes out. He slowly watches her silhouette turn around and fall back to the ground. He tries to run and catch her, but his feet are cemented to the ground. He tugs at one of his legs, trying to force it free. He watches as she plummets and smacks the ground, and then the dream rewinds to her back on the roof. It is like being stuck in an old VHS tape. A high-pitched squeaking rewinding sound would play, accompanied by squiggly black and white lines across his vision. When it is done, the dream repeats. Ben is stuck in the same spot, repeatedly watching the silhouette leap to her death. Fall, rewind. Fall, smack, rewind. Fall, smack, rewind. Before he wakes, he hears Jinni's voice.

"I always thought you would be the one to save me."

Ben jumps awake.

He looks at his phone, the display says 6:30 a.m. He wipes his forehead and finds it wet with sweat. Flopping his legs over the side of the bed, he turns on the bedside lamp. He rubs his face as he stands up. He walks towards the kitchen, turning on several lights as he walks. He can make out the sunrise creeping over the horizon. He grabs his electric kettle. Filling it with water from the sink, he plugs it in and flips the switch. He sits in his small dining chair and stares at the wall.

What are you staring at? His mother's voice plays in his head.

Nothing is Ben's usual reply. In truth, he liked to stare at the wall and zone out at times. It helped him to think about nothing for a minute. Blissfully stare at the wall. This time, though, his mind will not go blank. The images of his dream dance like a fire in his head. He tries to blank his mind, but his brain stubbornly will not let go.

The sound of the kettle boiling breaks him out of his trance. He gets up, grabs a cup, and makes himself some tea.

Ulysses calls him on Zoom at 9 a.m.

Ulysses starts, "Feeling better?"

"Yes," Ben replies.

"Great … Anyways, it's time to get to work. Jason emailed us today with the signed contract. I am having Dave review it this morning, and it all is copacetic; we begin tomorrow."

"That's great news, Ulysses."

"It is, isn't it." Ben watches Ulysses crack his back. "I am going to go do some yoga. Can you get in touch with Pavlov later today? After the debacle of questions yesterday, a little discord would do us well. Thanks, Ben." With that, he ends the call. Ben frowns and goes through his laptop, looking for Pavlov's email address.

The next few days are hectic for Ben. He has a few chats with Pavlov, and the increased incessant calls from Ulysses keep him very busy.

"Ben, Demetri is concerned with the security review and the prevalence of bad actors—" Ulysses states nervously.

"Ben, Pavlov is concerned with your scaling projections and what that means for the confluence of our two organizations—" Ulysses says with grave concern.

"Ben, Jason has some concerns with your proposed changes and what negative implications it will have on him and his cohorts—" Ulysses says in a panic.

And on and on it goes. By the end of the week, Ben is so tense that he grabs a pillow off his couch and screams into it.

Discord, cohort, confluence, actors. Ben increasingly can not stand Ulysses' continuous abuse of "Office Speak." *Just say what you mean, in plain easy to understand English*! Ben would often shout to himself when talking to Ulysses. When

Friday arrives, and Ben can finally take a moment to breathe, he realizes that he has not touched his phone all week other than answering Ulysses' calls. No videos were watched, no texts were replied to, and no social media notifications were viewed. He cradles his smartphone like a dead bird and walks to his kitchen table.

Pausing for a second, he unlocks his phone and opens the NikNak app. He scrolls through a few posts and sees pretty girls dancing (and advertising their "private" channels) and some reasonably funny videos of different users answering a question proposed by other users. (He particularly liked the one that asked: "Tell me how you are undateable, without telling me how undateable you are.")

A particular post makes him lean forward with attention. A skinny kid in a "Star Wars" shirt explains the different types of time travel:

"The first and most common form of time travel is the 'Fixed Timeline.' This is seen in movies such as *The Terminator* and *Harry Potter*." Short video clips of each movie follow this. "Basically, in this type of time travel," the skinny kid continues, "what has happened will always happen, and you can't change the future by changing the past.

"The next type of time travel is called the 'Dynamic Timeline.' This is seen in the movie *Back to the Future*." A short clip of the movie plays. "In this type of time travel, past actions have a definite impact on the present. So if you go back in time and kill your parents before you were born, you will fade out of existence since you were never born.

"And the final type of time travel is called the 'Multiverse.' This is seen in the movie *Avengers: Endgame*. This is where the act of time travel forces the universe into a different trajectory than the one you experienced before time travel." The skinny kid smiles. "I think the Hulk said it best: 'If you travel to the past, that past becomes your future, and your former present becomes the past which can't now be changed by your new future.'" The skinny kid laughs. "Hope you all learned something today. Don't forget to Nik, comment, and subscribe. I'm out, peace!" He flashes a "peace" symbol with his fingers, and the video ends. Ben frowns after watching the Nak. He feels the kid is missing something, but his mind cannot comprehend what.

Ben shuts down the app and leans back in his chair. A single thought had been occurring to him all week. He can not get the idea out of his head.

He shrugs and gets up off of his chair. He walks into his room and changes out of his work clothes and into his jeans. He puts on his best athletic shoes and a plain black T-shirt. He then walks back to his desk and grabs his phone. He reaches the middle of his living room, opens the NikNak app, and searches. When he finds the Nak he is looking for, he watches it. He takes a deep breath and presses firmly on the bottom of the screen. He closes his eyes.

CHAPTER 9 - AFK

The sunlight blinds Ben. He blinks his eyes open and takes a look around. His heart is thudding hard in his chest, but he calms down when he realizes his "second" is not there. Ben considers that and then realizes that the second time he "superimposed" in, the camera never captured him.

Directly in front of him is the dancing girl and her cinematographer, blasting the same music to the song that he did not know. *I should find out the name of the song,* he thinks. He quickly peers around them to see if his "first" is still there. He sees himself stumbling around in his pajamas. Ben notices that "first" Ben's face is red and puffy. The "first" Ben's eyes had dark circles around them as if he had not slept well in a while. A moment of sadness comes over Ben, but he quickly shakes it off and gets to his task.

He looks up and prepares himself—

Ben's favorite teacher in 9th grade was his Physics teacher Mr. Pettit. He had a graying beard, a chalky voice, and a glint of mischief in his eyes. Ben was fond of him. He generally hated most of his subjects in school and was not the best student, but he did well in Mr. Pettit's class. Ben could listen for hours to Mr. Pettit talking about Kepler's and Newton's laws. Mr. Pettit could even make angular momentum sound interesting.

One day in class, Mr. Pettit handed back an exam they had taken the previous day. Ben looked at Mr. Pettit's face as he placed the exam paper face down on his desk. Ben tried to read his expression to determine whether or not he got a good grade. Ben slowly flipped the paper. At the top was the score of 90%, circled in red. Ben silently pumped his fist. It was the first 'A' he had gotten all year. He did not even care if it was technically an 'A-'. He scanned the ten-problem test sheet, and on the final question, a red line was scratched through his answer. Below that, scrawled in red ink, were the words: "See me after class - Mr. P." Ben scrunched up his face, confused at the request. Teachers only asked you to see them when you did poorly. This was not the first time he had gotten the dreaded message on a test or quiz. But it was the first time he had gotten it on a test that was technically an 'A'.

Ben spent the whole class dreading the ending bell. *What does Mr. Pettit want to see me about?* he thought. His newfound pride in his grade slowly slipped into dread. *Does he think I cheated?* Ben wondered. *Surely Mr. Pettit doesn't think that.* He had heard stories of other students who purposely got at least one or two questions wrong while cheating to draw any suspicion away. Ben had studied hard for this test. He liked his physics class and felt compelled to do well. His hands started getting sweaty, and his stomach started tying itself into a knot. Ben looked up at the clock and realized he had forty minutes until the class was over. He let out a deep sigh and sat patiently at his desk, growing more nervous as he watched the seconds tick away.

After what seemed like hours instead of forty minutes, the class bell finally rang. Ben jumped in his seat, startled by the sound. His classmates gathered their things and prepared to leave. Mr. Pettit shouted out one final instruction that Ben did not hear. His heartbeat was pounding too loud in his ears. Ben gathered his things when most of his classmates were out the door and approached Mr. Pettit's desk.

"Uh, Mr. Pettit—" Ben said meekly as he cleared his throat. Mr. Pettit nodded towards the desk directly in front of him without looking up from the notes he was writing. Ben turned around and slowly slid into the desk.

After a few moments of silence, Ben blurted out: "Mr. Pettit, I didn't cheat on the test!" Strong emotions swept over Ben. He could feel the tears well up in his eyes. He did not know why he was so upset; maybe it was because the only teacher in his school he liked thought he was a cheater. Perhaps it was because, after a year of C's and D's, he had finally gotten a grade he was proud of, and now Mr. Pettit wanted to take that away. Ben could see Mr. Pettit's eyebrows raise before he lifted his face to reveal a smile. The smile turned into a chuckle.

"Ben, I know you didn't cheat on that test. That is not why I asked you to see me," Mr. Pettit said between smiles.

"Then why did you ask me to see you?" Ben asked defensively.

Mr. Pettit removed his thin-framed glasses and placed them on the desk. He clasped his hands in front of him and leaned forward. "I double as the school counselor here at Pacific Coast. With that role, I am privy to seeing all the students enrolled here and can look up their grades." Mr. Pettit reached into his drawer and pulled at a gray cloth. He began wiping his glasses lens with it. "You have always done well in my class, mostly getting B's and a few C's, but with the last test, you have gotten your first A. Every time I grade one of your tests, I shake my head in frustration." Mr. Pettit shook his head to emphasize this.

"I always say to myself, 'Wow, if Ben had taken a little more time and thought this through, he would have come up with the correct solution.'" Mr. Pettit placed one of his glasses lenses into his mouth, huffed out some hot air, and continued wiping.

"When I was grading your last test, I was excited. I was like, finally, Ben is going to do it; he's going to get a 100 percent!" Mr. Pettit motioned at Ben to hand over his test. Ben opened his notebook and passed the test to him. Mr. Pettit took the test from Ben's hand and flipped it towards him. He put his glasses back on and frowned at the paper in his hands.

"When I got to the final question, I knew it would be wrong before I even looked over it. You see, Ben, when you rush into a problem and try to solve it, you scribble hard and fast. All the other questions were written neat and tidy, but the last one—" He turned the page towards Ben and tapped the question at the bottom with his index finger. "The last one I could tell you rushed through without thinking about it." Mr. Pettit handed the test back to Ben.

Ben sat dumbfounded. He looked down at the test and tried to recall taking it. He remembered starting slow, double-checking his work on the first few questions. After they were done, he realized he had a firm understanding of the material, and all his studying was paying off. With a chuckle, he breezed through the next set of questions. When he got to the last one, his overconfidence was brimming, and he remembered rushing through that one, standing up, and confidently turning in the test.

"Like I was saying," Mr. Pettit continued. "Being a school counselor allows me to look up any grades of any student that attends here. After I graded that test, I pulled up yours. I thought to myself, 'Ben is probably one of those smart lazy students who get B's in all his classes when he should have all A's.'" Mr. Pettit puts his hands behind his head and leans back in his chair. He stares at Ben and continues.

"I was shocked, Ben, shocked to find out that you are getting C's in most of your classes, and you even have a D in math. This class is keeping your GPA at 2.0." Silence filled the room. Ben tried to talk, but no words came out of his mouth.

"You know, you remind me of my wife." Mr. Pettit rotated the ring on his finger. "She always liked to rush into things without thinking them through." Mr. Petit started to laugh. "Once she joined one of those pyramid scheme product things, I came home to a living room filled with boxes." Mr. Petit started laughing harder; he lifted his glasses to wipe the side of his eyes with his hand. "I said, 'Rose, how are you going to sell all this stuff?'" Mr. Pettit shook his head. "She said, 'Petty, don't you worry about it; I'll figure it out as I go along.'" Mr. Pettit slapped his knee as he laughed harder.

Ben sat there in silence; he felt like he was eavesdropping on a private conversation instead of being the center of it.

"You know what's funny?" Mr. Pettit looked at Ben, his face was slightly red, and his mouth was wide open. Ben shook his head uncomfortably. "Those boxes are still in the garage!" Mr. Pettit broke into hysterical laughter. He doubled over in his chair.

Ben was smiling uncomfortably, still not understanding what he was doing here.

After a few moments, Mr. Pettit calmed down and continued the conversation.

"The point I am trying to get out here is that you tend to rush into things without thinking. You knew the answer to the last question, but instead of sitting back and taking your time, you jumped right in and rushed to a solution. So please, in the future, take your time, and think things through; your life will be better for it."

Ben nodded in agreement and started to rise to his feet. He kept eyeing Mr. Pettit to see if his teacher had anything more to say. He quietly slinked out of the room. When he was about to exit, he looked back at Mr. Pettit, who now had his feet on his desk and was smiling and muttering. Ben could only make out a few words before he exited.

"Oh, Rose…" Mr. Pettit said with a chuckle and a shake of the head. "Oh, Rose."

Ben found out later that Mr. Pettit's wife had died of cancer years ago.

#

As soon as Ben looks up, the sunlight blinds him. He blocks the sun with his hand and tries to orient himself. He curses himself for not starting a countdown as he remembers he has but a few seconds before everything would be over. He shields his eyes with his hands and looks up. He can barely make out a silhouette of Jinni standing on the roof's edge. Her arms are stretched out in a T formation. Ben moves forward, keeping his eyes on her. He can see Jinni tuck her chin into her body and fall backward.

Ben moves quickly. He feels like an outfielder trying to catch a fly ball. He keeps his eyes on her as she falls quicker and quicker to the ground. He bumps into the girl filming, knocking her to the ground. He can hear a "What the hell!" come out of her mouth as he quickly pushes past her. He steps around the singing girl and moves in behind her. Ben has his arms stretched like a wide receiver trying to catch an over-the-shoulder pass. He is shuffling his feet in an attempt to stay under Jinni. One of the girls gasps. Ben ignores it and positions himself...

When Ben returns back to his apartment, he recalls Mr. Pettit's words. "Think things through, Ben, don't rush into things." Jinni had hit his arms going upwards of sixty miles an hour. She has broken both his forearms and dislocated his shoulders. Her sudden stop when she hit his arms ended up snapping and breaking her neck.

Ben looks down at her; his arms are bent the wrong way at his forearms. He looks down and sees Jinni lying by his feet, choking on her blood. Only one of her eyes is moving, and the other is filled with blood. She looks at Ben. She mouths his name before convulsing into shock. He stands there in disbelief. The dancing girl is screaming at the camera girl to stop filming and call 911. Ben can't hear them. He keeps staring at Jinni as the world around him disappears, and then he is standing in the middle of his living room with two badly broken and bleeding arms. His arms and shoulder scream in pain, and blood is pouring out of the wounds.

#

Ben opens his eyes. He is in the dark, surrounded by white and green lights and the occasional beeping. He panics as he tries to compute where he is. He attempts to pull himself into a sitting position, but his arms will not comply. His eyes start adjusting to the dark, and a cold white hospital room emerges around him. Ben starts piecing together how he got here.

He recalls standing in his living room in immense pain. Halfway up his forearms, he can see bones protruding from his skin, and his forearms bent at an awkward angle. He remembers seeing his phone by his feet and not being able to grab it with his hands as his fingers were not responding to his commands. In a moment of panic, he gets on his knees and prostrates himself on top of his phone. After a few panicked tries, he unlocked his phone (thank god for facial recognition) and used voice commands to call 911 (thank god for voice recognition). After that, his memory is blank.

Ben looks around the room. He is in a small, clean white bed, his forearms in thick plaster. He is tightly tucked under white covers, and his feet are parallel to the bed. His neck hurts as he tries to move his head to look around. Keeping his head as straight as possible, he rolls his eyes to see a clear plastic line protruding from his biceps. Without moving his head, he follows the tube to an IV bag above him, slowly dripping liquid.

The door to his room opens, and before Ben can move his eyes to look, fluorescent overhead lights turn on. Instinctively, Ben tries to use his hand to shade his eyes but settles for shutting them instead.

"Mr. White, glad to see you're awake." Ben blinks through the light; his eyes focus on the doctor standing at the base of his bed. He is around Ben's height and has dark hair with a few streaks of white. The doctor leans down at the bottom of his bed, pulls out a chart, and begins tapping it with his pen.

"Vitals look good, BP also—" Beside the doctor is a black nurse with a short crop top that is bleached blonde. Sparkling in the light is her bright gold hoop earrings. Ben stares at them. As if sensing what Ben is observing, the doctor turns to the nurse.

"Yvonne, what did I tell you about those earrings?" he asks impatiently. The nurse defensively touches one with her hand. "One day, a cardiac patient will get caught up on those and rip them right off your ear!"

"Sorry, Doctor," the nurse replies sheepishly and removes her earrings. The doctor gives her a nod and returns to Ben's chart.

"Mr. White, I am Doctor Kamal. I am the resident on for the night." The doctor moves towards the side of the bed and sits. "When you arrived, we sedated you as you were in hypovolemic shock due to the loss of blood, and I can imagine the pain of two open fractures on your arms. We anesthetized and moved you to the O.R. We reset your bones, addressed your dislocated shoulders, and placed four pins in each of your arms to help the healing process." The doctor walks to the front of the bed and removes some X-rays from the base. He moves to the back wall and flicks a switch. A backlight comes on, and the doctor attaches the X-rays to them. He begins to talk about the surgery and what was done, but Ben is not listening. His mind keeps wandering, wondering if what happened did happen. The broken arms were more than enough evidence that it did, but he was not convinced.

"...so after placing the pin in the Radius and the Ulna, you can see that the break was aligned correctly, and you should heal normally. At first, we considered amputation since the accident happened so long ago, but after seeing no nerve, vein damage, or infection, we decided to go with the normal process." Satisfied, the doctor shuts off the backlight and places the X-rays back in their envelope.

"So," the doctor asks somberly. "Care to tell me what happened here?"

Wait! Ben's face contorted in confusion. *Did the doctor say "so long ago"?*

"How long have I been here?" Ben asks.

Dr. Kamal looks up from his charts and says, "You were checked in last night." He checks his watch. "A little over twenty-four hours ago."

"Then what did you mean when you said 'so long ago'?" Ben asks. Dr. Kamal looks at Ben strangely.

"Mr. White, I was under the impression that these injuries were sustained ... almost two weeks ago." Dr. Kamal looks through his charts as if he is trying to confirm that information.

"No, they happened yesterday," Ben says, even more confused.

"Ok ... I must have gotten some wrong information. Regardless, did you want to tell me what happened here?"

Ben thinks about it for a few seconds. He does not know what is going on. He decides it would be best to play dumb.

"I don't ... remember."

The doctor frowns.

"You don't remember? Mr. White, you came in with both your forearms broken and your shoulders dislocated. You were in shock, bleeding profusely from each arm, and you don't remember?" Ben can see the confusion on the doctor's face.

"I don't remember what happened," Ben replies meekly.

"Ok … fine, you have been through a lot." Dr. Kamal turns to the nurse. "We will let you rest. Nurse Yvonne." The nurse looks up from the medical devices she had been inspecting. "Make sure Mr. White here is comfortable and see to it he gets some exercise later today." She nods at the doctor. "Oh, and Mr. White, the paramedics brought in your phone; it's on the bedside table in the top drawer if you need it. We had to turn it off as it was buzzing incessantly." The doctor whips around and leaves the room.

Ben stares at the nurse, and she stares back at him. After a few seconds, she began to smile, and so did Ben. She checks his IV drip, pats the bed, and exits after the doctor.

Ben drifts off to sleep.

CHAPTER 10 - WYA

Ben wakes up a few hours later. He tests his arms. He finds he can barely move his fingers, but his shoulders scream in pain if he tries to move his arms. He carefully tosses his legs over the bed, stands up, and, with some difficulty, opens the top drawer where his phone is.

It takes him three minutes to muster the finger strength to hold the power button long enough to turn on the phone. Ben lays back in exhaustion after he hears the familiar "boop be boop" sound of his smartphone powering on. When his phone connects to the network, a flood of notifications pops on his screen. He has six new messages from Ulysses, seven from Yumi, three from Jeremy, and five from his mom. He also has over thirty missed calls. Ben ignores the messages and looks at the date. Two days have passed since he "superimposed" himself into Jinni's video. He still does not understand why Dr. Kamal said his injuries had happened over two weeks ago.

"Better to get the shitty messages out of the way first," Ben says to an empty hospital room. He opens his Messaging app and clicks on Ulysses' name. He gently places the phone on his chest and starts going through his messages. The first one was back-dated two weeks ago.

"What the fuck?" Ben says out loud. One thing Ulysses had trained him on was to answer his messages immediately. Ben reads his messages:

Ulysses: *You didn't check into today's meeting. Are you sick? Call me.*

Ulysses: *FYI we have a big deal in the works, contact me in the morning, and I'll fill you in. Big things are happening!*

Ulysses: *It's been a few days, and we are all worried about you. We have that big meeting next week. WHERE ARE YOU?*

Ulysses: *Ben, you have been gone for a week. Technically and lawfully, I can terminate you after three days of no-shows. Please call or text me if you get this.*

Ulysses: *Ben, it's been over a week. I spoke with your mom, and we decided to file a missing person report. We are worried about you, and this is serious. Please contact us!*

Ulysses: *The meeting went well, I am sorry I threatened your job, but we need you, buddy. Please contact us or the local authorities.*

Ben pauses for a second and thinks things through. *Why did Ulysses think he was gone for two weeks? I just spoke with him a few days ago. And what was this big meeting he was talking about? Was it about NikNak? I was there.*

Ben, still confused, decides to read the messages from Yumi. The first one is dated two weeks ago:

Yumi: *I don't know what the fuck is going on, but please call me.*

Yumi: *Ben WYA?*

Yumi: *Why Ben, WHY? What happened? I need to know.*

Yumi: *I don't know what happened or why. I don't know why you were there but why are you not answering me?*

Yumi: *What happened? Please tell me.*

Yumi: *Why were you there?????*

Yumi: *The funeral is tomorrow. Jinni would want you there. Please come.*

Yumi: *Why didn't you come, Ben? Why?*

Ben puts the phone down. He attempts to rub his eyes, but the pain in his shoulder and the heaviness of his arms won't let him. Raising his hands to his chest is the furthest he could go. He grabs his phone and reads the messages from his mother:

Mom: *Hello, I haven't heard from you in a while. Are you ok?*

Mom: *Ben, your boss called me to look for you. Is everything ok?*

Mom: *Ben, the cops came by the house today looking for you. Is everything ok?*

Mom: *Ben, please call me. I am worried!*

The door to his room opens, and the headache-inducing fluorescent light flickers back on. In walks two people. One is a middle-aged man with a receding hairline and reddish-brown hair. The other female is in her early thirties with long, carefully colored nails. They both have "SFPD" masks on their faces. They walk towards Ben's bed, each standing on one side. The man stares at Ben and talks.

"Are you Ben White of 237 3rd Street apartment 808?" the man asks.

Ben blinks the light away and says, "Yes."

"I'm Detective Karl Bateson, and this is my partner Detective Susan Gonzales. How are you, Mr. White?"

"Ok ... I guess." Ben's heart starts to beat faster. The machine he is hooked up to begins to beep.

"Great," Detective Bateson says. "May we ask you some questions?"

"What is this about?" Ben asks, baffled.

"Well," Detective Bateson says as he walks around the small room. "What do you think it's about?"

"I have no idea," Ben shakes his head.

The other detective speaks. "Two weeks ago, Ms. Jinni Yoon jumped off a building to her death. Were you at the scene, Mr. White?"

Ben did not know how to answer that question, so he stayed silent.

"It appeared you attempted to stop that from happening and suffered some collateral damage for your efforts," Detective Bateson adds, nodding towards Ben's arms.

Detective Gonzales throws her partner a look and continues, "Ms. Yoon died from a broken neck when you attempted to break her fall."

"I guess my man here didn't study physics in high school," Detective Bateson quips.

Ben winces.

"Regardless," Detective Gonzales continues throwing another stare at her partner. "What you did or attempted to do was either an act of heroism or great stupidity."

"I put my money on stupidity," Detective Bateson chimes in. "Shit, if she hit him anywhere else, my man here would be long gone, and I could be at home with my family enjoying a nice dinner."

Detective Gonzales, ignoring his comment, says, "What we wanted to ask you, Mr. White, is why did you flee the scene? And why, only two weeks later, did you check into a hospital to take care of what looks like a pretty nasty injury?"

"We have been to your apartment," Detective Bateson adds, folding his arms. "You were not there the few times we came by. No one has been able to get hold of you. Maybe you fled the scene in fear or regret of what happened. Maybe you got scared and thought you would be the one blamed. Maybe you ran because you couldn't be the hero that day. But not answering our calls, not going home, and not getting obvious medical attention feels a little weird to me. Did you know Ms. Yoon? Was this some kind of game gone wrong? Were you two trying to create a viral video? The hero saves the day!" Detective Bateson throws his hands into the air. "The internet rejoices! Trending on Reddit, Facebook, YouTube, and Twitter!"

"No," Ben replies. His eyes are down, facing away from the detectives.

"Then what the fuck, Mr. White? Where have you been?" Detective Bateson asks.

Ben sighs. He is slowly piecing this all together. He has to think fast, but Ben can only think of one thing to say between the medicine and the pain: "I don't remember."

"You don't remember?" Detective Bateson asks, confused.

"No."

"Well," Detective Bateson chuckles. "Looks like we might have a Kathy Bates-type situation here. Did someone take you in an attempt to heal you back to health in a secluded cabin? Maybe tied you to a bed so you couldn't escape? What was the name of that movie, Susan?"

"*Misery,*" Detective Gonzales says as she continues to eye Ben.

"Right, *Misery*, is that what happened here, Mr. White? You ran from the scene into an old lady's house, where she kept you prisoner until you made your dramatic escape two weeks later. Is that what happened?"

"I don't remember," Ben replies. He stares at his lap, continually avoiding eye contact.

Detective Gonzales rubs her forehead and face. "We are getting off-topic here. Leaving a scene is a serious offense, and saying you don't remember it is not helping."

"Am I in trouble?" Ben asks.

Detective Gonzales moves away from the bed and places her back on the wall.

"We considered charging you, but ultimately the girl was dead either way. If this was some stunt, you guys did it verbally, which we cannot prove unless someone steps forward and claims it, which they haven't. We checked the text messages on her phone and could find no evidence of this being a prank or stunt. It appeared you two had no contact before the incident, so the D.A. decided this was an act of a 'Good Samaritan' and dropped the felony charge. We are charging you with a misdemeanor for fleeing the scene. On the other hand, her family may consider a wrongful death lawsuit, but who knows? As I said, she was dead either way."

Jinni's family wanted to sue him? Ben could not believe that.

Detective Bateson paces back and forth. He looks at his partner, and they share a telepathic look. Detective Gonzales turns towards Ben and says, "She was your ex-girlfriend, wasn't she, Mr. White?" Ben's head snaps up. She looks Ben in the eyes. "We talked to her sister, and she said you two dated a while ago. Did she tell you she was going to commit suicide?" Ben keeps staring past the Detectives. Silence filled the room for a few moments.

"No," Ben says quietly. "We haven't talked in a while."

"Ok," Detective Gonzales sighs. Detective Bateson looks at his partner and shrugs.

"Next time, Mr. White," Detective Bateson starts, "do not flee the scene. Do that again, and we will find a reason to arrest you." He glares at Ben. "Now, let's get the fuck out of here ... Susan." He motions towards the door.

Detective Gonzales reaches into her pocket and pulls out a card. "Call us if you remember anything." She places the card on his bed.

"Just remember, Mr. White," Detective Bateson says as the two detectives make their way out. "No good deed goes unpunished."

#

Ben is released the next day. Dr. Kamal warns him to take it slow and not to use his hands if possible. Ben checks out, looks over his ten thousand dollar hospital bill (technically, it was thirty thousand dollars, but his insurance covers two-thirds of it), and grabs an Uber home. On the way, he calls Ulysses and lies about getting into a car accident and being in a coma for the last few weeks. Ulysses incredulously accepts his lie but not without asking if he feels up for a status meeting the following day to catch him up. Ben agrees. He then calls his mom. He tells her the same lie. She tells him that she is worried about him. He tells her that he is ok.

Ben wiggles his finger on the ride home, testing his hands. While they were stiff, they seemed to be functioning normally. His casts are attached to his arm like white evening gloves. They came up to his elbow, and he appeared to have some freedom of movement. The pain in his arms is not too bad, and the doctor has prescribed him some extra-strength aspirin.

Ben arrives home, thanks the driver, and goes to his apartment. A new lock had replaced the lock when the EMT had broken into his apartment to get to him. His key did not work. He goes to his super's apartment, where he receives a set of new keys and a bill for the new lock and installation.

Ben opens the door and looks around. There is a large blood stain on the carpet near his couch that would most likely not come out, and his table, where he passed out, is destroyed. Ben makes a mental note to clean that up later. Right now, he wants to check one thing and only one thing. He had been too scared to do so in the hospital as he had already caused a ruckus, but now that he is home, he feels much safer.

He sits down on his couch and opens the NikNak app. He goes to his saved Naks section—where only one Nak should be saved—and is startled to see that it is blank. Confused, he opens the search bar and types: koryBrewer.

After scrolling through her feed, Ben is surprised not to find the Nak titled "OMG, a suicidal woman almost kills us!" but instead, "OMG, you will never believe what happened to us! A GHOST?" Ben presses play. Instead of seeing the girl dancing through the street, Ben sees two faces on his screen.

"Guys," one of them starts. "We had the most insane day today!"

"It was insane!" the other girl agrees.

"Kory and I were filming a Nak when all of a sudden, this guy barges through us—"

"He knocked you to the ground." The other girl points to the first girl, who nods vigorously.

"Yeah, and he knocks me to the ground. Then, out of nowhere, this lady comes flying down from the skies, and this guy tries to catch her!"

"It was crazy," the one Ben thinks is Kory cuts in.

"Yeah, and I am on the ground; my phone is on the sidewalk, so I scream at him and go to pick up my phone and point it at him—"

"Then," Kory breathlessly cuts in again. "His arms are out, and 'boom,' she bounces right through his arms and hits the ground hard. We could hear her neck snap." The girl snaps her fingers, simulating the sound.

"So I am holding my phone, and Kory screams at me to 'call 911, call 911!' I look up and see the lady lying on the ground and the guy standing with his arms bent weirdly." The girl takes a deep breath. "So I am like, 'What the fuck?' I stop recording and dial 911. I put the phone to my ear and look back at the scene—"

Kory cuts in again. "Guys, the guy was gone—poof." She mimics the sound with her hand. "I mean, he nowhere in sight."

"And I am just standing there—" This time, the other girl cuts in. "I'm standing there with my mouth open. The 911 person is saying, 'Hello 911, what's your emergency?' and I totally freeze up. Like five feet away from me is this dead girl; Kory is running to me, and this guy who was there a second ago is not."

"Anyways," Kory cuts in again. "I see Makena is not talking to 911, so I pull the phone away from her and tell the dispatch what happened. She asked me where my location was, and I looked around to see what street we were on; that's when I noticed the guy was gone. I look at Makena—"

"And I am looking at Kory, and we were both like, 'What the hell is going on?'"

"Anyways," Kory continues. "The cops arrive, and we try and explain what happened."

"Yeah, they were all confused and shit," Makena explains.

"Yeah, and I am like, 'Look, we have it on video,' and we show them the Nak we were trying to record."

The screen goes blank for a second, and the Nak plays. It starts as it always does when the one girl (Kory) lip-synched to the song that Ben still hasn't bothered to look up, and the camera girl (Makena) follows her as she dances backward. The song goes:

"Try again tonight ... If you want my light ... I can hold you, hold you."

A few seconds later, the camera violently shakes, and the video twists upward and then back down to the ground, where it goes black. A distinct "Hey!" can be heard, followed by a snapping sound. The camera rumbles as the camera girl runs towards her friend. The camera rises off the ground moving quickly up. Ben catches a brief glimpse of himself standing there with two broken arms. A voice can be heard screaming, "Call 911, call 911." The phone rises away from Ben. A moment later, the video ends, and the two girls return to the screen.

"So we went through the footage and got a screen grab of the guy." A screenshot of Ben appears. The picture was the side of his face, and he had a look of disbelief.

Ben leans back on his couch, lays his head back, and closes his eyes.

"So if anyone recognizes him, please DM us so we can inform the police," Makena finishes. "Thank you, and we love you all!" they both say in unison. With that, the video ends.

Nak by:
@koryBrewer
1,231,236 views
124,134 Niks
NikNak©

Ben scrolls through the comments. The top comment is by @JerBear69. *"Hey @koryBrewer, I think I know that guy. DM me!"*

Ben walks to the kitchen to make himself a drink.

CHAPTER 11 - ILY

Over the following weeks, Ben dives into his work. He is re-introduced to Pavlov and Demetri and proceeds to work on NikNak's S-1 document and do the security review. Ulysses is annoyed with him but is glad to have him back working. Ben meets with Pavlov many times over the following weeks to try and prepare them technically for their public offering.

Ben meets with Mark Fischer, FrontSpark's VP of Finance, who is doing the financial due diligence for the S-1. Ben asks him what he feels the value of NikNak will be when they go public.

"Around ten billion plus or minus two or three billion," Mark says matter-of-factly. "The founders own 51% of the voting stock, so both Pavlov and Demetri will be worth about two and a half billion each when they go public."

Ben lets a high-pitched whistle slip through his lips.

"How is that possible?" he asks.

"Well," Marks says through the Zoom call as he shuffles papers on his large desk. "They are projected to make around five hundred million in total revenue this year; they have a fairly small staff of around sixty people for a company making that much money. They are fully remote, so they do not have any office expenses. Plus, they have done this organically with very little marketing. Imagine what they could make if they had the capital to market and improve their product."

That night, after Ben's fifth or sixth drink, he finds himself with his phone in his hand. In the last couple of weeks, other than for work, Ben has rarely touched it. He sits on his couch and thinks about what has happened. *Why did everyone think he was missing for those two weeks?* The weird thing is that all evidence, things like emails and text messages that Ben knew he had sent, had vanished. He watches the @koryBrewer's video again, and other than the one-second shot of him, he is nowhere to be seen in that video. That one second wiped out two weeks of his life. Ben looks at his arms. The pain is mostly gone, and Dr. Kamal told him that Ben could get the casts removed in a few weeks. He has always been a fast healer. What bothers him the most is how ineffectual it all was. He did not save Jinni; he did not become the hero.

"Jinni," a drunk Ben says quietly. "I am so sorry...."

The first few months of their relationship had been so good. It was that novel-like cinematic rom-com bliss that you read about in books or see in the movies. She liked him, and he adored her. Although he was concerned about the age gap, the massive ego boosts it gave him from dating someone ten years younger caused him to ignore his concerns.

The first few months of their relationship consisted of dinners, bars, the occasional nightclub, and intense sex. Drinking was usually involved. For Ben, she provided a reprieve from work and life. She was sexually free and adventurous and did not seem to have the hang-ups of most women Ben had dated before. She was just the fun that Ben needed in his mundane and boring life. Some of the best times he had with her was when she would tell him in detail about a dream she had when they woke in the morning. She would lay in the crook of his arm and whisper in his ear. Nearly two months after their first encounter at the party, she had moved in with him, and Ben could not have been happier.

His friend Raj had said they were moving too fast, to which Ben countered that he and his fiancée were in an arranged marriage that his family and her family had set. Raj kept his thoughts to himself after that. The fun continued the first few months; the drinking accelerated, the partying more prominent. Jinni loved to party.

During this time, Jinni and he got to know each other. He told her stories that he had not shared with anyone. He told her about how he was severely bullied in junior high and how he dreaded going to school. He told her about his father's passing when he was twelve and how it burdened and broke his mother, who had relied on his father financially and emotionally.

Jinni spoke little about herself. Ben knew she immigrated from South Korea at a young age. She did not give him any more detail other than she had some family here and an uncle who had passed away. As they lived longer and longer together and became more and more comfortable with each other, Ben felt himself opening up, but Jinni mainly stayed distant. Still, the mystery enticed Ben; he kept feeling she would open up to him with some patience and love.

One night, after a rough week at work, Ben recommended a night out to blow off some steam. Jinni and he got blistering drunk that night. They were sitting at the bar, laughing and enjoying themselves. Ben excused himself to go to the bathroom. As he returned from the restroom, he spotted Jinni across the room. Standing beside her, whispering in her ear, was an older man with graying white hair. The older man showed her something on his phone, then gave her a smile and a nod.

Ben watched this interaction as he moved closer and closer to Jinni. He watched Jinni shake her head no. The man laughed and said something else and pointed towards his phone. Ben watched as Jinni jumped out of her chair and started swinging her fists. Her hands were balled up, striking the man's chest and arms. Ben started to run towards her. When he arrived, security had already separated the two of them. The older man argued with the security guards, claiming, "I didn't do anything." A large guard was holding Jinni, and she was screaming at the man, spitting and cursing at him.

Ben watched in shock. He had never seen Jinni act like this before. He moved towards her. A security guard stopped him and told him to back up. He pushed the guard's hand away and told him she was his girlfriend. Not hearing or caring, the security guard pushed Ben away and told him again, "Back the fuck up!" Ben looked around. He could see Jinni still struggling, still shouting obscenities at the man who had a smirk on his face. Ben pushed past the first security guard and went up to Jinni. When she saw him, she stopped struggling and went limp. Ben asked the guard to let her go. He obliged, and Jinni ran into his arms. Ben looked around again and asked what had happened.

"This your girl, man?" asked one of the security guards.

"Yes, what happened here?" Ben demanded.

"Y'all need to go," he said as he crossed his arms. "Now!"

Ben started patting Jinni on the back as she began to cry in his arms. Ben felt the anger and confusion rise up. "What happened here?" he asked angrily.

A more diminutive security guard came and stood next to the larger one. They stood directly in front of the older man. The smaller one pointed at Jinni.

"This one attacked this one here," he said, gesturing with his thumb pointed at the man behind him. "Like big boy said, y'all need to go."

"Can we just go?" Jinni asked through her tears.

Ben stared at the guards for another couple of seconds and walked Jinni out.

On the Uber ride home, Jinni, somewhat regaining her composure, sat with her body on the other side of the car, legs crossed away from Ben, staring out the window. She had not spoken since she had asked to leave. Ben drew up the courage and asked her what had happened. She sat motionless, staring out the window. Ben asked her again.

"What happened at the bar?" She did not move or acknowledge his question.

"Jinni?"

"Jinni!"

"What!" she hissed at him.

Her response surprised him, and he recoiled.

"What happened back there? I go to the bathroom and come back to you pounding some old man." Ben paused for a second, softening his voice. "Babe, what happened?"

Jinni slowly turned her head towards him. Her eyes and face were dark with anger and mistrust. She looked at him and stared him down, unblinking. For a moment, she looked at him like he was the enemy.

She turned her head back to the windows and said one word: "Nothing."

They rode the rest of the journey in silence. She popped out of the Uber and moved silently to their apartment when they arrived home. When Ben opened the door, she headed to the bathroom and locked herself in. Ben waited hours for her to emerge. Finally, with sleep overcoming him, he walked towards the bathroom door. He was about to knock but instead pressed his ear to the door. Through the muffled sound of the bathroom fan, he heard her weeping.

Things would only get worse for them from there.

CHAPTER 12 - NAGI

After his arms have healed and his casts removed, Ben brings up Jinni's video again. He plans on entering one more time and trying anything different, but when he plays the Nak, he realizes he cannot "superimpose" in. He panics and wonders if he has lost the power just as quickly as he has gained it. He tests this out by playing an innocuous video of a new park that had opened up in Oklahoma. The video is about two minutes long, and he soon finds himself in the middle of a lovely garden. When he tries the same with the Jinni video, it will not let him in. Ben considers why and realizes that his chance has come and gone. He can do no more. After that, Ben enters a stage of deep depression.

Ben sits angrily drunk on his couch. His feet tap rapidly on the ground. He can feel the anger on his cheeks. He hates his life right now. More so, he is tired of it. He is tired of the pain, loss, isolation, and being locked down. *Three-plus years I have spent alone in this apartment,* Ben's mind races. *Three years!* All week he had been thinking about the bad things that had happened in his life: Jinni's suicide, his father dying, and getting bullied at school.

"Fuck you all!" he shouts into an empty room. "I fuckin' hate you all!" He screams as he stomps around the apartment and begins to shadowbox the air, punching an unseen enemy.

"I hate you!" he screams as he punches the air. "You think you can pick on me, make me feel like shit? Huh! I will show all of you! I will show—" Ben pauses mid-sentence. An idea pops into his head. He grabs his hair and combs it back with his fingers. His hands lay resting on his head. A smirk enters his lips. He starts giggling like a crazy person. "That would be fuckin' hilarious!" He laughs out loud. "Could it be possible?" he asks himself. "Let's find out."

#

"Hello, Mom," Ben greets her when she answers the phone.

"Ben! Is that you?" his mother asks.

"Yes."

"Oh my goodness, Ben, where have you been? You never call your mother. I am here all alone. You know you are only a few hours away, and you never come to visit." She pauses and asks. "Where have you been?"

Ben sighs. Talking to his mother is always a chore. He misses her, but her guilt trips always make him feel bad.

"You're right, Mom." Ben closes his eyes. "I'm sorry."

"It's ok; I am just worried about you. You never call or write me one of those email things. I even tried downloading that Inter-gram thing so that I could see pictures of you, but I was scared it would steal my information. I saw something on Fox News saying all these things were stealing your personal information and selling it to bad people. I didn't want to take the chance." Ben's mother continues speaking breathlessly. "When are you coming to see your mother?"

"That's the thing, Mom. I was calling to see what you were doing this Saturday. I thought I would drive down and visit you."

"Will you stay for dinner, or will you head back the same day?" she asks.

"How about I stay overnight?"

"Yay!" His mom squeals like a seven-year-old girl. "I'll make you your favorites, and I can prepare your old room."

"Sure, Mom, why not?"

The following Saturday, Ben gets into his car and takes the five-hour trip to see his mom.

Ben arrives at his old house late in the afternoon. He parks on the curb despite an open spot on the driveway. He turns off the car and leans back in his seat, staring at his old house. The house looks the same, only smaller than he remembered. They called these kinds of dwellings "Rancho" style, but Ben never understood why; it looked nothing like a ranch. He considers looking it up on his phone but realizes he does not care. Supposedly it was designed by some guy who would later go on and become a famous architect. He could still remember his mom excitedly telling any guest who visited about it. Ben would watch their polite but confused faces nodding in approval, but like him, they did not care. The house is a standard three-bedroom, two-bath affair with a small attic. Ben's parents always planned on having a second child, but after Ben's messy birth, his mom could not have any more kids.

"Even in birth—I am destructive," Ben mutters.

After a few rings and a knock, his mother opens the door.

"Ben!" she whispers, excited, her eyes wide. She rushes towards him with a slight hobble (knee replacement surgery) and wraps her arms around him. She sticks her face into his chest; at this point, it is closer to his abdomen. Ben has noticed his mom getting shorter and shorter every time he sees her. Where she once almost came up to his shoulders, now her chin touches the bottom of his chest.

"Ben," she whispers louder, still holding him in her bear hug.

Ben starts patting her on the back with his free hand. "Hello, Mom," he says softly.

Her hair is getting increasingly white, and her skin, which used to be smooth and vibrant, is now leathery and eggshell-thin. Ben smells his mother's hair. He always enjoyed her hair smell. A combination of hair dye and sweet shampoo. This time he only smells shampoo. His mother had finally let her hair go to its natural color.

"Well," his mother demands, hands on her hip. "Don't just stand there. Come inside. You will catch a cold. And take that stupid thing off your face." She turns around, opens the door wider, and ushers him into the house. When Ben enters the house and stands in the living room, his mom stares at him. She points at her mouth and then at Ben's. Ben, giving in, removes his mask. His mom tells him this is all about government control and that no son of hers will be a puppet.

They sit in the living room, sipping on iced tea. Ben looks around the living room and realizes not much has changed. Shaggy brown carpet that his mother keeps meticulously clean. Old pictures of Ben and his dad on the wall. The oakwood coffee table is still shiny but chipped at one corner. Ben smiles as he recalls the scolding he received when he damaged the table. He was around eleven years old and was practicing his basketball moves in the living room, screaming, "Kobe!" as he practiced his fade-away shot. His leg hit the coffee table, causing it to tip over. Ben tried to catch it but only successfully caught one side. The other corner hit the floor and chipped. His mother was furious at the time. He recalls his dad patting her on the shoulder, calming her down, and telling her it was only slightly damaged and that he would get it fixed. He never did. He died a few months later.

Ben takes another sip of the homemade iced tea. His mother is stirring hers with a spoon. She always liked it sweet.

"So ... Tell me what's new."

Ben places his glass on the coffee table (this time, remembering to use the coaster). "Nothing much, Mom, just working and trying to get by in these trying times."

"Oh," she replies with disappointment.

Ben raises his eyebrows and continues talking. "We signed a big client at my job," he offers hopefully. "I have been extra busy, which is a good thing with everything going on." He looks at his mother, who is staring at the ground. "If everything goes well, I might get a raise, so hopefully, more money ... more problems." He smiles, knowing she will not get the joke but hoping she will ask him what he means. His mother continues to stare at the ground. "Mom, what's wrong?" He slides towards her and places his hand on her bony shoulder.

She is silent for a few seconds before finally speaking. "Well," she starts, finally looking up. "You haven't seen your mother in a long time, and suddenly you call me and ask to come to see me. I thought you had some big news like you were engaged or something."

Ben has to stifle his laugh. "Why would you think that?" he asks. "I mean, I am not even dating anyone right now." He reaches for his glass and takes a sip of his tea.

"I just thought," his mother continues, "that maybe you got back with that nice Oriental girl I had met a few times."

Ben sinks back into the couch, nearly spilling his iced tea. "First off, Mom, you shouldn't use the word 'Oriental,' that is a type of rug; second, she's Korean," Ben replies, his voice a little louder than he wanted. "Third, she passed away a few weeks ago." His voice softens. "She committed suicide."

"Oh," his mother says as she covers her mouth. "Why did she do that?"

Ben sighs and runs his hands through his hair. He has a good idea why. But it would be too vulgar, too grotesque to discuss with his mother.

"I don't know, Mom … She just did." It is the only thing he could think of to say.

"Such as shame. She was a nice girl."

"I know, she was."

As the evening ends, Ben and his mom sit at the kitchen table, finishing dinner. When his mom gets up and starts to clear the plates, Ben rises to help her.

She waves a hand in front of his face to stop him. "Now sit down and let your mother take care of you."

Ben, embarrassed, sits back down. He watches his mother clear the table and place the dishes into the sink. Ben remembers she used to move gracefully like a swan, but after her knee surgery, she shuffles around like a wounded duck. *I should come to see her more,* he thinks. He begins to wonder why he doesn't. The drive is a pain (five hours each way), but it is more than doable. Ben and his mom have had issues in the past. Ben wonders if he has moved past them. After his father passed, Ben was forced to do more; he bore more responsibility and had hoped his mother would do the same. In the end, she didn't. Ben wonders if he still holds some resentment towards her for it.

Ben watches as she grabs a sponge and starts wiping the table down. She moves her hand to the edge of the table and catches the crumbs with her free hand. Ben notices her hand has the slightest shake to it. He looks away. He realizes it is not that fact that he did not love his mother; he hates seeing her get old.

Around ten o'clock, Ben's mother announces that she is going to bed and asks Ben if he needs anything. Ben replies that he is ok. As she walks away, he calls out, "Mom, do you mind if I go into the attic for a bit?"

"Why would you want to go in there?"

"Just wanted to look at some of my old stuff."

"Sure," she says, hobbling away. "Knock yourself out."

"Oh, and Mom," Ben calls out to her again. "Do you still have that old TV of mine in the guest room?"

His mom looks at him, confused, and chews on her lower lip, something she always does when thinking.

"I think it's in the closet," she replies after thinking about it for a moment. "Why do you want that old thing? If you want to watch TV, watch it in the living room."

Ben decides not to press any further. He gives her a thumbs-up gesture.

After she leaves, Ben watches a little TV. After some time has passed and he is sure she is asleep, he quietly heads to the hallway, grabs the rope above his head, and slowly brings down the ladder to the attic.

The attic is dark and dusty. Ben fumbles around until he finds the light switch. He crouches slightly as the support beams running along the roof are right next to his head. Looking around, he sees a bunch of boxes and some shelves with old electronics and appliances. His parents never liked to throw things away. His father had fancied himself an amateur handyman, while his mother always feared the occasion when something like a cupcake maker would once again prove useful.

Ben is looking for two things. He finds the first almost immediately. It is a gargantuan VHS device that is fashioned from another era. He blows off the many years of dust and carefully brings it down from the shelf. He then places it near the ladder for easier access to it later. The second item he is looking for is in one of those many boxes in the corner. He walks over to them, careful not to hit his head, and sits down cross-legged near them. He pulls one down off the stack, brushes off the dust, and opens it up. It is a pile of his mom's old clothes. He carefully and quietly goes through each box until he finds the one he is looking for.

On top is an oversized glossy hardcover book. Ben pulls it out and reads the cover:

P.C. Year Book 1996 Grades 6-8
Go Falcons!

Ben smiles despite himself. Good old Pacific Coast or, as the kids called it, "Piece of Crap" junior high. Ben opens the book and starts leafing through it. He can not remember what grade he is in that year, so he starts from the beginning. When he gets to the seventh graders, he starts recognizing some faces. Finally, he gets to his photo. Below his picture is the caption:

"Don't try to be a great man, just be a man, and let history make its own judgment." - Commander William Riker.

Ben grins. He had been a huge *Star Trek* fan and loved the movie *First Contact*. Consequently, that is what first drew the ire of his bully. Ben backs up a few pages to the "O" section and scans the page. In the second row, he finds the person he is looking for.

"Sean O'Fucking O'Connell," he whispers angrily. He looks at the picture of Sean. He had black hair, slinky black eyes, bad skin, and a thick neck. He is not smiling in his picture. Below his photo is the caption:

"Welcome to the Jungle!" - GNR

Ben stares at the picture; as he stares, he remembers the day when his life in junior high school through the beginning of high school would become a daily hell.

Ben was walking down the hallway in his new Star Trek "First Contact" shirt; he was around eleven at the time. He had watched the movie two times over the Thanksgiving holiday and begged his dad to buy him the shirt when they left the movie theater. He loved *Star Trek: The Next Generation* and spent many days after school watching it at night with his dad. As he walked down the hallway in his crisp new white shirt, he heard some laughing and someone calling out to him.

"Hey ... hey ... you!" someone shouted. Ben stopped and looked back at a bunch of much bigger boys.

"Who me?" he asked.

"Yeah, you, come here," the biggest one demanded.

Ben slowly walked over, stopping halfway. "What do you want?" he asked.

"Just c'mere," repeated the biggest one. Ben moved a little closer. The biggest one looked him up and down, stopping at the title on his shirt. "*First Contact*, huh," the biggest one said. Ben nodded meekly. Without warning, the biggest one slapped him hard, almost knocking him over.

"How's that for 'First Contact'?" he asked as his two friends laughed.

Ben put his hand to his face and slinked off. His cheek and nose were stinging, and his eyes started to water. He quickly broke into a jog and heard the laughter drone off behind him. He walked into the bathroom to look at his face. His nose was bleeding, and the blood was dripping all over his new shirt.

Throughout the day, when his teachers asked him about the blood on his shirt, he lied and said he had walked into a pole. When his parents asked him the same, he told the same lie. His mother told him to be more careful; his father eyed him suspiciously.

As the week went on, the biggest one—whom Ben had discovered was named Sean—started a new game with Ben. Every time Ben walked past him in the hallway, Sean would punch him in the arm, kick him in the ass, or slap him in the back of his head. Every time he did this, he called out, "Second Contact!", "Third Contact!" and so on. This continued for the next month until he finally reached "Thirty-ninth Contact!" That's when Sean got bored with the game, or Ben had just gotten better at avoiding him. Ben always wondered if Sean couldn't count any higher.

One day, his dad laid a hand on Ben's shoulder, and Ben whelped in pain and slid under his dad's hand. His father raised both his eyebrows and asked him what was wrong.

"Nothing," Ben replied, looking down at the floor. His father moved closer to him and gently pushed the collar of his shirt to the side, where Ben had a massive bruise on his right shoulder.

"Ben," his dad asked. "What happened here?"

"As I said, nothing," Ben replied defensively, his head down.

"Come," his dad said softly. Ben followed his dad into the garage. His dad opened up the freezer and grabbed a plastic bag off the shelf next to it. He filled the bag with ice and handed it to Ben. "Put that on your shoulder. It will help with swelling." Ben gently put the bag of ice on his shoulder. "So," his dad continued. "Do you want to tell me what happened?"

Ben shook his head and said, "I don't remember."

While the days of yelling "'Some Number' Contact!" were over, Sean still made Ben's life miserable. Today he ran up behind Ben and clapped him hard on the shoulder, so hard that he brought him down to his knees. As he walked past, he said, "Hiya, Ben." Then he and his cronies walked away laughing, leaving Ben crumpled on the floor, holding his shoulder.

"Am I in trouble?" Ben asked his dad quietly.

Ben's dad sighed, grabbed a beer from the freezer, and opened it. He took a long swig and offered the beer to his son. Ben shook his head.

"Drink it," his dad commanded.

Ben took the bottle with his free hand and took a sip. He made a face at the beer's bitter taste and handed the beer back to his father.

"You know, Ben, there are always trying times in our lives," his dad said as he took another long pull of the beer. "People always try to fuck with you." Ben's eyes shot up. He had never heard his dad curse before. "And it is up to you to decide how much you want to take." His dad took another swallow before walking over to throw the beer away. He grabbed another from the refrigerator and twisted open the cap.

"My brother and I came to this country when I was only eighteen, and your uncle Basil was only sixteen. It was hard for both of us. War broke out in my country, and my father didn't want your uncle and me to join the army, so he sent us here." Ben's dad took another drink and continued. "It was hard for us here. We barely spoke English, and people didn't like us very much. After I graduated college, I decided I had had enough. I was tired of the racism and off-putting comments, and I decided to make a change." Ben watched his dad in fascination. His dad was not an emotional man and rarely talked about his first days after he immigrated to the U.S. His dad continued, "I decided to make some drastic changes so people would stop messing with me. My brother was not happy with what I had done, but in the end, he understood."

Ben's dad stared at his son and continued, "I don't know what going on with you lately, and if you don't want to talk to me, that's fine. Just remember that there is always a breaking point, and it's up to you to decide when that point comes. For some, it's sooner. For others, it's later. The thing is that it's always in your hands to decide when."

Ben stared at his father. He was not what you considered a handsome man. He had thinning black hair, a stocky slight shoulder build, and he was fifty pounds overweight. He was a local airline commercial pilot and was usually gone half the week. He was forty-five at the time. He stared at Ben with his arms crossed, waiting for a response. Ben shrugged, unsure what to say; he could feel his eyes watering up, so he blinked away the tears. They stood there for a while, not talking.

"Keep in mind, son," his dad continued. "Once someone knows you're willing to stand up and fight, they will back down. Even if you lose and maybe get hurt, that person will gain respect for you. It's something to think about." Ben, still looking at the floor, nodded silently. They stood in the garage for a few more minutes, not talking. Ben knew his dad wanted him to say something, but he could not find any words.

Finally, his dad sighed and smiled. "C'mon, son, let's go inside before your mother gets worried." He ruffled Ben's hair, something he had not done in a long time.

A few days later, he was dead.

Ben sat silently, looking straight ahead, trying to avert his gaze from his dad's casket. His mother sat beside him, silently sobbing. His dad had always loved flying. "Flying is my second wife" was a phrase he was prone to say. He and his buddies would rent a small plane once a year and fly off somewhere. One time it was Vegas. Another time, it was Catalina. They called it the "mile-high trip." Halfway through the trip, something went wrong, and the plane crashed into the mountains (the "mile-high trip" this year was a camping trip to Yosemite). The autopsy claimed that his dad had a myocardial infarction while flying and lost control of the plane. When Ben asked what that meant, his mother just shushed him. Later, when he looked it up on the internet, he discovered that it was just a medical term for a heart attack. All four passengers died that day.

Ben did not know his dad's friends that well. They had been over to the house occasionally. Ben generally greeted them and then went off to do whatever he was doing that day (usually playing video games but sometimes homework). He overheard his mother talking about two of his dad's friends not being married, and one of them married, but thankfully they had no kids. Ben, his mom, and the other guy's wife got the short end of the stick.

Ben sat with his hands folded in his lap, listening to the preacher talk about something. He was uncomfortable, and his suit was itchy. He badly wanted to go home.

After the day's events, Ben lay wide awake in bed; he tried to imagine what it had been like on the plane with his dad. His dad slumped over the yoke, the aircraft veering to the left in a nose dive. Ben wondered if he was sitting next to his dad, as he had done a few times, would he take over? Be the hero, land the plane? Or would he just sit there in shock as he watched the mountainside creep closer? He did not know.

After a couple of weeks, he went back to school. A few of his classmates came over to him to offer their condolences. He meekly and quickly thanked them before going off to be alone.

One day Ben was sitting alone outside with his lunch. He was absentmindedly picking at it while trying to complete his homework assignment that was due for his next class. He found it hard to concentrate at home and preferred to do his homework at school whenever he could. It also stopped people from talking to him. He heard a shuffle of feet in front of him. Ben kept his head down, ignoring well-wishers who wanted to talk to him.

"Hey, Ben!" Sean shouted, trying to get his attention. Ben ignored him. "Ben!" Sean called again. Ben clenched his teeth, hoping that Sean and his two cronies, who never spoke, would go away. "Ben! Watch this!" Sean shouted. Ben could hear Sean making a mock plane engine sound with his mouth. "WHIRRRRRRRRRR!" Ben peeked up. Sean had both hands in front of him, holding a fake flight stick, and was running around in circles while making airplane sounds with his mouth.

"WHIRRRRRR BRUP BRUP BRUP!" Sean was now simulating an airplane engine dying as he quickly moved to the wall. Ben raised his head and watched him.

"BRUP BRUP BRUP … BOOOOOM!" Sean ran straight into the wall and came crashing down onto the floor. His two cronies broke up in laughter. Ben stood up. He had decided that he had reached his breaking point. He walked towards Sean, who had picked himself up off the floor and was dusting himself off, laughing. He saw Ben approaching and cracked a smirk onto his face. Ben had never thrown a punch at anyone before, but he decided that he was going to wipe that smile off of Sean's face once and for all. In his mind, he imagined a punch so fierce that it would break Sean's nose and knock out two of his front teeth. Sean would then be the laughingstock of the entire school and one day would come up to Ben and apologize for everything he had done.

When Ben threw his punch, he arched his fist over his head to slam it down on Sean's nose. Instead, he hit Sean in the chest.

Sean didn't budge.

Time froze for a second. Ben looked at his fist and then at Sean. Sean looked confused, but slowly his face was morphing into anger. He grabbed Ben's arm and twisted it. Ben screamed out in pain. Then he punched Ben hard, once in the gut, then in the face. He grabbed Ben and hoisted him against the wall by his neck. Ben could feel the air being choked out of him as he struggled with both hands to unlock Sean's grip.

"Sean?" said one of his cronies. "Sean!" The crony shouted louder. "You're going to kill him!" Sean was not paying attention. He was looking up at Ben, a snarl on his face. Ben saw a black fog starting to creep around the edges of his eyes.

"Listen here, you little retard," spat out Sean. "You ever touch me again, and I'll kill you ... Do you understand?"

Ben somehow managed to nod his head. Satisfied, Sean released Ben. Ben crumpled to the ground, gasping for breath.

"Don't let me ever see you again," Sean whispered, his mouth close to Ben's ear. "I don't know if I can stop myself next time." With that, Sean kicked him in the ribs, and then he and his cronies walked away.

#

Ben puts the yearbook down. Even after all these years, the memories still hurt. The worst part was knowing that his dad's last piece of advice was wrong. Standing up to a bully only lets them know they can beat you. Ben should have ignored Sean; maybe he would have gotten bored and started on another kid.

The bullying did not stop after that day. Even if Ben got very good at avoiding Sean, run-ins were inevitable. They did go to the same school and lived in the same area. One day when Ben was waiting for the bus, Sean and his cronies happened to turn the corner. Ben didn't see them, but they saw him. He heard, "Have a good flight, retard!" before being lifted by the seat of his pants and tossed into traffic. He almost got run over by a car but luckily found his footing enough to slow him down, so the car just missed him. The side mirrors broke one of the buttons on his shirt. It was that close.

"Sean O'Fucking O'Connell," Ben repeats. He puts down the yearbook and digs back into the box. A further quick search reveals the item Ben is looking for. He pulls out a few VHS tapes labeled "P.C. Year in Review." Each dated with a different year.

It took him half an hour to set everything up. The TV is where his mom said it was, and he had to watch a couple of "P.C. Year in Review" tapes to find the right one. The "Year in

135

Review" tape was a forty-five-minute video the school released yearly. It was akin to a digital yearbook; if Ben remembers correctly, it costs about ten dollars. Despite Ben's protest that he was not in that edition, his mom always bought one. Still, he would occasionally appear in some background shot, and his mom always squealed in delight when she saw him. It was like her own game of "Where's Waldo."

He watches three tapes: 1995, 1996, and 1997. He briefly remembers Sean dropping out of school one year but is unsure exactly when. *Was it the spring of 1997 or the fall of 1997?* he thinks, but he cannot remember. He decides his best option is to stick with the 1996 tape where he knew he and Sean were in the same grade and Sean was definitely at that school.

Ben stretches out his arms. He looks at the paused blurry image on the screen. It shows a schoolyard in either mid-fall or mid-spring; he could not tell which. The day is slightly overcast, and the announcer talks about all the improvements they had made to the schoolyard that year. Ben finds a good stopping point, pauses the video, checks that his mom is still sleeping, and mentally prepares.

He was not sure how this would go. Last time he was gone for two weeks. *Does this time mean I will be gone for twenty-seven years?* he wonders. Somehow he did not think it worked like that. His mistake last time was being seen; this time, he would be much more careful and avoid the camera. Last time he got directly involved, locking the timeline by getting in front of the camera. He will stay out of the camera's view; this time, he will do it differently.

He chooses a somewhat quick left-to-right panning shot of the courtyard. Judging by the shadows in the video, he estimates it is mid-afternoon. He presses "Play" on the tape player and touches the far bottom left side of the TV screen. He closes his eyes.

He can see the light flood the back of his eyelids, so he opens them. He breathes deeply through his nostrils, inhaling the cool air. He peeks behind him to see the three-person camera crew. One kid is turning the camera on a tripod, one is holding the mic narrating, and the other is standing behind them with a clipboard. He does not recognize any of them.

He quickly moves away from the camera crew towards the northwest side of the school. The school's ugly orange/brown and white colors still make him cringe. A few kids walk past him, but they are deep in talk and do not even look in Ben's direction. His memory of the school has not faded even after all these years, as he heads towards the northwest stairs to get to the second floor. Where Ben wants to go is the southeast stairwell. He thinks it best to get off the ground level. This approach will take him where he needs to go.

He climbs up the steep flight of stairs to reach the second floor. He pauses at the top to catch his breath. He starts walking around the classrooms towards the southeast end of the building. None of the doors had windows, so he could not see inside the classes. He tries to remember which class he would have been attending now but cannot.

He takes a left and then another left and starts walking towards the pedestrian bridge that connects the current building with another staircase that goes back to the ground floor. Then to another pedestrian walkway that takes you to the southeast building. As he approaches the corner, he can hear his heart thumping in his head. He considers that Sean may not be there. He may have called in sick or been in class. He can hear some kids talking and laughing as he approaches the corner. He stops himself just out of their view.

"… so I tell this kid to fuck off or else I'll hit him so hard his mother's pussy will have a bruise on it!" This is followed by laughter from two other kids. Ben moves closer to confirm who it is. He sees Sean perched on the railing, legs dangling above the ground. One of his cronies is standing beside the stairways leaning against the support beam. And the other kid is sitting on the floor next to Sean, partially blocking the walkway. Ben always went to great lengths to avoid this section of the school when he was a kid. This is where Sean and his crew liked to hang out.

Ben stares at Sean. He had expected a flood of anger to engulf him, but now he only feels pity. Sean is much smaller than he remembered, his clothes cheaper and dirtier too. He looks poor, has a bad haircut, and is obese with a terrible case of acne.

Ben chuckles to himself. *What did I come here to do? Beat up this poor stupid kid? Wouldn't life do that to him eventually?* Ben laughs out loud. That gets their attention. They all fall silent and look his way. The taller, long-haired kid in the back looks at Ben with a confused look.

"If you're a teacher, we are on our lunch break and do not have to be in class until 2 p.m.," the kid with long hair shouts towards him. Sean drops off the railing onto the floor. He is maybe five feet tall and perhaps a hundred pounds. He looks up at Ben with a defiant look in his eye.

"I am not a teacher," Ben manages to say.

Sean looks at Ben, confused. He looks Ben up and down. "So why are you here? Are you some kind of fag?" Sean asks. His two friends giggle.

Ben's smile starts to fade from his face, and then he looks down at what he is wearing. He has the same outfit that he wore when he came to visit his mom. He has on skinny ripped jeans and a black V-neck. He stares back at the kids; they are all dressed in baggy jeans and loose flannel button-ups. Fashionably, he must have looked out of place.

"No … I'm not." He pauses, looking at Sean, almost cracking up in laughter again. "Sorry, I think I went the wrong way." With that, Ben turns and starts walking away, shaking his head.

"Yeah, faggot!" Sean shouts at him. "Go back to your boyfriend so he can fuck you up the ass through them ripped jeans … Retard!" Sean's crew breaks up into laughter.

Ben feels his eyes twitch. The anger he expected to engulf him earlier rolls into his body. He turns around, blinks twice, and moves towards a still-laughing Sean. Ben stops directly in front of him.

"What did you call me?" Ben asks, staring the little kid in the eyes.

"Sean, c'mon, let's go." The long-haired kid grabs Sean by the shoulder, looking slightly scared.

"You want a kiss, fag boy?" Sean asks, puckering his lips at Ben. "That's why are you hanging around our school? You some kind of kid fucker?"

"What ... did ... you say?" Ben asks again; his hands clenched up into fists.

Sean pauses for a second. He looks towards his crew, who are now standing up. Ben can see a flash of uncertainty cross his face, but once Sean sees his friends looking at him, he turns towards Ben defiantly. "I. Called. You. A. Kid. Fuc—"

Ben grabs him by the shirt and armpits and lifts him off the ground. He walks a few feet towards the stairs.

"Hey! Hey! What are you doing—" Sean flails around in his grip.

Ben throws him down the stairs.

#

Ben stands aggressively tapping his finger on the edge of the TV screen. He is sweaty and breathing hard. The courtyard pan shot is again playing on the old TV. Ben removes his hand and wipes his face with his shirt. He hears the door creak open.

"Ben?" His mother asks. "Are you still awake?"

"Yes," Ben replies, turning towards her. He moves away from the TV screen.

"Are you ok? Do you need anything?"

"No, I'm fine."

"I thought I saw a light and heard some noises, and I just wanted to check in on you." His mother looks at him through her sleepy eyes.

"I am fine, Mom. I am just about to go to sleep," Ben assures her.

"Ok." Ben's mother looks at his shirt. "Why are you all sweaty?"

Ben thinks fast and says, "I was doing some light workouts before bed, you know, got to watch my physique." Ben playfully pats his stomach. This gets a smile from his mother, and she wishes him a good night.

The following day over breakfast, Ben asks her a question.

"Mom, do you remember Sean O'Connell?"

His mother looks at him apprehensively and says, "Sean? You mean Mary O'Connell's kid?"

"Yeah," Ben replies.

She stirs her coffee and sits there for a moment, thinking. "Oh … They moved away years ago." His mother goes back to stirring her coffee.

"Oh." Ben watches her stir.

"That poor boy," Ben's mom says with a sigh.

"Why do you say that, Mom?" Ben leans forward.

"No … it's nothing; I just remembered her poor son. Some crazy guy attacked him at your school … Don't you remember, Ben?"

Ben shakes his head.

"Well, it was a long time ago. It was the gossip of the whole neighborhood. If I remember correctly, Mary said her son described him as some sort of alcoholic lunatic … a crazed pervert. The poor kid broke his ankle, suffered a bad concussion, and was in a cast for months. After that incident, his mother pulled him out of school. I considered pulling you out of that school too. They never caught the guy, and Mary feared he would come back. So they left that same year. It was such a tragedy." She finishes stirring her coffee and takes a sip. Ben looks at his mom. He peers into his mind. In his head, there were two versions of the events. One is where Sean tormented him up to high school and the second is Sean suddenly disappearing in junior high. Ben does not know which one is true.

Ben looks at his phone and tells his mom he has to get going. After grabbing his things, he hugs her tightly at the door and vows to come to see her more. His mother kisses him on the cheek. Ben gets in his car, waves goodbye, and starts driving home. During the drive, his mind wanders to the previous night's excursion.

After throwing Sean down the stairs, Ben ran away from the school as fast as he could. He kept running until he was out of breath. Without realizing it, he finds himself on the street where he had lived. He catches his breath and starts walking. A few minutes later, he finds himself near his house. Outside is a man trying to start a lawn mower. It is his dad. Ben starts to call out to him, but as soon as he raises his hand and shouts, he is back in his old bedroom. Ben tries to enter the videotape again. He wanted to forget about Sean and talk to his dad instead. Tell him not to take the trip with his friends. Beg him if he needs to. But like Jinni's NikNak video, the tape would not let him back in. He tries and tries again until his mom walks into the room.

Ben puts on his turn signal and enters the freeway. He drives for a few hours when tears start pouring out of his eyes. A few moments later, he cries so hard that he has to pull over to the side of the highway for fear of crashing his car. He cries like a twelve-year-old boy who has just lost his father.

CHAPTER 13 - WYD

Ben drunkenly stumbles to bed. He collapses on the bed face down, not bothering to remove his shoes. He snores loudly and dreams intensely.

He dreams of Jinni.

Their relationship started slow, then moved fast. After their first date, he waited three days before texting her again. She did not reply. After three more days, he then contacted her on Instagram. She still did not respond. He gave up and moved on. A week later, he checked his Instagram messages, and there was a message from her. She explained that she had been swamped and would love to get together sometime. They made tentative plans for a future date, but nothing materialized. A few weeks later, he got a text from her at almost midnight.

Jinni: *Hey wyd?*

Ben stared at his phone in disbelief. He was not doing anything. It was Friday night; he had a long day at work and was working on his fourth vodka and soda. He shook his head violently, trying to shake the alcohol out of his system. He counted sixty seconds and then texted her back.

Ben lied: *Just having a drink with some friends, wyd?*

Jinni replied playfully: *Oh, so you are busy :)*

Ben started to panic; he took a deep breath.

Ben: *I could not be. Why?*

Jinni: *Since you are already out, come and meet me for a drink.*

Ben started to run towards the bathroom, ripping off his clothes as he turned on the shower. He got the details of their meeting place as the shower water heated up. He said he would be there in twenty minutes while he shaved. Thirty minutes later, he exited the Uber and walked up the stairs to the bar.

#

Ben blinks his eyes awake. He reaches around his bed for his phone and looks at the screen. It is two in the afternoon. He tries to get out of bed, but his head and body will not cooperate. "Ow," he cries out and grabs his head and temples. He rolls over on his back, keeping his eyes shut. After a few minutes, the headache and dizziness subside enough for him to focus. He closes one eye and looks at his phone. He had twenty-seven missed messages and four missed calls. "Fuck," he mutters. He checks his Calendar app and sees that he has a meeting in twenty-one minutes. He gets up from bed and gently steps forward to test his balance. He wobbles towards the wall and grabs hold of it to keep himself from falling. He slaps himself hard across the face. He stumbles towards the bathroom. He enters and turns on the light. Immediately he regrets it and shades his eyes. He waits a couple of seconds for his eyes to adjust and makes his way towards the sink. Ben turns on the tap and ducks down to wash his face with cold water. He straightens up slowly, grabs the towel next to the sink, and wipes his face. He removes the towel and checks himself out in the mirror.

"I am so done with you," he tells himself. His eyes are bloodshot, and he sways like there is a strong wind in the bathroom. He reaches into a drawer underneath the sink and

144

pulls out some eye drops. He uses them, takes a quick shower, brushes his teeth, shaves, and combs his hair. After he is done, he quickly gets dressed into his standard work outfit—a shirt and shorts. Before logging into his meeting, he checks the bedroom mirror. He still looks hungover but is a little more presentable. He sits at his desk and joins the meeting only a few minutes late.

After the meeting, he eats, takes some aspirin, and feels better. He checks his Calendar app and realizes he has a one-on-one with Ulysses in a couple of hours. He groans as he sits back at his desk and returns to work. He opens the NikNak app and starts doing the analysis that Ulysses wanted.

The app is simplistic in its presentation. The landing page is a short video, usually of someone lip-synching to a song, working out, or offering life tips. You tap the screen once to move on to the next Nak, and a new video appears. There is a little heart in the top right corner where you could "Nik" the video if it appealed to you. If you wanted to go to a particular content creator's channel, you held down on the screen for a second, and you could see all the videos ("Naks") they had curated for their specific channel. Some individuals were "live streaming," in which they participated live with their audience. In a few of the Naks, when you held down, you were taken to the "Subscribe" screen, where you have to pay a monthly fee to view the channel content or participate in the live stream. Monthly fees can only be paid in crypto, and there is no option for credit cards.

Ben scrolls around the app; he comes across Kitty Josephine's newest video. She wears a see-through white dress and a blonde wig. She has her camera on a selfie stick, moving it up and down her body. A gust of wind blows up her dress as if on cue, giving the audience a quick flash of her undergarments. She quickly puts one hand to hold her skirt down, mimicking the famous Marlyn Monroe pose.

Curious, Ben holds onto her Nak, where he is hit with a subscribe page. It costs the equivalent of fifteen dollars a month in crypto to subscribe. Below the subscribe button, there is a line that exclaims:

Be a member of the Pussy Army, which is 28,453 soldiers strong!

Ben quickly does the math in his head and whistles softly. *This girl makes over four hundred thousand dollars a month! Well, less the twenty percent cut NikNak takes, but goddamn!* he thinks. Ben also notices that the algorithm keeps adapting to his tastes. When he watches some sports clips and "Niks" them, it shows him more sports clips. Same with other genres like movies and video games. He goes back through his history and finds the Kitty Josephine clip. He taps on the heart and becomes one of the two-point-five million "Niks" she has on that Nak. Within a few taps, he notices his feed recommendations have changed. He sees more female Naks advertising their private and public channels as he progresses through the different clips until he stops on one that confuses him. A young girl, maybe four or five, is climbing a tree in a short dress. As she climbs the tree, her underwear briefly shows, and she sits on a branch. The camera zooms into her face. She smiles. Text appears on the screen:

"Join The Red Ballon now!"

Confused, Ben holds onto the Nak. A large subscribe button appears. Below the button is the channel's cost—$100 in crypto per month. Ben mutters, "Damn." Ben taps the subscribe button in curiosity. *What kind of things would people pay one hundred dollars a month for?* Some additional text appeared on the screen:

"Before being granted permission to view this channel, you must answer the following five questions correctly. Fail any questions, and you will not be allowed in."

1. *"What is Sarah's real name?"*

Below the question is a text input box where you can type in the answer. Ben has no idea who Sarah is and does not know the answer, so he closes the app.

Later he has his one-on-one with Ulysses.

"Where were you this morning?" Ulysses asks. "I messaged you like twenty-six times."

"Twenty-seven," Ben corrects him.

Ulysses shoots him a look through the screen so cold that Ben can't help but flinch a little.

"Seriously, what the fuck?" Ulysses questions. "I need you more now than ever."

Ben shuffles in his chair.

"I wasn't feeling well this morning," Ben replies.

"What is it this time, Monkey Pox?" Ulysses asks sarcastically.

"No," Ben responds. "Just some stomach issues, but I feel better now."

"Good ... good. Now about NikNak, have you had some time to do the risk analysis? Are we good here?" Ulysses asks impatiently.

Ben rubs his hands together uncomfortably. "Ulysses … are you sure we want to get into business with these people?" Ulysses' eyebrows raise. "I mean," Ben continues. "There is some 'questionable' content on their platform … Stuff that I am not entirely comfortable with…."

"What kind of content?" Ulysses puts both palms on the desk and leans forward.

"I mean … There is this girl who has like three million followers and twenty-eight thousand subscribers and…" Ben inhales deeply. "She doesn't look of age, to be honest." Ben exhales.

"And—you can confirm she is underage? You saw her identification?"

"Well, no." Ben clears his throat. "She just looks young."

"We can't make multi-million-dollar decisions on hearsay." Ulysses looks around his room. "I once dated a girl in her thirties who looked like she was barely in her twenties. The girl you are talking about could just look young for her age." Ulysses leans back in his chair. A motion he always does when he feels like he's won an argument.

"But … what if she not?" Ben retorts.

"Ben … Ben … Ben," Ulysses always says Ben's name three times in a slow, punctuated fashion when he feels Ben is being unreasonable. At first, it was madly irritating, and now it is positively infuriating. "There are always bad actors on any platform," Ulysses proceeds to monologue. "Section 230 protects any content provider against those bad actors." Ulysses leans forward. "Let me put it this way, if you go into a gun shop and buy a gun, then use that gun to kill people, is the gun shop owner liable?" Ulysses stares at Ben. "Should he be charged as an accomplice just because he sold you the firearm?" Ulysses stares directly into the camera at Ben, awaiting a response to his bulletproof argument.

"I guess not," Ben sighs.

"Right." Ulysses slams his desk with his palm, another gesture of victory. "Look, if bad things are happening, the authorities will deal with it. Our role here is to support NikNak in going public. They can do whatever they want with their platform, and we are here to support them!" Ulysses reaches for his water pitcher and begins pouring. "We stand to make a lot of money from this, Ben," he says softly. "Let's try not to screw this up." He nods at Ben and ends the video chat.

Later that evening, Ben is washing the dishes after making dinner. When he and Jinni lived together, they decided that if one person cooked, the other did the dishes. Dinner was the best part of their relationship. Ben is not a bad cook in his own right, but Jinni made dishes he had never heard of. She explained to him that she would often help her aunt with the cooking when she was younger.

Ben's mind wanders back to his second date with Jinni.

He remembered walking up the stairs to the bar where she told him to meet her, half drunk and nervous. He scanned around and saw her sitting at the end. A guy was standing close to her, talking to her. Ben scratched his neck and contemplated leaving. He had already saved her once from a drunk guy; he did not like conflict. He was about to turn around and leave when he heard a voice shout.

"Honey ... Honey!" Ben looked to where she was seated. Her hand was up, motioning him to come over. He walked over slowly. As soon as he got close, she grabbed his arm.

"John, meet my boyfriend, Ben," she told the guy hovering over her. John took a step back in disgust. "Babe," she continued as she patted the seat. "I saved this seat for you." She removed her purse from the seat adjacent to her. Ben squeezed between them and sat down.

"Whatever," the guy muttered before walking away.

Ben turned to her, his eyebrow raised.

"Boyfriend?" he asked.

She smiled at him, and then they both burst out laughing.

"Yes, Ben," she said, flashing her eyelashes. "You're my boyfriend—" She smiled as she placed her hand on top of his. Ben smiled back, then called over the bartender and ordered drinks.

#

Ben comes back to himself in the kitchen, smiling over the memory. He finishes the last dish, washes his hands, and sits on his couch, drink in hand.

Over the next couple of days, Ben drowns himself at work. FrontSpark has promised NikNak that they would complete the required information for the S-1 by the beginning of the next quarter, which is about sixty days away. Ben is tasked with reviewing their management structure from the technical side and providing the security review. He frequently meets with Pavlov and Demetri, trying to decipher their organization. To his surprise, there is little of a structure in place.

Sitting on top is Demetri, the company's president and CEO. Beneath him are Pavlov, the CTO, and Jason, the COO. Pavlov has a staff of engineers, but most of the complex programming is done by him. Ben finds him increasingly difficult to work with. When Ben suggests hiring a director to help him run his engineering team and offers a few candidates, Pavlov scoffs at each resume. He criticizes their technical acumen, the companies that they came from, and almost anything else about their credentials. The conversation tended to go like this:

"Pavlov, I have a candidate from Facebook. She —"

"Facebook? Facebook!" Pavlov screams at him over the video chat. "Those guys are a bunch of hacks."

Or:

"Pavlov, this candidate has some excellent experience; he graduated from Berkeley with a master's in Computer—"

"Pass," Pavlov says as he is typing into his phone. "Berkeley graduates are a bunch of idiots."

Or:

"Pavlov, this candidate is exciting; he's a Senior Engineering Manager at an early-stage start-up." Ben watches as Pavlov's ears perk up. "He's been there for three years and was their Senior Principal Software Engineer—"

Pavlov raises his palm to stop Ben. "What kind of start-up?"

"Umm," Ben takes a look at his notes. "Fin-Tech," Ben replies. Ben hears a weird noise come from Pavlov. When he was a kid, he used to love the show *Batman: The Animated Series*. In that show is a character called the Joker, whom the famous Mark Hamill voiced. The sound coming from Pavlov is a direct facsimile of the Joker's laugh.

"Fin-Tech?" Pavlov asks as he bangs the desk in hilarity. "You want us to hire a guy from FinTech?"

"Well, he has excellent credentials, and I think—"

"Pass!"

Finally, after about fifteen candidates, Ben gives up and asks Pavlov precisely what he is looking for.

"Hmmm," Pavlov says, rubbing his chin and leaning back in his chair. After a few moments, he turns and faces Ben. "I am looking for someone who can establish a torrent network, set up a crypto coin, or be an expert in compression algorithms. Do you have anyone like that?"

Ben runs his hands through his hair.

"Pavlov, those kinds of individuals are not easy to find. Most of them don't have corporate experience and are usually freelancers. Wouldn't you want someone with a little more management experience who has previously worked at a mid-to-large size company?"

"Ben," Pavlov says softly, folding his hands in front of his body. "I want a Ross Ulbricht, and you keep giving me Ross Ul-Shit."

"Didn't Ross Ulbricht get convicted of two life sentences plus forty years?" Ben asks.

Pavlov ends the call.

It is around eight in the evening at Ben's apartment. He has just finished a grueling workday and has nothing to do. He ignores his phone like it has the plague, only using it for work-related stuff and responding to texts from his mom. He sits on his couch, drumming his fingers on the arm of his sofa. He has not had a drink in a few nights, either. He is sitting on his couch with nothing to do. It is Friday night. He considers going out but realizes the pandemic is still happening, and most of the bars are closed or only allowing a limited number of people inside. His TV doesn't have cable, and most of the stuff he watches is streamed through his phone. He sighs and reaches for his phone. He unlocks it and begins browsing through his social media feeds. Nothing, in particular, interests him, just his friends and acquaintances, all living the life that dreams are made of. He cannot fathom how everyone looks so happy, well-dressed, and fit. He sees pictures of birthday parties with magnificent spreads. He sees people he used to party with in hot air balloons taking breath-taking selfies. He sees old classmates trekking through the forest with beautiful mountain backdrops—people socializing in pristine parks.

"You all are not supposed to be doing that," Ben says softly. "Don't you know we have a lockdown going on?"

Ben locks his phone and starts pacing around his living room. He used to be one of those people. He used to go out, party, socialize, get drunk, and have fun. Those days are far behind him.

His mind wanders back to Jinni.

He and Jinni started hanging out more and more after their second date at the bar. He found it complimentary and thrilling that someone so young would be interested in him.

"Goddamn you, Ben! You lucky son-of-a-bitch!" Raj would say to him, shaking his head in admiration and disbelief after Ben told him about his latest exploit with Jinni. This was late into their friendship, which would soon be over. Things were changing between them ever since Raj had gotten engaged. His soon-to-be wife, Indra, disapproved of his and Ben's late-night drinking excursions. So they were hanging out less and less these days. Ben did not mind so much lately as Jinni was filling in the gap that Raj had left. He was happy for Raj but felt a little disappointed. By this point, they had been good friends for many years, but Raj wanted to grow up, and Ben wanted to keep the party going.

It had become increasingly difficult for Ben and Raj to find time for each other. Raj resigned from FrontSpark a few weeks back. He took a higher-paying corporate job as a Senior Security Engineer for a large multinational bank. His rationale was that he was to be married soon and needed to be in a better position financially for his family. Today was his last day at the office, and Ben made him join him for an after-work drink. Raj looked at his phone.

"You have somewhere to be, big guy?" Ben asked playfully. "The new ball and chain got you locked up pretty tight, huh."

Raj smiled and shook his head. "No, Indra is just making us dinner, and she wants me home before it gets cold."

Ben patted his friend on the shoulder.

"Enough about my boring life, Ben; tell me about this twenty-two-year-old Asian girl. How are things between you two?" Raj asked, trying to change the subject.

Ben took another swig of his drink.

"She's moving into my place tomorrow," Ben replied coyly.

Raj opened his eyes wide. "Wow, that was fast. How long have you been dating, around two months or so?"

"Six weeks," Ben corrected him.

After seeing each other for over a month, Jinni dropped a bombshell on him. They met up at a bar after Ben got off work. Jinni seemed distracted and not her usual jovial self. When Ben got the courage to ask her what was wrong, she told him that she was being kicked out of her apartment and was moving to another city about an hour away. This floored Ben. She shrugged and stared at her drink when he asked her what had happened. They sat in silence for a few minutes. At this point in their relationship, they already had pet names and regularly introduced each other as their "boyfriend/girlfriend." He met a few of her friends (well, one, Jayne) and her little sister. They were officially a couple.

Ben sat there thinking for a bit; he could not believe what he was about to propose.

"How about you move in with me?" he asked shyly.

Jinni, who was stirring her drink, suddenly stopped and stiffened. She slowly turned on her stool towards him. "Just for a short while," he added. "You know ... until you get back on your feet."

Jinni's eyes widened, and a smile crawled on her face. She wrapped her hands around Ben and embraced him tightly.

"You would do that for me?" she asked softly.

"Sure, baby bear," he said as he wrapped his arms around her waist. "Why not? We get along well, and my apartment is lonely without you."

She released him and smiled at him. She waved down the bartender and ordered shots.

"To us!" she shouted. They clinked glasses and downed their shots.

#

Ben drunkenly tries to get up from the couch to go to the bathroom. He knocks over the half-filled drink on the coffee table next to him. As it falls, Ben tries to grab it, but being reasonably tipsy, he misses the glass, slips, and finds himself on the floor next to his couch. To add insult to injury, his phone crashes down on his brow.

"Ouch!" he screams at the phone. Ben looks further along the floor at the fallen glass, where the liquid is slowly spilling out and pooling towards the phone. "Good, now you die, you piece of shit!" he shouts at the phone. He watches as the liquid gets closer and closer to the phone. Ben quickly picks it up off the floor when the spilled drink is about to touch his phone. He sits up and leans on the foot of the couch. He grabs some tissue from the coffee table and cleans up the mess.

He looks at his phone, which is still unlocked and is playing a short video from his social media feed. The playing video looks like it was filmed at a country bar where a bunch of the patrons—respectfully six feet apart—are doing a line dance in sync with the music. Ben closes one eye so he can focus and read the poster's name.

"Darren, you sell out, son of a bitch," Ben whispers. Darren is an ex-colleague of his at FrontSpark. Ben and Raj once took a weekend trip to Tennessee with him. They were all around twenty-eight years old, and Ben remembered how Darren loved his hip-hop. Ben and Raj always messed with him, proclaiming that Tupac was better than the Notorious

156

B.I.G. This would set off Darren into a spew of mini rants about how "Biggy" could do any style and despite his relatively short career, his music was more timeless than Tupac's. He would list his songs and achievements, and Ben and Raj would start cracking up. It was always funny to see the quiet Darren get so worked up. On that trip, Darren met his soon-to-be wife, Amanda. Two years later, they were married. Ben did not go to the wedding. They lost touch soon after that.

Ben could feel the anger starting to boil inside of him.

"Fuck you all!" he screams at his phone. "Fuck your line dancing, mountain climbing, social distancing asses."

Ben stands up; he is raging now.

"What, you all think you're better than me?" Ben asks the empty room, pointing his finger at his chest. "Well, you're fuckin' not; you call that fun?" Ben is now pacing angrily around the room. "I'll show you fun! I'll show all of you miserable fucks what fun is—"

Ben's voice trails off. He has a thought; a smile crosses his face.

He runs to his kitchen table and grabs a sheet of paper from his notebook. He grabs a pen, sits down, opens his laptop, and types some words into Google. As he clicks on links, he starts writing stuff down. After about thirty minutes, he looks at his list and chuckles. He stands up from the kitchen table triumphantly.

"I need clothes!" he proclaims loudly. Ben looks up a particular type of store on his phone and saves it. He checks the clock and decides to go to bed. *Tomorrow I will show those fucks what fun is,* he thinks.

CHAPTER 14 - FML

The next day is a Saturday, and Ben sets his alarm to wake up early. He gets in his car and drives about thirty miles out of town. His destination is a store called *Vintage You*. He parks his car, puts on his mask, exits the vehicle, and opens the door to the shop.

"Hi, I'm Kim. Can I help you?" He is greeted by a small girl as soon as he steps into the store. A mask covers her face; she has soft brown eyes.

"Umm, yes," Ben mumbles. He brings out his phone. "I am looking for something like this?"

Kim takes a look at the photo on his phone. "Oh," she proclaims.

In the picture is a blond man wearing a pinkish (fuchsia? Ben did not know how to describe the color) oversized jacket with a large lapel, a black shirt, and oversized sunglasses.

"Hmm," Kim mutters. "I think we have something like that in the back. What European size are you?"

Ben thinks for a moment, then says he is not sure. Kim walks out from behind the counter with a flat tape measure. "Hold your arms out, and I'll measure you."

Ben stretches out his arms. Kim gently touches him with the tape and writes down some numbers on paper. Satisfied with his measurements, she goes towards the back of the store and starts pulling clothes off the rack. She then lays them down on the counter next to Ben.

"I think these should fit you," she says confidently. "Is this for some '70s party?"

Ben smiles and nods. He looks over the clothes. "Can I try them on?"

"Sure, the fitting rooms are in the back."

After trying on a couple of different outfits, Ben is satisfied that he has the right look. He puts the clothes on his arm and goes to the cashier to pay.

"That will be $865.34," she says, looking at the register.

Ben's eyes shoot open. "That's a lot more than I was expecting to pay," he says as he digs through his wallet for his credit card.

The cashier looks up at him. "History does cost." She smiles at Ben, who, despite the hefty charge, smiles back.

Ben spends a long time getting ready. He constantly looks at the mirror, then back to his phone and the mirror again. After a few more minutes of combing his hair, he feels he is as ready as ever. He steps out of his bathroom and into his bedroom and looks at himself in the large mirror behind the bedroom door.

"Wassup, cool pimp, daddio," Ben blurts out loud as he admires himself in the mirror. He walks towards the living room couch, where his phone sits next to his notebook. He looks over the list he had written the night before. The list contains five entries. The list's title is *Five Greatest Parties of all time*. Number one on that list is *Bianca Jagger's birthday, Studio 54*.

It takes Ben almost an hour to find the right video; it is about an hour-long documentary. In the documentary is a brief section that shows the inside of Studio 54 at the peak of its popularity. He pauses the video and looks at himself in the mirror.

He is wearing a pinkish (fuchsia?) colored coat with oversized lapels, tight white pants, and a black shirt. He also bought big oversized glasses with yellow-tinted lenses. He has to admit that he looks good. He pours a drink and dissolves it in a couple of gulps. Ben mentally prepares himself. *Am I really going to do this?* he thinks. *This is crazy.* Ben reconsiders for a few seconds before recalling all the Instagram Stories and Facebook Reels of all his "friends" doing cool and exciting things. *Fuck them, there is no going back now.* He goes to the middle of his living room, presses play on his phone, holds his breath, closes his eyes, and touches the screen.

The heat of the club hits him first. The smell, second. It is hard to describe, but it's a combination of weed, sex, cigarettes, perfume, body odor, alcohol, and a strange peppermint smell. He positions himself to "superimpose" in the back of the balcony overlooking the dance floor. The cigarette smoke overwhelms him, and he grabs his chest and starts coughing. He waves his hand in front of his face and clears the air. Ben looks around.

He has seen his share of drunk and fucked up people, but this is at another level. The music is so loud that it is almost headache-inducing. Ben pushes his way to the front of the balcony and peers over the edge. He leans over and sees lights flashing, many people dancing, and what appears to be a ballerina troop dancing ballet to the disco beats. Ben decides to go downstairs to the bar and get a drink. After finding the stairs (where a couple is having sex on the bottom step), Ben slides around them and emerges into the main room. One thing that surprises him is how relatively small the club is. Ben always had pictured Studio 54 as more grandiose, larger than life.

The club has one square wrap-around bar, a few tables, and a dance floor. There are column lights that extend down and flash in different colors. The energy of the setting more than makes up for its size. It is a pulsing, driving, electric vibe that makes Ben crack a smile. Everyone appears to be drunk, high, or both. The look on their faces is one that Ben has not seen before. It is a look of pure joy and freedom. Ben makes his way to the crowded bar. People in colorful outfits walk past him as he patiently waits to get his drink. As she walks by, a pretty black lady in a beautiful rainbow dress strokes his cheek and chest. She turns and gives him a wink and a smile. Ben looks away and cracks a smile. As the line moves slowly, he peers at the VIP section and is surprised to see a young Cher dancing on top of her table. He is taken aback by how pretty she looks. He had only known her from some movies he had watched. While he never found her particularly attractive, seeing her pre-plastic surgery and in her early twenties, he finds her exceptionally beautiful.

Ben makes his way to the front of the bar and orders a vodka and soda from the shirtless bartender. The club is getting hot, and Ben can feel the heat starting to build up in his body. The bartender makes his drink and tells him the price is three dollars. Ben smiles at the lower price than he is used to and reaches into his pocket to pull out his wallet.

His wallet is not there.

Ben sheepishly grins at the confused shirtless bartender. "I … um … seem to have forgotten my wallet," he says, patting his pockets.

"What?" The shirtless bartender shouts at him. "It's three dollars, pal; c'mon, I got people waiting." The shirtless bartender impatiently puts his hands on his hips.

Ben shrugs and starts walking away from the bar drink-less. Before he exits the crowd, two large bouncers converge on him. They put their hands under his armpits, gesture towards the bar, and point at Ben. The shirtless bartender nods. They lift a surprised Ben off his feet and carry him to the club's side. They nod at another bouncer, who takes one look at a confused Ben and smirks. The bouncer lets them pass. Ben enters a dark room, where he sees lighters heating spoons, and people sitting on the floor with needles at the ready. The light emitting from the lighter is flickering on their desperate faces. Ben finds the courage to speak.

"Where are you taking—oof." Ben doubles over. The bald bouncer on his right had released him only to clock him in the abdomen with a giant fist.

"Shaddap," he says.

They lift Ben again and head towards the door to the side. They open the door, and Ben feels the cool New York wind on his face. Like in a cartoon, they toss Ben into the trash pile, dusting off their hands and telling him never to return. Ben lays among the garbage, doubled over, holding his gut.

It takes him a few minutes to get up. He carefully walks towards the street, covered in garbage, his new vintage pants ripped, and he has a hole in his jacket. He sits on the curb away from the large crowd trying to get in. While he sits, he ponders something.

Ben and his friends laughed at its comical design when the new hundred-dollar bill was released a while ago. They called it Monopoly money. Ben and his work friends were sitting in a living room, smoking weed and drinking. One of his friends, Jay, stands up.

"Looky looky," Jay shouted as he stood in the middle of the group. He reached into his pocket, pulled out his wallet, and flashed a brand-new, one-hundred-dollar bill.

"Is that—" someone asked.

"Yessir, it is," Jay said, beaming.

"Can I see it?" a girl in their group asked. Jay thought about it for a second before handing her the bill. The girl looked at it in wonder before the guy next to her asked to see it.

"It looks like Monopoly money!" she exclaimed, turning the bill in her hand.

"Lemme see!" the guy next to her demanded. She passed over the bill as an ever increasingly nervous Jay watched. The guy raised the bill to the light to see the watermark and then mime-ed, putting it in his pocket to the crowd's laughter. Finally, Jay got his money back.

"You know why they changed the design," said a voice from behind. Ben was sitting next to a girl whose name he could not recall; all he could remember was that he badly wanted to sleep with her.

"Yeah, why?" Jay shouted back.

A bearded figure arose from his chair. Kevin, or, as his friends called him, Special K because he was usually high, drunk, or both. He was about to give an epic monologue.

"Because think about it," Kevin said as he pointed at his head. "If someone invents a time machine and goes back to the late '70s or early '80s and brings like a thousand dollars with him," Kevin circled his hands in the air, "which in the '70s was like a million dollars—" Jay shot Ben a look. Ben rolled his eyes. "What happens if that person takes that money and buys tons of shares of Apple? He would be a billionaire, man … a billionaire. The government can't have that. So they got to change their money all the time to protect themselves. That's why they want us to use credit cards!" At this point, Kevin was shouting. "It's all about control, man, control!"

#

Ben sits on the curb, recalling. He wonders if that is why he cannot bring anything with him other than his clothes. Something as simple as bringing in a few hundred or a few thousand dollars, opening a bank account and letting the interest accrue, or even buying up stocks could significantly impact his world. He can only make changes that he personally can make. Nothing that could cause massive financial, social, or technological changes is allowed. No smartphone, no wallet, no watch, just the clothes on his back.

Ben lifts his head off his chest. A guy in a motorcycle vest and no shirt and two girls are walking up to him. They step around him and start heading towards the club.

"Get yourself a slice, bum." The guy throws a dollar bill at Ben's chest. The girls snicker loudly as they walk away. Ben walks around '70s New York City until he finds a pizza place. He uses the dollar, gets a slice, and eats it. It is the best pizza he has ever had.

Ben wipes his hands with a napkin and looks at his wrist at the watch that is not there. He knows time is almost up; he had always been good at estimating the passage of time, but now he has gotten even better at it. He stands up, walks towards the door, and exits when he sees the light flashing in front of his eyes. He is now standing alone in his living room. He can still smell the pizza place on his clothes.

"Those mother fuckin' '70s pieces of shit!" he screams to an empty room. He had a list of places he could have gone instead of Studio 54. *P. Diddy's White Party*, the *2014 Met Gala*, and *Alexander Wangs's 2017 #WANGFEST*, but he chose the '70s because all those parties had lots of cameras at them. He didn't want someone he knew browsing YouTube one day and seeing his face pop up.

You know, his mind suggests. *You changed nothing; you can always try again.*

Ben looks for his phone and finds it on the floor. He unlocks the screen and restarts the video. He fast-forwards to the section where he had entered previously. In the dark, grainy film, he can make out his silhouette in the background. Ben knew that he would be there, but he did not care. He can touch the other side of the screen and enter on his left or behind his second self. But first, he needs a few drinks and to clean his clothes.

Five vodka sodas in, Ben is ready. He washed and cleaned his clothes while he drank. Besides some small rips down the side of his pants and a small hole in his jacket, he looks the same. He downs the remains of his drink and takes stock of himself in his bedroom mirror. *Clothes, check. Drunk, check. Ready, check.* Ben stands in the middle of his living room, this time putting a pillow directly under his phone. He takes a deep breath and starts up the video. He touches the left side of the screen and closes his eyes.

He "superimposes" himself; he breathes in the smells of the club and opens his eyes. He looks around until he finds his other "self." He watches himself stumble around the balcony towards the edge. Ben follows "himself," being careful to stay out of "his" vision. He watches "himself" lean over the edge of the balcony and look around awkwardly. Ben smiles. *Rookie*, he thinks and laughs.

"What are you laughing at, baby?" says someone to his left. Ben turns slowly, not wanting to take his eyes off his other "self." His eyes meet the eyes of the pretty black lady who had smiled at him at the bar last time.

"Nothing," Ben replies, glancing towards the other "Ben."

"Who are you here with, baby?" she asks, slowly bringing her drink to her lips. Ben notices she has on dark red lipstick that stains the straw as she sips. Ben glances at the other "Ben," who is leaving the balcony to head downstairs. Thinking fast, Ben answers her question.

"You know." He shrugs. "I came with a date, but they wouldn't let her in."

The pretty black lady laughs. "Yes, they are pretty strict about who they let in." She stares him up and down. She reaches for a vial around her neck and unscrews it.

"Here, baby," she says as she brings what looks like a little spoon filled with white powder. "Take some of this, and you'll forget all about that pretty little thing you left behind." She places the spoon under Ben's nose and closes one of his nostrils with her other hand. Ben almost flinches but instead inhales instinctively.

Ben is no stranger to drugs. When he was younger, he had done ecstasy, weed, and acid. At twenty-five, he stopped and preferred to focus on alcohol instead. Jinni had introduced him to the white powder. This girl reminds him of Jinni. When he inhales, it feels like he is hit by a ton of bricks; he takes a step back and begins to lose his balance. The pretty lady takes his arm and steadies him. She laughs.

"How was that, baby?"

Ben shakes his head hard. "Whoa!" is all he can muster.

The lady grabs his arm. "C'mon, baby, let's go downstairs; you can meet some of my friends."

Ben nods his head agreeably; he blinks hard. Whatever he took hit him hard. He feels very, very floaty. The pretty lady leads him towards the stairs. The stairs are packed. Moving down is slow, more so because of the couple having sex at the bottom.

"Where you from, sugar?" she asks. "You don't seem from round here."

Ben opens his mouth and quickly shuts it. He almost tells her he is from San Francisco but decides against it. Instead, he winks and smiles and says he is from out of town.

After a few minutes of squeezing through people, they finally exit the staircase. The lady asks him something, but he can not hear her. She moves up close to his ear.

"Isn't this place groovy?" Her lips flicker against Ben's ear.

Ben smiles and nods. He looks towards the bar. He can barely see through the crowd and makes out the back of his other "head." He watches himself fumble with his pockets, looking for a wallet that would not be there.

"Did you want a drink, honey?" the lady asks him.

Ben looks at her. Now that there is light from the dance floor, he can truly see her. She has a fabulous rainbow dress that looks like it has been made of individual strips of cloth. It hangs from her body via two straps. She has soft light-dark skin that glows from the lights coming from the dance floor. Her hair is in an afro and glistens. Her dark red lipstick fits her face and features well. She is almost as tall as him, but he also notices that she is not wearing any shoes. Ben shakes his head as they proceed to walk past the bar. He asks her where they are heading. She tells him that some of her friends are on the other side of the dance floor.

As they walk closer to the bar, Ben watches as the shirtless bartender shouts at the other "him" and nods towards the two large bouncers in the back. They start making their way towards the other "Ben." Ben stops the girl from going further by asking her name. In reality, he does not want his other self to see them.

"Destiny," she says, smiling. "But you can call me Des." She asks for Ben's name, and he tells her. Out of the corner of his eye, he watches as the two large bouncers hoist the "other" him up from his armpits and begin carrying him out. Ben nods towards the commotion, gently pushes Destiny back, and shields her from the two bouncers and "himself," effectively blocking her view. As the two bouncers pass, he looks into her eyes. She keeps her smile, and Ben feels one emerging on his face. She looks towards the bouncers and the other "him."

"I wonder what that was about?" she asks.

Ben watches "himself" being dragged out.

"No ticket!" Ben says as he breaks into laughter. The drug Destiny had given him made him feel floaty and goofy. Destiny looks at him, confused. *In a few years*, Ben thinks, *you will get that joke.* "Let's go." He gestures for her to lead.

She leads him towards the back of the club, where three of her friends are sitting at a tiny table. At the table are two stunning-looking women and a creatively dressed man. In the middle of the table are a few joints and a couple of lines of white powder. Destiny introduces Ben to her friends, but they barely seem to register his existence. They nod at him and offer him a line. Ben accepts the rolled-up dollar bill. He still feels woozy from the first hit Destiny gave him. *When in Rome,* he thinks. He leans over and quickly inhales. He immediately grabs his throat and starts coughing. The back of his throat feels raw, and his eyes water.

"What the fuck is that!" he shouts between coughs. The two women at the table immediately start giggling. The well-dressed man stands up and slaps him on the back.

"That was just some LBJ, my man," the well-dressed man says. "My name is Jack, but most call me Wolf Man."

Ben wipes the tears from his eyes.

"Why do they call you Wolf Man?" Ben asks, finally composing himself.

"Because ... OOWWWWWWWW!" he responds and then proceeds to howl like a wolf at the moon. The women at the table hold their sides because they are laughing so hard.

These people are high as fuck! Ben thinks. He manages to control the coughing, but the drip in his throat is starting to irritate him.

"C'mon, Ben," Destiny says, grabbing at his shirt. "Let's dance."

"Hold on there one second, Des." Jack, aka Wolf Man, picks up one of the rolled-up cigarettes. "Do you want to do a hit of this Joy Stick with me?" Jack, aka Wolf Man, asks, putting the rolled-up cigarette in Ben's face.

Ben glances at Destiny, who smiles at him encouragingly.

"Ok," Ben says.

Jack, aka Wolf Man, lights the cigarette, closes his eyes, and takes a long deep drag. He exhales into Ben's face, forcing Ben to stifle a cough again.

"Your turn," Jack, aka Wolf Man, says as he hands over the cigarette to Ben. Ben looks at Destiny and the two girls sitting at the table. All of them are staring at him. Jack, aka Wolfman, reminds him of people like Ulysses and Bobby Chitz. They always need to be in control. Jack, aka Wolfman, is a rich, powerful, and controlling man. These girls are his; this place in the club is his; if Ben wants to invade his turf, Ben needs to prove himself worthy. Ben grabs the cigarette from Jack's hand. Destiny grabs his hand; at first, Ben thinks she will protest and try to stop him from smoking it. But instead, she guides his hand towards her mouth, wraps her lips around the joint, and inhales, then exhales deeply. She gives Ben a coy smile. Ben shrugs, closes his eyes, takes a deep puff, and repeats what is slowly becoming his mantra, *When in Rome—*

The next time Ben opens his eyes, he is on the dance floor with Destiny. He shakes his head furiously, trying to recall how he has gotten out here. He is drenched in sweat, and Destiny is furiously dancing around him. He feels that his head is detached and floating above his body. He looks down and finds his arms and legs moving furiously to the beat. He is dancing, something he does not usually do, and not only that, he is in the middle of a sea of people. All are moving to the music in a synchronized, chaotic rhythm. The loud disco music is blasting in his ears. He looks towards Destiny, who dances in front of him, and vibrates to the beat so fast that it seems like she is in the midst of a stroke or seizure. Ben blinks hard and looks around. The classic song "Last Dance" booms onto the speakers. Bars of lights drop down from the ceiling, engulfing the dance floor. Ben looks towards Destiny, and she is dancing up a storm. A small crowd has begun to encircle her.

Ben watches her dance, her face a granite slab of emotionless fury. She seems to stare through the crowd, the sweat glistening off her cheeks. She is lost in the moment. The song plays:

Last Dance,

Last Dance, Last Dance for looooooooooove!

Ben feels dizzy. Destiny is dancing, and the circle around her grows. Streaks of light fly past Ben's eyes. *What the fuck was in that Joy Stick?* he wonders. The crowd begins to turn ugly. All their faces appear to be looking at him, mad and hungry. They seem to have vampire teeth, their mouths covered in blood. Ben tries to look above the crowd, away from their faces. Their hands in the air become disjointed and distorted. The streaks of the lights start to become blades, moving towards the hands of the crowd. Ben looks at the blades in shock. He tries to shout to warn them.

"Watch out!" he screams, but no one pays attention to him. Ben watches as the blades of light cut into the hands of the unsuspecting patrons. Fingers, blood, and body parts fly everywhere. Ben tries to move away, but the blood and body parts splash around him. He again shouts, "Watch out, the lights are dangerous!" but again, no one hears him. He furiously points at the light blades, but the crowd keeps dancing. Ben tries to escape, but the group keeps pushing him back towards the dance floor. Ben looks for Destiny and finds her on the floor, covered in blood and fingers, grinding to the song's beat. He can not take it anymore. He pushes his way furiously through the crowd, trying to escape.

When he emerges from the dance floor, he spots a light and is drawn towards it. He enters the room; the buzzing of fluorescents replaces the music. He moves towards the back of the bathroom, desperate to escape the music. As he passes the first stall, he looks inside. In the stall are two people, a man and a woman. Both look overly skinny, and the light did them no favors. Ben sniffs. He can detect a slight peppermint-like smell in the air. In the stall, the two people are holding a lighter under a bent spoon. They bring out a syringe and draw the syrup-like liquid into it. They place the spoon on the floor and gently flick the needle. Ben stands there, watching. Not noticing him, the woman sticks out her arm and ties a tourniquet around it. The man taps her arm and injects her with the brown liquid. Her eyes roll into the back of her head. The man sees Ben and flinches. He smiles.

"Did you want some?" he asks, smiling. He is missing three teeth.

Ben turns towards the door and runs. He moves as fast as he can through the club towards the door where he had been previously thrown out. He dodges the two massive bouncers who shout, "Hey! You can't go that way!" as he flies by them. He enters the dark room, unlocks the back door, and exits into the night. He stops and catches his breath at the same garbage pile he had been thrown on earlier. The back door reopens, and he sees the two hulking bouncers.

"Stay out!" one of them screams at Ben as they slam the door shut. Ben waits until the door is closed before flashing them the finger. There are streaks of light flashing all over his vision. He feels he is going to be sick—

He emerges into his apartment, drops to his hands and knees, and throws up all over the floor.

"What the fuck was that!" Ben says as he kneels over his vomit.

CHAPTER 15 - TTYL

Ben tosses and turns as he tries to force sleep. Shadows around his room keep coming to life. The drugs are coursing through his system, and the only way he can sleep is to cower under the blankets like he is seven years old again.

The next day goes on as usual; Ben goes to his meetings, has lunch (which he promptly throws up), and tries to do some work. He keeps seeing trails of light outside his eyes, but he figures it is the residue of the drugs he had consumed. Later that night, Ben goes to the kitchen to make himself a drink. He opens the freezer and realizes he is out of vodka. Cursing, he grabs his jacket and mask and heads outside. The cold wind feels good on his face. He walks one block to the liquor store. As he walks, he passes a masked homeless man. The homeless man stops and stares at Ben. He begins to point.

"You fat fuck … You fat fuck!"

The homeless man screams and points at Ben as he walks by. Ben moves away from the man and continues to walk towards the liquor store.

"Ben!" screams Sam through his mask. Ben was hoping Sam would be off tonight as he always roped him into small talk when all Ben wanted to do was purchase his vodka and leave. "The usual?" Sam asks, already turning around to grab Ben's favorite vodka brand. He has it on the counter and is ringing Ben up before Ben can even reply.

"You look tired," Sam says with a hint of concern. "You getting enough sleep?"

"Yeah," Ben replies, pulling out his phone and moving it towards the P.O.S. system on the counter.

"How come I never see you with that pretty girl you used to come in with?" Sam asks.

Ben's eyes shoot up to meet Sam's. When Ben's eyes hit Sam's, Sam takes a step back as if Ben had physically nudged him. He holds Ben's gaze for a microsecond before averting his eyes downwards.

"Cool … you're all set. Did you want a bag?"

Ben shakes his head but will not look away. Sam keeps his gaze down and only glances up to see if Ben is still watching him. Ben holds his gaze a fraction longer, then grabs the bottle and walks out of the store.

As soon as Ben arrives home, he opens the bottle, leans his head back, puts the bottle to his lips, and drinks. He watches the vodka exit the bottle and enters his mouth. He finishes about a quarter of it before his eyes sting, and his throat begins to hurt. He pulls the bottle away and lets out a deep breath and a cough. He wipes his mouth, grabs a glass, and makes himself a drink.

Hours later, he is sitting on the couch. His mind wanders. He thinks about Jinni and the times they have had together. He remembers surprising her with tickets to Disneyland (she had always wanted to go). How much fun they had on that trip. He recalls the first time they had made love and remembers how she snuggled next to him when she slept. Always a hand on him as if to prevent him from flying away. They had many amazing dinners, great nights out, and fun conversations.

One day it all changed.

Jinni came home one night and immediately went to their shared bedroom. Ben was sitting on the couch watching a basketball game. He did not remember who was playing. He looked at the bedroom door in confusion as Jinni usually greeted him and planted a kiss on his lips whenever she returned home. He got up from the couch and went to the bedroom, where she was lying away from him over the covers on her side. He walked to her and got on the bed.

"Hey babe," he said playfully. Jinni did not answer. He reached over and gently touched her shoulder. She violently shook his hand off.

"Ok … Ok," Ben said, retreating from the bed with his hands in a defensive position in front of his chest. He started walking out of the room, waiting for her to call him and apologize. He stepped out of the room and looked back; she was lying in the same position. He quietly closed the door. Ben went back to the couch to continue to watch his game. He figured Jinni had a bad day and would eventually come out to talk to him.

She never did.

Things started deteriorating after that. Jinni quickly lashed out at Ben for even the slightest concern. Questions like "Are you ok?" or "What's wrong?" were met with a hard stare and hostile language. She would say things like "Nothing's wrong!" or "Leave me alone!" Ben felt isolated and confused.

One night a few days later, Ben was watching TV, and Jinni entered the room dressed up. Ben lifted one eyebrow and peeked in her direction.

"I'm going out," she claimed as she put on her shoes by the door.

Ben took a quick look at the clock on his smartphone.

"Babe, it's midnight on a Tuesday," he said to her with concern. "Where are you going?"

Jinni looked over at him with hostile eyes. "Out," she said calmly. "I am going out," she repeated.

Ben got up from the couch and walked towards her. She started putting on her second shoe. He stopped by the door.

"Honey," he started. "You've been in a bad mood for the last couple of days. I am here if you want to talk about it." He was doing his best to remain calm and rational but was fuming inside. The last few days had been strenuous, and he was tired of it.

Jinni paused to consider his proposal but continued putting on her shoes. She stood up, looked at Ben, and opened the door.

Growing increasingly fed up, Ben stuck out his right arm and pushed the door closed. Jinni jumped back. This was the first time Ben had shown any aggression towards her.

"I am going out!" she said in a low growly voice. She stared hard into his eyes.

"No, you're not until you tell me what's been going on with you lately!" Ben shouted back.

She proceeded to open the door again, only to have Ben shut it. Jinni's whole body tensed up. She slowly moved closer, her hands rising as if she was going to embrace him. Ben, sensing victory, relaxed and lowered his voice.

"Babe, please talk to me and tell me what's—"

Jinni, quick as a cat, pushed Ben hard in his upper pectoral area. While she might have been smaller than him, the sheer force that emerged from her surprised Ben. He reeled back, placing his feet behind him, trying to regain his balance. His right leg got caught on the table near the door that held Ben's keys and wallet, and before he could comprehend it, he was on the floor. Ben looked up at Jinni; for a second, her face seemed to soften, but almost as quickly, she had a stern look on her face again.

"I am going out," she said quietly this time. She opened the door and stepped out of the apartment. Ben didn't see her again for two days.

#

Ben's head snaps up, waking from his dream. He reaches for his almost empty glass and downs the remaining content. He gets up and stumbles his way towards the kitchen. He opens his refrigerator and makes himself another drink. He places his hands on the kitchen counter and takes a deep breath. The dream disturbed him. He remembers that day vividly.

He recalls that for the next two days, he was worried sick.

He woke up abruptly the next morning and instinctively reached for the other side of the bed. Jinni was not there. He tried texting her, but she did not respond. He showered and drove to work. He tried to focus on his work, but there was a bad feeling in his gut. He kept texting and calling Jinni but got no response. When he got home, the apartment was empty. He messaged Yumi and asked if she had seen her sister or if Jinni was staying with her. She responded that she had not. After a long, worrisome day, he tried texting her one

178

more time before bed, and still no response. The next day, Ben repeated the process only to get the same results.

He woke up to the doorbell ringing loudly. He grabbed his phone off the nightstand and checked the time. It was 5:45 a.m. He stumbled out of bed and went to his front door. His heart raced. The doorbell rang again, this time in three loud successions. He walked towards the front door and slowly opened it. Jinni was still in the same clothes she had left the apartment in. She was leaning against the door frame, wobbling. It seemed like it was much effort for her to stand.

She looked up at him and gave him a tired smile. "Hi, baby," was all that she said before moving forward and collapsing in his arms.

He caught her and dragged her inside. She stunk of alcohol, and she badly needed a shower. Her eyes were bloodshot, and she had white powder residue around her nostrils.

They stumbled to the bedroom, where Ben laid her down. "Where the hell have you been?" he asked.

Jinni opened her eyes halfway, smiled, and then fell asleep. She slept for the next two days.

#

Ben pushes himself away from the counter. He realizes he has been standing in the kitchen for a while. The ice in his drink is already half melted. Ben grabs his glass and slides down to the floor. He places the drink next to him. He stares off into the distance. It dawns on him how miserable his life has been. The last six months with Jinni had been terrible. After they had broken up, the pandemic hit, and three years later, Jinni killed herself. Ben crumples on the floor of the kitchen. He is almost forty, lonely, and depressed. It just does not make any sense.

After Jinni had come to visit him that one time long after they had broken up, he found it hard, in retrospect, even to blame her. After what she had told him—*No!* Ben screams in his head. He did not want to think about that. His mind again wanders back to when he found Jinni crying on his doorstep —*No!* he screams again in his head, shaking it violently to wipe away the memories. *I am not going there!* He pushes himself off the floor, but his hand slips and knocks over the glass, spilling its contents.

"Goddamnit!" he screams out loud in the empty kitchen. He grabs some paper towels off the counter and cleans up the mess. He returns to the fridge, discovering that, once again, he is out of vodka.

"Jesus fucking Christ!" he growls under his breath. He looks over at the kitchen clock and finds it is past midnight, and the liquor store closest to him is already closed.

"Shit!" he says out loud. "Where the fuck am I going to get a drink now?" All the stores near him are closed, and he is in no condition to drive. *There is a bar open somewhere, someplace,* his mind tells him.

He laughs out loud. He runs into the living room and grabs his phone. He finds a short three-minute video from years back of people celebrating a birthday at a bar. He puts on jeans, shoes, and a shirt. Ben grabs his phone, presses play, and "superimposes" in. He walks up to the bartender and orders three chilled vodka shots. He sits and waits, watching a ballgame on TV and ignoring the "Happy Birthday" singing behind him. When the shots arrive, Ben downs them and ignores the bartender's request for payment. One of the players hits a home run. The bartender turns around. When he looks back towards Ben, Ben is gone.

When he emerges back into his apartment, he repeats the process over and over and over again. Finding different people at different bars and made sure the videos were short enough so he could order his drinks and "leave" before they demanded payment. After the seventh trip, an incredibly drunk Ben starts giggling to himself.

"Now this," he proclaims loudly, "is what I call bar hopping!"

One more time! Ben tells himself *One more time!* But he passes out before he can finish searching for the next video.

Over the next few days, Ben works on the NikNak app. He starts checking off his tasks as his organization pushes forward on creating the S-1. Ben spends a considerable amount of time on the app. Today he is greeted with the latest Kitty Josephine Nak, showing her in a wet white one-piece bikini licking on a red lollipop, asking him to join her channel for the price of $15 in crypto per month. Occasionally he would see the little girl in a black-and-white video with a red balloon tied to her wrist. She is climbing the tree, asking him to join "The Red Ballon" for $100 in crypto per month. Curiosity again gets the best of Ben, and he presses on the Nak. The same test came up, this time with different questions. What is new is a warning on the top.

You have two attempts left.

The question reads:

How many videos did Molly appear in?

Below is a selection of six options, each with a different value. Ben clicks on one at random. A flashing red screen appears.

Wrong! You have one attempt left. Try again?

Below that are two buttons:

Yes / Cancel.

Ben mutters to himself and clicks on the cancel button. He can not comprehend why they would want to screen out people willing to pay $100 a month. It does not make sense, but he knows that there is something terrible behind that assessment.

CHAPTER 16 - IIRC

Ben gets into a rhythm. He works all day, submitting his reports, meeting with his co-workers, and talking to the founders of NikNak. At night, he sits on his couch and searches for a couple of specific videos. He goes to his room, changes into a time-appropriate outfit, and "superimposes" himself. Most of the time, it is going to parties, grabbing free drinks, and talking to random people. Occasionally he visits places he always planned on going to but never got around to. He visits the Nasam tower in Seoul and places a lock he stole on the tower fence with "B+J" written on it. He sees Obama's inauguration speech live as he joins the crowd. He goes to Bali to watch the Komodo dragons. He goes to Sydney and has a beer with the Australians. Each time he invades someone else's memory, he feels less and less genuine. It is like using a cheat code to beat a game.

Ben receives a phone call.

"Mr. Ben White?" the caller asks.

"May I ask who is calling?"

"This is Detective Karl Bateson. Is this Mr. White?"

Ben freezes and nearly drops his phone. "This is him," Ben says meekly.

"Mr. White, I hope you are well." The detective continues without waiting for a response. "We were wondering if we could ask some follow-up questions regarding the death of Ms. Yoon."

Ben's heart skips a beat. "What did you want to know?" he asks.

"My partner and I will be in your area at 3 p.m. Does that time work for you?" Detective Bateson asks.

"Am I in trouble?" Ben asks as he switches the phone to his other ear.

"Let's discuss that when we meet, Mr. White," Detective Bateson says. "We will be at your residence at three o'clock. Please be home at that time."

The phone clicks off.

Ben sits nervously on his couch. At 3:01 p.m., his doorbell rings. He wipes his sweaty palms on his pants and opens the door.

"May we come in?" Detective Bateson asks, his voice muffled by the SFPD mask on his face.

Ben moves from the door and gestures for the two detectives to enter the fray. Detective Bateson enters and starts walking around. Detective Susan Gonzales follows him. She stops and talks to Ben.

"How're the arms?" she asks.

Ben shrugs and instinctively touches his arm. "It gets stiff sometimes, but it healed pretty well."

She nods and stands waiting by the door with Ben until he guides her in. Ben sits on the couch, and Detective Gonzales sits on one of the armrests on a chair across from him. Detective Bateson continues to wander around Ben's apartment. Ben stares at him suspiciously.

"Ignore him," Susan says. "Do this job long enough, and you think everything is a clue."

Detective Bateson stops when he finds something interesting and begins to reach out to touch it but pulls his hand back at the last moment.

"So," begins Detective Gonzales, pulling out an iPad from her bag. "My partner and I wanted to go over the case of Ms. Jinni Yoon's suicide with you one more time." She taps what looks like an electronic pencil against the iPad's case.

"Ok," Ben replies.

"We would like to officially close the case on Ms. Yoon's death. The D.A. is still unhappy about how you fled the scene and asked us to follow up with you. Currently, it's labeled as a 'Death by suicide,' but we are here to ensure this wasn't a viral video stunt gone wrong, and you had no part to play. It's still a weird coincidence that you happened to be at the exact spot where she attempted suicide."

"A real coincidence," Detective Bateson says, emphasizing his words.

Detective Gonzales, ignoring her partner, flips open the cover on her iPad.

Ben swallows hard.

"Mr. White," she continues. "We are here to ask you some questions. You are not under arrest or anything, for now. You are still a person of interest. If you'd like to have a lawyer present with you, we could end this conversation now—"

"Or you could just answer our questions, and we can put this whole matter behind us," Detective Bateson interjects.

"What will it be, Mr. White?" Detective Gonzales looks at her partner, then at Ben. "Do we finish this here, or would you like a lawyer present?"

Ben rubs his eyes and takes a moment to process the situation. While he felt he did nothing wrong, he could understand why they felt there was much weirdness in this instance. Of course, he could not come clean; they would think he is a nut job.

"Let's just finish this here," Ben sighs.

"Excellent." Detective Gonzales starts typing on her iPad. "We reviewed Ms. Yoon's text messages, social media profile, and phone calls. Unless you two were communicating subconsciously, it appeared you have had no communication in the last few years or so. Is that correct?"

Ben sits there for a minute. He feels both of the detective's eyes burning a hole in him.

"The sooner you answer, the quicker we can be out of here," Detective Bateson barks behind Ben which startles him.

"Yes … That seems about right," Ben finally speaks.

Detective Gonzales places the iPad on her lap and begins typing. She continues. "You and Ms. Yoon dated for how long?" she asks.

"About two years."

"And how long ago was that?"

"Over three and a half years ago," Ben replies.

"Right about when the pandemic hit?" Detective Bateson questions.

"Yeah," Ben confirms. "About three months before."

"Bad timing," Detective Bateson says while looking through Ben's shelf.

"And when did you last see Ms. Yoon?" Detective Gonzales asks.

"You mean before her death?"

"Yes, before her ... suicide." Detective Gonzales furrows her brow.

Ben sits back in his seat. The painful memory of his last encounter with Jinni starts to replay in his head. He did not want to go to that memory. Ben sighs audibly.

"About six months ago," Ben says quietly.

"And where did you see Ms. Yoon?" Detective Gonzales asks as her head perks up.

"Can we just call her Jinni?" Ben pleads.

"Sure, if that makes you feel better, Mr. White."

"And can you just call me Ben?" Ben asks. Detective Gonzales nods. Ben points towards the door. "She was outside in the hallway when I last saw her."

Detective Bateson stops moving around Ben's apartment and sits in the chair next to his partner.

"Can you describe the events that happened with Ms. Yo— with Jinni?" she asks.

"Well," Ben begins. "The pandemic at this point had been going on for almost three years, and everyone had enough. I hadn't dated in a while, so I put up my profile on Tinder, and after a few hit and misses, I finally secured a date." Ben stops and takes a sip of his water. "The date goes well, and I invite her back to my place for a drink." Ben pauses for a moment. This is a painful moment that he had hoped to forget.

"Officers ... is this really..." Ben stammers.

"It's detectives," Detective Bateson corrects.

"Detectives," Ben restarts. "Is this necessary? I mean, this is not going to bring her back—"

"Ben, first of all, you can call me Susan, and this is Karl," Susan cut him off. "Second, there is a lot of strangeness in this case. Like how you were in the exact place where she jumped and how you disappeared for what, like, two weeks?"

"Thirteen days, to be exact," Karl corrects.

"Yes, thirteen days. Now, unless your memory of those days has improved, please answer our questions so we can be confident that these coincidences are just that." Susan again begins tapping her iPad with her pen.

"Ok," Ben continues. "I am coming back with my date to my apartment, and we are walking down the hall talking, laughing—we were both a little drunk by then. When we turn the corner to get to my door, I see Jinni sitting by the door crying. I drop my date's hand and move towards her." Ben takes another sip of water. "Can I get you two anything to drink?" he asks the two detectives.

"No, we are fine; please continue."

"Jinni is sitting with her back against my door, audibly crying. She looks up when I call out her name and sees me and my date."

"Did she say anything to you?" Karl asks.

"We all kinda froze ... It was awkward. Finally, she spoke and asked me if we could talk. I look at my date with an expression like, 'What the hell?' My date nods at me and says she will message me later, leaving Jinni and me alone."

"What was the name of your date?" Karl asks, pulling out a pen from his jacket pocket.

Ben noticed he now had a small foldable notebook in his hand.

"I think her name was Carol ... or Caroline ... no, it was Carol."

"Can we contact Carol?" Susan asks.

Ben shakes his head. "She blocked me after that night, and I didn't get a chance to get her number."

"Ok, go on," Susan encourages.

"I tell Jinni to come inside, and at this point, I am livid. I had not seen or talked to her in over two years, and she had just ruined my date, and I wanted to know why. Jinni stands there, turned away from me. So I touch her shoulder, gently turn her around, and start asking her what the hell is going on." Ben folds his hands in his lap. "When I turn her around, I realize how terrible she looks. She stunk of alcohol, and it looked like she hadn't taken a shower in a week or so. Her eyes were bloodshot red, maybe from crying or something else. She has cuts all over her arms; it looked like it was from self-harm." Both detectives were staring at him intently. "I ask her a little more quietly, 'What's wrong?' She collapses in my arms and begins crying. I carry her to the couch and go and get her some water.

"After a while, she calms down and starts talking to me. I could tell she was super drunk because she slurred her words and could barely keep her head up. She tells me: 'Ben, I want you to know why we broke up. It wasn't about you; I want you to know that.'"

"Can you tell us what she meant by that?" Susan asks.

"Maybe we should take a step back." Ben raises his hands in the air. The words have begun to flow out of him. He has been keeping this inside for a long time. "The last few months with Jinni were hell. She didn't want to be touched; she would disappear for days. We were arguing all the time. We go out for her sister's birthday, and she disappears again. I have had enough at this point, and after a huge fight, I break up with her." Ben pauses to catch his breath. "The weird thing was that this happened so suddenly. One day, we were fine, happy, and doing well. Then Jinni returns home one day, and suddenly, she is changed."

"Got it, Ben; thank you, now please continue with the events of that night," Susan says.

Ben ignores her and says, "Jinni was an extremely private person. She didn't like pictures taken of her and was cryptic about her past. Whenever I asked her, she would tell me she had moved here from Korea and was sent to live with her uncle. She never provided any further details. That night she started talking to me about when she first came to the U.S. and how her father was having trouble back in South Korea, and he needed his brother to take her in until he got back on his feet."

"How old was Ms. Yoon at this time?" Karl asks.

"She was twelve at that time."

Susan writes something down and nods for Ben to continue.

"I noticed her shoes were muddy, and I wanted to ask her why but she was talking, and I didn't want to cut her off. She was telling me about her life during that time. She moved in with her uncle, his wife, and their two sons. Since they felt it was unfair to move one of the boys out of their rooms, they created a small space in their basement for her to sleep. They put in a bed and a desk for her. She told me her unemployed uncle didn't want to enroll her in school until she learned some English. So for the next year, while his wife was at work, her uncle would teach her English … and more."

Karl raises his eyebrows.

"She told me that her uncle called them her 'lessons.'" Ben cringes when he says the last word. "She told me that when his wife and kids left the house to go to school and work, they would go down into the basement, and he would grab various parts of her body and tell her the English words. Like touching her breast and saying, 'tits' or grabbing her bottom and saying, 'ass.' While teaching her English, he would sit close to her in her makeshift classroom and rub her shoulders or legs." Ben looks at both the detectives; they are staring at him in silence.

"I see where this is going, and Jinni starts to get quiet. I am also a little creeped out to hear more. I told Jinni that she didn't have to tell me anymore and that I was very sorry this happened to her. She continues like she didn't hear me and tells me that her uncle started grooming her further. The touching moves to kissing, the kissing to undressing, and finally, the 'lessons' move to her bed."

"Jesus," Karl whispers.

"Jinni goes quiet, and I sit there, not knowing what to do. I touch her on the shoulder, but she shrugs me off. I started talking and telling her that I was very sorry that this had happened to her. I asked her why she didn't talk to me about this earlier, and maybe I could have helped her out. Gotten her therapy and whatnot." Ben finishes his water and sets the glass back on the table. He strongly felt the urge to drink something much stronger than water.

"She continues like she hadn't heard me again," Ben continues. "And she said one day her uncle told her that since he had been out of work for a while, the family was in bad shape financially, and she would have to help out." Ben fiddles uncomfortably on the couch. "She told me her uncle told her he would have to take pictures and videos of her and sell them on the internet to make money. She told me that when the filming started, the abuse started to get worse."

"Do you think this was the reason for her suicide, the abusive memories?" Susan asks.

Ben exhales loudly and shrugs.

He continues the story. "I am sitting there with her, unsure what to say. I asked her: 'What did he do to you?' And she finally looks me in the eye and says, 'Anything he wanted.'" Ben takes a deep breath. "I asked her for how long did this happen, and she told me it was about two years of this before she ran away. I asked where she went, and she said she didn't remember. She just ran and slept wherever she could. Finally, the cops found her and wanted to return her home. Luckily one of the cops was Korean and could talk to her. She told him what had happened, and they arrested her uncle the same day. Jinni was fourteen when this happened." The room goes silent. Both detectives were holding their pens—one digital and one real. Neither of them was writing. They both knew the story was not done.

"She said it was a significant event in her community. Her uncle had many friends, and not everyone wanted to believe that he had done something like that. After the arrest and after the police had left the house, the first thing her aunt did was slap her. Her aunt asked her why she would make up a lie like that after they had welcomed her into their home. If it wasn't for the mountain of evidence the cops found when they seized his computer, she wasn't sure if anyone would have believed her. She told me that at the trial, she found out her uncle was part of some underground ring that traded pictures and videos of underaged girls. She told me what upset her the most was that none of this was for money; her uncle was just showing her off to his online friends.

"Jinni's parents got wind of this back home, but her dad was in jail then, and they couldn't do anything. After the trial, her aunt told the court that she could no longer support Jinni, so they placed her in the system, and she lived in a foster home until she was eighteen. By then, her dad had been released from jail, and he migrated her family here. When they arrived, she had left foster care and was living with some rich older guy in Malibu.

"I am listening to her, pretty mortified. I knew something was up, and this explained a lot." Ben goes to grab his glass of water but sees it is empty. Both detectives are silently watching him. "She asked if I remembered the night she came home and didn't want to talk to me. I said I did. She told me that a few years before we met, the FBI asked her if she wanted to testify against some pedophile they had caught, and he had all of her videos on his computer. They asked if she wanted to give a statement at his trial and help them prosecute him. She told me how they kept pressuring her to testify. She always refused. Before the FBI left her alone, they asked her if she knew her videos had been downloaded over three million times from the dark web. She told me that until then, she hadn't realized how many people had watched her abuse and how she got increasingly paranoid about people finding out about her past." Ben badly needs a drink. He wipes the sweat from his brow. He feels sick and dizzy. He looks at both detectives, who remain silent.

"Jinni tells me that every so often, she will catch someone looking at her; she will see a hint of familiarity in their eyes as if they recognize her but are not sure from where. The day when our relationship started falling apart, Jinni was at the mall shopping or something." Ben has never told anyone this story before, he wants to stop, but he realizes that if he does, he will not be able to continue later.

"At some point, she realizes someone is following her. This guy goes into a store when she goes into a store. She goes to Starbucks for coffee, and he is standing on the other side of the store, looking at her. Finally, she leaves the mall and hears someone call out to her as soon as she is outside. This guy apologizes for bugging her, but he needs to ask her a question. Jinni asks him what he wants, and the guy pulls out his phone and starts playing a video of a young Jinni and her uncle. He asks her: 'Is this you?'"

Susan shifts uncomfortably in her chair. "Did she notify the authorities?"

"No, she ran from him and came home. We didn't talk for two days. I was going crazy trying to figure out what was wrong. After that, she started going out and not coming back for a few days. When she did come home, she was usually drunk or high out of her mind. That's when things started falling apart for us." Ben ran his fingers through his hair. "Had I known what was happening, I might have handled it differently, but I didn't, and now I have to live with it." Ben leans back in his chair, defeated.

"And what happened after she told you all this?" Susan asks.

"She looks at me and tells me that she just wanted me to know that it was not my fault that we broke up. She then comes over to me and hugs me. She whispers into my ear and says, 'I always thought you would be the one to save me.' before letting go and walking out my door." Ben sits there quietly, his head hanging. "I was too shocked to move; after I regained my composure, I went after her. But she was gone."

Both detectives sit silently, watching Ben. Susan stares at her partner and back to Ben.

"And do you recall why you were there when she committed suicide and why you fled the scene?" Susan asks.

Ben shakes his head.

Susan looks at her partner. Karl looks back and shrugs his hands. She stands up. "Well, we are sorry for troubling you. We will submit our notes to the report and let you know the outcome."

"We will show ourselves out," Karl says.

Ben watches the detectives walk out of his apartment. When they leave, he puts his head in his hands.

CHAPTER 17 - BFF

"What!" Ben screams as he answers his phone. He is lying face down on the couch. He had just gone through the bender to end all benders. He had spent the last few nights and days "superimposing" himself through the internet, primarily in bars or nightclubs. When he is home, he usually has a drink in one hand and his phone in the other, looking for the next adventure. He has called in sick a few days, much to his boss' chagrin.

"Ben," his mother replies softly. Ben sits up on the couch and forces his eyes to focus. Through his blurry vision, he sees the face of a worried mother staring back at him. In his drunken stupor, he had not realized that she had FaceTimed him.

"Mom?" Ben asks in a cracking voice. He had spent last night at a New York nightclub in the '90s, and the cigarette smoke had hurt his throat. Ben quickly tries to fix his hair and blinks his eyes awake. He starts to stand up but decides that it is not a good idea.

"You look terrible," his mom says in a voice only a concerned mother could pull off.

"I had a long night, Mom." Ben lets out a yawn. He looks at the time and realizes it is almost noon.

"Oh," his mom responds. Both of them go silent for a few moments.

"Well," she continues. "I was checking to see how you were doing. You haven't called or texted me in a few weeks. I was worried."

"I have been busy with work," Ben lies. Ben's part of the work is almost done. Despite his protestation to Ulysses about some of the potential shader practices of NikNak, Ulysses told him those were no reason for concern. Ulysses is excited at what the Initial Public Offering of NikNak could do for his company.

"Your eyes are red."

"Mom … As I said, I had a long night. I am tired." Ben has to force himself not to shout.

"I've been worried about you." His mom looks on the verge of tears.

Ben softens his voice. "I'm fine, I promise."

"Ok … I just wanted to check on you."

Ben apologizes to his mom again and gets off the phone. He leans back on the couch and covers his eyes with his hands. He stays in the position for a minute before sitting up and checking his phone. He has one message from Ulysses.

Ulysses: *We just submitted the S-1. The IPO is next! We're in the big leagues now, baby! I hope you feel better.*

"Great … Just great." Ben walks into his bedroom to go back to sleep.

That night (or day, Ben has lost track of time), Ben has his first dream in a long while. He is on a cliff out in the mountains. He wears brown cargo shorts, a brown explorer hat, and a black shirt. He is sweating. In his right hand is a silver walking stick. He is standing on the cliff's precipice with one foot in front of him, stabilizing his weight. He looks around and sees nothing, no animals, no people, no trees. He listens and hears nothing, no birds, no wind, no sounds. He brings his hand to his forehead and wipes his brow. He starts inching his body closer to the edge of the cliff. *Don't look down*! his mind screams. But still, he leans closer and closer to the edge. As he peers over, he sees a body at the bottom. He pulls his hat down lower to block the sun from his eyes. He focuses on the body below.

He can barely make out the body of a young woman. She is mangled and twisted, her legs broken, and her arms at odd angles. A pool of blood is forming beneath her head.

Ben!

Ben steps back from the cliff and turns around to look behind him. There is nothing there.

Ben! A voice shouts again.

This time the sound comes from beneath him. He carefully inches his way towards the cliff's edge and looks down again. The body is gone. He leans over further, and a gust of wind catches his back. He whirls his arms backward, trying to regain his balance, but the gust is too strong. He tumbles over the edge face-first into the abyss. As he falls, he hears: "I always thought you would be the one to save me."

Ben wakes a few inches from the floor and grunts as he hits the carpet around his bed. He has fallen from his bed, something he had not done since he was six. He lies there on his cheek for a moment before slowly getting up. He touches his face and chest to ensure nothing is bruised or broken.

It is the weekend, so he does not have work. He sits in his pajamas in the living room. He tries to watch YouTube but cannot find anything that entertains him. He tries playing video games but keeps getting owned by kids half his age, who proceed to curse at him and crouch up and down over his face. He shuts off the game console and sits in the dark. His mind wanders to his conversation with the detectives. He had not lied to them per se, but he had excluded some of the truth.

The last few months with Jinni were trying. Between her drinking, her disappearing, and the constant fighting, Ben truly started to hate her. At the time, he did not understand what had changed between them. Things before were going well. They were laughing, making love, drinking, and enjoying life together. After she had disappeared from Yumi's birthday party, Ben had had enough. When she finally showed up two days later in the middle of the night, she drunkenly crawled into bed and attempted to cuddle with him. Ben released his anger. He started screaming at her. He had always had a gentle tone with her, but this time the angry words spewed out of his mouth like bile. He called her names he had never called her before, and all she did was stare back at him with a blank expression.

When he completed his tirade, Jinni spoke a few words. "Babe, I'm so tired—" she said as she passed out.

Fueled by anger (and the bottle of vodka Ben had dusted off earlier), he did what any irrational man would do and began packing her things. Ben was already sitting on the couch when she awoke, fuming with drunk anger. As soon as she emerged from the door, he verbally attacked her. Ben held nothing back, spitting angry words on a hungover and already defeated Jinni, accusing her of everything from cheating on him to lying. Jinni stood there taking the abuse, eyes glued to the floor. Ben told her to take her stuff and get the fuck out of his house. When he was done, his breathing was heavy; his eyes were wet. Jinni looked at him with fear, sorrow, and betrayal. During the whole time, she never muttered a word. She quietly moved towards the door, picked up her bags, and left Ben's apartment.

#

Ben stands up from the couch. He has done many wrong things in his life, and maybe he could do something right. He needs help, and he knows only one person who can help him. He takes his phone out of his pocket and calls an old friend.

"Ben … Is that you?" Raj says tepidly.

"Yes … Are you home?"

"I am—you never did like to say hello." Raj laughs. "Always straight to the point."

Ben ignores him. "I'm coming over."

"Ben … What the hell? We haven't talked in years, and now you want to come over? What's up, man?"

"It's important; I need to ask you something."

Raj sighs audibly into the phone. "You can't just tell me over the phone?" Raj asks.

"No, it's important … It's about Jinni."

Raj sighs again and says, "I heard about that … I am sorry, sure, come on over. I am home. I'll text you the address."

Ben stands at Raj's door for what feels like an hour. Twice he comes close to ringing the doorbell, and twice, he pulls his hand away at the last second.

Things did not end well between Raj and him.

They were hired at nearly the same time at FrontSpark; Ben was employee number 16, and Raj number 22. Ben was

200

hired as a junior software engineer, and Raj as a junior security engineer. Both had limited job experience. They came from similar backgrounds, suburban kids who had enjoyed a quiet nuclear family (until Ben's dad had died). They had both gone to schools in the suburbs and had degrees in Computer Science. The only difference between the two was that Raj was from the Bay Area, and Ben was not.

On Raj's first day, he sat in a cubicle directly in front of Ben. He sported a long beard and a red hoodie and wore large headphones. Before sitting at his desk, he looked at Ben and gave him a quick nod as he sat down. For the first couple of weeks, neither spoke to the other. They started every day at roughly the same time, each giving the other a nod and a "hey" before getting to work. They continued this routine for the first couple of months.

One day Raj came to Ben's desk.

"You have a bug in your code," he told Ben nonchalantly.

"What?" Ben asked.

Raj motioned for Ben to move over, which Ben obliged. He pulled up a code file with a few keystrokes and pointed towards the problem area.

"Right here," Raj exclaimed, pointing at the screen. "You didn't escape your inputs. That is a security violation." Raj fiddled with the laces of his hoodie. Ben looked at the code on the screen. He smiled and then laughed.

"No, man," Ben said. "That's not a bug."

They spent the next couple of minutes arguing. Raj was immovable in his assessment, Ben resilient in his skills, until finally, they made a bet. Ben would buy him a drink if Raj could prove that the code was buggy. After a few minutes of typing, he turned to Ben triumphantly.

"I'll take a rum and coke."

#

Ben stands nervously at the front door of Raj's apartment. He replayed the conversation he wanted to have with Raj in his head a hundred times. He had a counter for every objection, a comeback for every complaint. He plans to place his hand on Raj's shoulder and look him in the eyes when the time comes. He is as ready as he ever would be. He rings the doorbell.

Raj's wife, Indra, opens the door. Ben hadn't seen her since a few nights before their wedding. She is a small woman with long black hair, hazel eyes, and a killer smile. When she opens the door, her eyes widen. Ben can not tell if she is smiling or frowning because a mask covers her mouth.

"Ben?" she whispers.

"Hello, Indra," Ben says quietly.

The last time he had seen her, they were at a bar a few nights before their wedding, a few weeks before the pandemic. Indra was sitting on Raj's lap in a corner booth at a local bar they frequented. Indra was asking what Ben was going to wear for the wedding. Ben sighed.

"I don't do weddings," Ben said, taking a sip of his drink.

"Why?" Indra asked.

"Ben has issues, babe," Raj said, snuggling up to her neck.

"Ben! Stop joking; you know you are coming." She pushed Raj's head away from her neck. "You and Raj are best friends.

I hope you are not mad because Raj's brother will be the best man?"

Ben shook his head. He honestly could care less about who was the best man. He hated weddings, and he had excellent reason to. *Happily ever after is bullshit,* he thought. *No one lived happily ever after. It was all a pipe dream.* He had experienced the dreadful truth firsthand. Indra reached down and grabbed her drink. She took a sip.

"You have to come," she whined. "I have some really cute friends who will be there."

Ben had recently broken up with Jinni, and Indra was always trying to find him a date. Ben looked towards the front of the bar where some rock band was playing. He shot Indra a sideway glance, shook his head, and looked away. He had already made up his mind months ago not to go. He hated weddings.

"You'll be there," Indra nodded confidently. "I know it."

#

Indra looks up at him from the frame of the door. She motions forward to hug him but stops herself short. After over three years of lockdown, no one knew how to do personal space anymore.

"Come in." She widens the door and takes a step back. Ben walks into the apartment, and they both stand awkwardly at the door. After a few moments of silence, Indra speaks.

"Raj is in his office," she points towards a door. "I have to get back to work." She closes the door and goes into their bedroom.

Ben walks over to the office and notices the door is ajar. He knocks quietly and opens the door a bit more to peer inside. Raj has a headset on and is on a Zoom call. He looks up and sees Ben and motions for him to come in.

"No … no … no," Raj says abruptly.

Ben freezes in place. Raj smiles, points towards his headset, and signals for Ben to sit down. Ben sits on the corner of the small couch in the back of the room.

"Look," Raj continues. "All I am saying is our latest scan of the dark web found three hundred eighty-five credit cards that belong to our clients." Raj looks at Ben, makes a gun gesture with his hands, and proceeds to mock blow his brains out. Ben smiles.

"Yes … yes … yes," Raj rubs his eyes. "We shut down those accounts … no … no … no … The other cards are not part of our clientele, so we left them alone." Raj laughs. "I guess they should have banked with us … Ok … Sounds good. Talk to you later, Frank." Raj presses a couple of keys on his keyboard.

They both look at each other for a few moments. Ben notices Raj's long bushy beard has a few gray hairs intertwined in it. He had also gained about thirty pounds since they last saw each other. Raj shakes his head and smiles.

"Ben … you son-of-a-bitch … How have you been?" He extends his hand for a fist bump, which Ben slaps eagerly. The first few moments are awkward, but they slowly regain their groove. Raj has never been the one to hold a grudge. They discuss old times and current times. Ben slaps his knee in laughter as Raj regales old tales of former colleagues at

FrontSpark. Indra pops in with a couple of beers, still wearing her mask. Ben side-eyes Raj, who shrugs. They continue their conversation.

"... so I tell Robbie, don't do it, do not do it!" Raj takes a sip of his beer. "But Robbie is shit-faced; I mean, he's hammered to the bone." Ben's smile widens. "So there we are, standing on the sidewalk in front of Ulysses' house, and Robbie looks around and starts unfastening his belt. I am pleading with him not to do it, but he is not listening." Ben starts to chuckle.

"He starts walking to Ulysses' door, and I am like, I am out of here. I want no part of this. I get about thirty feet away, and suddenly bright blue and red lights light up behind me. I continue walking but turn my head to see what's happening." Raj starts to laugh but catches himself finishing the story. "And I see two cops with their flashlights pointed at Ulysses' front door, and Robbie is squatting down, taking a huge dump at Ulysses' doorstep!" Raj throws his head back and lets out a loud laugh. Ben could not stop himself from laughing too. Between laughs, Raj continues. "Then, as I walk away, I see Ulysses at his front door in his robe, looking out towards the cops where they are handcuffing poor Robbie, his pants are still around his ankles, and Ulysses is staring down at a massive shit on his porch!" Raj slaps his knee and doubles over in laughter. Ben could not help but follow suit. After a few minutes, they calm down and begin finishing their beers.

"Wait," Ben asks incredulously. "you were there the night Robbie got caught taking a shit in front of Ulysses' house? How come you never told me?"

"I told no one, Ben-San. I was scared shitless that Ulysses had seen me or made me out, and I didn't want to get fired too," Raj explains.

"Oh, man." Ben lets out a chuckle. "Those were the good old days of FrontSpark."

"Yes, they were." Raj wipes tears of laughter from his eyes. "What's going on now? There are rumors on the street that you have a huge deal. Something to do with NikNak?" Raj raises an eyebrow at Ben.

Ben ignores the question and starts. "You know, Raj, things were hard for me after you left. You were one of the only people I could relate to there." Raj nods in agreement. "I was despondent and upset when you left."

"Blame old man Ulysses, the cheap bastard. When we first started, there were, what, thirty people in the company? When I left, we had over two hundred. We were no longer a small company, so I asked for a ten thousand dollars a year raise and the sucker said he could only do three. After I had been there for ten years, he had the gall to lowball me. After that, I decided it was time for me to move on."

"I know," Ben agrees.

"I got this great job with Franc Bank as a Senior Security Engineer, and look, five years later, I am Director of Security, married, a few pounds heavier but a lot more well off. That place is a cul-de-sac, Ben. I am surprised you stayed as long as you did." Ben shrugs.

"I'm loyal, I guess."

"Loyal to a fault. That's something I always liked about you, Benny." Raj leans back in his chair.

"So, Mr. White ... if that is your real name," Ben smirks at their old inside joke. "What brings you to my side of town after all these years?"

"I know you are a good security engineer."

"A great security engineer," Raj corrects as he smiles.

"I overheard you talking about the dark web. Do you know much about it?" Raj puts his beer down and leans forward.

"What I do is incredibly complex. The bank I work for has some of the highest-end clientele in the world; sometimes, those clients get hacked, and they steal their PII data. We have software that can crawl many parts of the web, or the dark web if you will, that finds this information and sends us reports. For clients who pay for our service, we immediately close their accounts, issue them new cards, and alert them. If we can, we scrub their information off the web also."

"So, let's say hypothetically, I need you to find something on the web or dark web. Could you do it?" Ben asks.

Raj leaned back in his chair and took another swig of his beer. "Ben, my boy, I can do anything."

"Good, then I need a favor."

"Sure, what it is."

"I need you...." Ben hesitates, trying to find the right words before deciding just to say it. "I need you... to help me find some ... child porn."

Raj's mouth drops open. The room goes silent for a few seconds before Raj laughs. He doubles over and slaps his leg. "Ben, you asshole, you got me!" He laughs. "Damn, I always fall for your stupid jokes—this one was a little weird—but damn, you got me good." Raj looks up at Ben, who is not laughing.

"Wait … You're not serious, are you…." Raj's voice trails off.

Ben takes a large gulp of his beer. "You are the only person I can trust to do this, and more importantly, you're the only person who knows how to do this. Things in my life have gotten weird lately, but I think I understand the purpose of why they are happening. I need your help."

"But … but … I mean, this is ludicrous." Raj downs the rest of his beer and uses the back of his hand to wipe his mouth. "Why would you want something like that? You're not one of those—"

Ben raises his hand to stop Raj. "You remember Jinni?"

Raj nods.

"And you know what happened to her, right?"

"Jeremy told me about that. I am truly sorry," Raj says as he lowers his eyes.

"What's done is done. A few months before she died, she showed up at my apartment. She told me a story about how her uncle had sexually abused her, recorded it, and uploaded the videos to the internet. Supposedly there are multiple videos of her and her uncle on the dark web. She was only twelve years old." Ben grabs his beer with a shaky hand and takes a large drink.

"Jesus Christ," Raj proclaims.

"I need to find those videos, but I don't know where to start. I need your help."

"But why?" Raj asks. "She's already gone. Is the person who abused her still alive?"

"No, he died years ago."

"Then why?"

"Raj." Ben pauses, searching for the right words. "It's ... it's ... complex. If I told you, you would think I am crazy. I need you to trust me, and I promise I will tell you everything when all this is over."

Raj swivels his chair around to face his computer. The room grows quiet.

"Raj?"

"This is a lot to process; I need to think about it. Can you give me a couple of days?" Raj asks.

"Sure." Ben checks his phone.

"Thanks, sorry, but I got a lot of work to do; it was good seeing you, pal." Raj begins to type on his keyboard.

"Thanks," Ben says as he walks out of the room. He lets himself out.

A few days later, Raj calls Ben. "Hey."

"Hello, Raj."

"So about that thing we talked about ... Yeah, man, I can't do it."

"Oh?"

"Oh? Oh!" Raj fires back. "All you have to say is 'oh'?" Raj's voice starts to increase. Ben has to hold the phone a few inches away from his ear. "I haven't seen you in years, man. You come to me asking me for this shit?" Raj shouts.

"Raj, I—" Ben starts.

"Don't 'Raj' me. I knew we were close at one point, and maybe back in the day, I would have done anything for you. But now—" Raj's voice softens. "Now ... we are just acquaintances." Raj goes silent.

Ben is about to say something but thinks it is best to shut his mouth.

"You know," Raj continues. "I always thought you were joking when you said you wouldn't come to my wedding. I knew you had some weird hangups with weddings, but I thought you would surely show up—You kind of told me what happened with your mom—I just thought you would get over it for me...." Raj trails off.

"Raj ... I'm—" Ben starts.

"Don't, Ben, don't. Like you said: What's done is done." The call goes silent.

Goddamnit! Ben curses himself. He knew he had hurt Raj by not going to the wedding. Ben never got around to telling Raj the whole reason why. *Fuck,* Ben thinks, w*ithout Raj, this is not going to work.* Suddenly his brain wakes up. *Wait a second, wait a goddamn second*—Ben's mind screams at him.

"Raj, I don't know how to tell you this, but ... I was at your wedding," Ben lies.

After a few moments of silence, Raj chuckles. "C'mon, let's not bullshit each other. I know for a fact you were not there."

"I came secretly, and I can prove it."

"How?"

"Did you take a video of the wedding?" Ben asks.

"Yeah, it's on a flash drive around here somewhere, but c'mon, I know you were not there," Raj says defiantly.

"Find the flash drive. I will be over in a couple of hours."
Ben grabs his mask, runs out of the apartment, and gets into
his car. He speeds to the local business park and rushes into
the men's suit store.

"Welcome to the Men's—"

"I need a tuxedo!" Ben cuts him off.

"Sir?" The staff member asks.

"I need a tuxedo now! Please?" Ben lowers his voice.

"Ok…" says the very confused staff member. "Right this
way."

#

An hour and forty-five minutes later, Ben rings the
doorbell of Raj's apartment. Raj opens the door and sees Ben
dressed in a tuxedo. Raj's eyebrows raise, and then he breaks
out in laughter.

"Ben—What the fuck?"

"This is the tuxedo I wore at your wedding," Ben claims.
"Did you find the video?"

"Yeah," Raj says, still chuckling. He pulls a flash drive out
of his pocket.

"Where is Indra?" Ben asks.

"She went out to run some errands. We have the place all
to ourselves." Raj walks to the living room and sits on the
armrest of a chair.

"Look," Raj begins. "You know, and I know, you weren't at
my wedding. Can we stop the charade?"

211

"Plug in the drive," Ben commands. Still shaking his head, Raj walks over to the TV and plugs the flash drive into the side.

"This is ridiculous…." Raj says quietly. He walks to the coffee table and grabs the remote. Ben walks near the TV screen.

"Can we cut the bullshit? You and I both know that you weren't—"

"Play the video," Ben cut him off.

With a shrug, Raj presses a button on the remote, and the wedding video starts. The first scene is Raj and Indra getting ready for the big day. A few minutes in, the video shows people arriving at the wedding hall that Raj's family had rented out. Ben knew that over three hundred people showed up at the wedding and that Raj was very drunk by the end.

"Can you fast forward a bit until after the ceremony?" he asks. Raj fast-forwards to where the wedding is going in full force. Ben takes a deep breath.

"How long is the rest of the video?" he asks.

Raj brings up the information screen.

"There is a little over an hour left."

"Good," Ben says quietly under his breath. Ben walks closer to the TV screen. On the TV is a party in full swing. The ceremony is over, and people are dancing and drinking. The party has moved outside onto the grass lawn. Raj is seen taking shots with his cousins. Ben decides it is time.

"See, Raj," he says as he points at the LCD. "I am right there."

"Where?" Raj squints, trying to find Ben. Ben walks up to the flat screen.

"Right here." Ben touches the screen and closes his eyes.

CHAPTER 18 - MFW

It always amuses Ben that no one is looking in his direction when he "superimposes" himself. Every time he "superimposes" himself, all eyes are looking elsewhere. It was like the universe was opening the tiniest windows for him to appear. It is only a fraction of a second, and he startles a few people who were either in mid-blink or just turned their heads away for a second.

This time he arrives at the back of a crowd with all faces turned away from him, looking towards Raj and his new wife. Ben stands at the back. He looks for the cameraman and ensures he gets into his line of sight. If Raj ever plays back the video, Ben wants to ensure the cameraman captures a shot of him.

While Ben was driving over, he outlined in his head what he planned on doing. He would first actually go to Raj's wedding. He had always felt bad about missing it. He never dared to tell Raj the whole story of why he hated weddings so much. He just told him a little about what happened to his mom. His second goal was to ensure the cameraman had a few shots of him in the background. Finally, he wants to avoid Raj at any cost. Ben is concerned about changing anything too much. He has already learned his lesson about messing with the past.

Ben slips away from the crowd and heads towards the bar. It is relatively empty as most party-goers are taking pictures with the bride and groom. He walks up to the bartender and orders a vodka and soda.

"Coming right up, sir," the red-vested bartender chirps.

As Ben leans on the bar, he turns back towards Raj and Indra. They both look so happy. They are on a slightly elevated stage. People are lining up to take photos with them. Raj has a slight red glow around his face that he only gets when he drinks. Raj, who always sported a beard, is cleanly shaven. His usually messy hair is nicely combed.

"I love these gigs," the red-vested bartender says.

Ben turns. "Huh?" he says as he turns to face the bartender.

"Weddings, man." The bartender places his drink on the counter. "Serving at these events always makes me happy." Ben nods in agreement.

"Except when the bride or the groom doesn't show up. Then it's not so fun." The bartender gives off a hearty laugh. Ben winces and takes a sip of his drink. As he starts to walk away, he asks the bartender the time.

"It's 10:02, sir," the bartender states, looking at his watch.

Ben nods and walks away.

When Ben started his adventures, the one thing that bothered him was that he could never bring anything that told time. He assumed it could not be brought in if it did not exist in that period. So he tried various things like carrying old phones, vintage watches, and even an hourglass. But whenever he "superimposed" himself, those things always disappeared. What it did improve is his sense of time. By this point, he could count the minutes in his head. He recalls the one time he "jumped" into a four-minute clip of some friends drinking in a bar (he could not remember which country it was in) and ordered ten shots as soon as he "arrived." Ben downed the tenth one just as the bartender told him how much he owed. Ben winked, and on the TV, some soccer team (he thought they called it football there, so maybe it was in Ireland or England) scored, causing the bartender to turn around and look, and poof, Ben was gone.

It is now 10:04, Ben thinks. He walks towards the back, staying on the crowd's periphery as they gather to watch the newlyweds taking pictures with their guests. Ben watches in silence. He considers just walking away, taking a long hike down the road. He has pretty much accomplished his goals. He knew where he was and had around fifty minutes to kill. He is sure there is a bar about a ten-minute walk away from here. He would have killed to have Google Maps right about now. *Hell, even Apple Maps would do*, he thinks. He has not been to a wedding since he was seventeen, and he is fascinated by how much fun it seems. Everyone seems to be having a good time, taking selfies, laughing, and drinking. His last wedding had been in a crusty run-down hall.

The speeches start, and Raj's father strolls up to the podium. He is a slim, tall man with graying hair and a small mustache. He tells a story about how Raj would be locked in his room playing with his computer all day. How he was scared his son would die a virgin. He then turns and thanks Indra for not making that come true. This garners a huge laugh from the crowd. Someone, presumably one of Raj's cousins, yells out that Raj is still one, which gets a burst of even louder laughter and some cold stares from Raj. It even gets Ben to smile.

Ben casually looks around to see if he recognizes anyone; he sees some people he knows, others from Raj's new job whom he had seen in Raj's Instagram posts. There is a sprinkling of family members, some he recognized, others he has no idea who they are. Ben figures now would be a good time to go; he thinks it best not to get recognized, and he has proven to Raj that he was there, even if he is being deceitful. Raj's father finishes his speech and hugs his son and his new daughter-in-law. Ben turns around and begins to walk away. As he does, he hears Raj's voice on the speaker.

"Friends and family!" shouts an inebriated Raj. "I thank you all for coming to get free food and drinks!"

The crowd cheers at this. Ben stops in his tracks and turns back towards the stage.

"And to witness me and my lovely new wife, Indra," Indra stands by his side as Raj lifts her hand. "On this holy day of matrimony!" The crowd cheers and whistles even louder. Raj lets go of Indra's hand and grabs the podium like a president giving a victory speech.

"You know I have a friend—this friend hates weddings." The crowd begins to boo. Ben swallows hard. "This friend always tells me that marriage is the beginning of the end. I always argued with him that marriage is the end of the beginning! I love my new wife!" The crowd cheers. "To this friend, wherever you are, this one is for you...."

Raj grabs Indra's hand and clumsily leads her onto the dance floor. The crowd parts and creates a circle around them. Curious, Ben walks towards the group to see what is happening. What happens subsequently shocks him. Raj and Indra are doing a choreographed dance, part Indian and part Western. The DJ keeps changing the tunes to match their dance style. Ben watches in awe at their precision and coordination. Raj grabs Indra by both arms, twirls her around, lifts her off the ground, and grabs her by the back of her legs. They continue spinning as the crowd eggs them on. Ben realizes he has a huge grin, and his eyes start to water.

He had never dared to tell Raj why he hated weddings so much.

After Ben's father died, his mother was very lonely. She would sit around the house all day, drinking wine and crying. She had little to no skills outside of the barely over-minimum-wage job she had (Ben's father had been the breadwinner of the family). After a few months, Ben decided to step up and do all the tasks that his father used to do. He paid the bills, cut the grass, and took out the trash. As a thirteen-year-old boy (his birthday had passed with little fanfare), it was tough for him, but he did the best he could.

After months of filing claims, talking with the insurance company, and meeting with insurance representatives, Ben's mom had finally received the life insurance payout from his dad's company. It was a little over a hundred thousand dollars, and his mom told him that if they cut back on a few expenses, the money should last them for a while. Ben was greatly relieved to hear this as he kept an eye on the growing "past due" bills they had been receiving lately. He told his mom that he would handle the past due accounts and for her not to worry. His mom hugged him.

A few years went by, and one day at the dinner table, his excited mother told him that she would like Ben to meet someone from her work, and she had invited this person over for dinner the next day. Ben raised his eyebrows at her but said nothing. His mom had continued her low-paying job at the drugstore, and Ben wondered what that meant.

The next day at dinner, his mom's "friend" came over. He was in his late thirties with long hair, a ripped shirt, and small neck tattoos. He liked to call Ben "Benny." He was very different from Ben's father.

"That's not my name," Ben told him at dinner.

"Huh?" the man replied.

"My name is Ben, not Benny."

"Sorry, Benny boy, I'll try and remember that in the future; I'm James, but you can call me Jamie," James said with a grin.

Ben's mom gave him a stare. Ben decided to focus on his food for the rest of the dinner. James, "Call me Jamie," kept looking around and commenting on their lovely house. Ben was fifteen at the time.

A few more months and many awkward dinners later, James "Call me Jamie" moved into their house. Ben argued with his mom, stating that this was their house and asking why he was moving in. His mother replied that James, "Call me Jamie," was having a hard time and needed a place to stay. So for the next few years, James "Call me Jamie" occupied their household. He was not abusive or unpleasant to Ben; he just treated him like an accessory, as if Ben had just come with the house.

Most nights, James "Call me Jamie" would sit on the couch drinking beer, watching one sports game or another. Occasionally he would scream at the TV, urging his team to "Hit the shot!" or "Run the ball!" but mostly, they stayed out of each other's way.

One day Ben came home from a friend's house (he was spending more and more time outside of the home) to find James, "Call me Jamie," sitting at their kitchen table with an open checkbook, paying their bills.

"I usually do that," Ben said, pointing at the stack of bills on the table. James "Call me Jamie" looked up at him, perplexed.

"Benny, my boy, I didn't hear you come in," he replied. He ignored Ben and went back to writing a check. Ben moved closer to see what he was doing. Ben noticed he was using checks from his mom and dad's joint account. Ben felt the anger rise into his face; he clenched his hands into fists and moved closer.

James, "Call me Jamie," sensed this and looked up. He stared Ben up and down and rose from the table. "What's up, kid?" he asked quietly, staring Ben down.

Ben froze for a second. He looked up at him and backed down. He turned around and walked to his room.

"From now on, I will do this!" he shouted as Ben left the kitchen. "You go be a kid, and I'll take care of the man's work."

Ben slammed the door to his room.

That night, Ben watched an old video of his tenth birthday party. Ben was sitting in the middle of the table wearing one of those stupid pointy hats. His mom was filming and directing everyone at the party. His dad walked out of the kitchen with his birthday cake as his mom started singing "Happy Birthday" at the top of her lungs. Ben smiled and laughed as the few guests at his party sang along. His dad set down the cake in front of him and hugged him with one arm while simultaneously singing. Ben looked up at his dad and started singing along.

Later in the video, Ben opened his presents. Most were boring things like new T-shirts, socks, and some toys. Ben thanked each of his guests every time he opened a gift but inside, he could not help but feel a little disappointed. After all the gifts were opened, Ben's dad asked him what was behind the couch. A confused-looking Ben gingerly walked around the sofa to check. He pulled out a large box covered in red wrapping paper. There was no card on the gift. His dad said he wondered who that could be from. He had a smile on his lips. Ben ripped open the present and found a brand new Nintendo 64, the gift he truly wanted. Ben screamed in delight as he jumped up and down.

"I guess you are also going to need this," his dad said as he whipped out a cartridge box from under his shirt. It was "Super Mario 64," the game Ben had been dying to play. He ran over to his dad and wrapped his arms around his waist, crying tears of joy.

As a teenager, Ben watched the video on his desktop. He wished he could return to that party to spend one more day with his dad.

A few months later, James, "Call me Jamie," grabbed Ben and took him outside. He looked very nervous. Ben hoped he wanted to talk with Ben privately because he was moving out. Things between him and Ben's mom had been strenuous lately. They were fighting a lot, and Ben occasionally had to sleep under his pillow to drown out the noise. Ben stood proudly, awaiting the good news. Instead, James "Call me Jamie" directed him to stand at a specific spot and hold his camera. He told Ben when he gave him the signal to start filming.

"What's the signal?" Ben asked.

"Huh?" James "Call me Jamie," grunted.

"The signal, what is the signal you are going to give me?" Ben repeated.

"I don't know," he said hurriedly. "Use your best judgment."

"Angie … dear, Angie," James "Call me Jamie," sang inside the door, calling for Ben's mom. "Can you come outside for a moment?"

"What is it, Jamie? I am busy right now," Ben's mom shouted back.

"It won't take but a second. Come outside, honey." He turned and nodded at Ben. Ben, assuming that was the signal, pressed record on the camera. Ben's mother came out, drying her hands on a towel.

"Jamie, what is it—Oh." She stopped in her tracks. What happened seemed to happen in slow motion. As Ben's mom emerged from the backdoor, James "Call me Jamie," took a small box out of his pocket and bent down on one knee. Ben's eyes widened, and he felt his stomach rise to his throat.

James "Call me Jamie" opened the box. "Angie, my love … Will you marry me?" he asked.

For a second or two, they all froze. Everything stood still. Finally, Ben's mom spoke up. "Of course I will!" she shouted as she ran towards him and embraced him.

Ben almost dropped the camera.

Over the following months, things were hectic in the household. There were halls to book, invitations to send out, flower colors to be picked, and of course, a cake and wedding dress to be bought. As the wedding date drew nearer and nearer, Ben noticed that James "Call me Jamie" was withdrawing more and more. He spent less time at the house, going to the local bar to watch his sports. He would stay out later and later, sometimes coming home before sunrise. Ben's mother, on the other hand, was on cloud nine. Ben had never seen her more happy or content than she was when she was planning the wedding. But James "Call me Jamie" barely seemed to care. When a decision was to be made, he usually went with the cheapest choice.

One day in the living room, Ben and his mom looked at cake designs. Ben decided to talk to his mom.

"Mom, Jamie seems to be spending a lot of time at that bar," he said.

Ben's mom looked at him. "Jamie is enjoying the last days of being a single man. Let him have his fun." She turned the page of the cake book they were looking at. "Now, what do you think of this one?"

Ben stood at the front of the church uncomfortably in his new suit. He had recently turned seventeen a few weeks back with little excitement. James "Call me Jamie" had given him a card with ten dollars in it, and his mom had bought him this suit for his birthday. There had been no cake, no singing of "Happy Birthday," and no father filming the events with a goofy smile. His mother had sold their video camera soon after Ben's dad had died to pay some bills. Ben had grown quite a bit in the last year, so the suit his mom got him was a size too small. His old dress shirts were also getting small on him, causing them to choke him whenever he moved his head.

Standing next to him was his cousin Kairo, Kairo's dad, and Ben's uncle, Basil. Across the pew were Kairo's sister Esra and their mom, Hala. Kairo was tapping his feet. They had been standing there a good part of twenty minutes. Ben looked up at the large clock on the wall. The wedding was supposed to begin at four, and it was already twenty after. Ben looked at Kairo, who just shrugged. Ben stared out at the room where the guest was sitting. Most were fanning themselves in the hot hall, looking bored and murmuring amongst themselves. Kairo's dad looked at his watch and stared at his wife, who had a look of concern on her face. Kairo's dad motioned his head for his wife to check what was happening. She nodded and started walking towards the back of the wedding hall where the changing rooms were. Ben started to follow when Kairo grabbed his arm. Ben shook him off and started to follow his aunt down the aisle. As they made their way towards the back, Ben had a bad feeling in his gut. They found the door and opened it to his mother in her white dress, crying while her makeup artist was drying her tears while simultaneously trying to fix the damage the tears were causing.

"Mom, what's wrong?" Ben asked as he ran to her side. He noticed the phone in her hand.

"He's not coming," his mom said blankly. Tears began to stream down her face.

"Whose not—oh." Hala brought her hand up to her mouth. Ben looked at the phone in his mom's hand, and on the screen were the words: "Sorry."

After all the guests had left, Ben took his mother to their car. He had his arm around her waist and her arm around his shoulders. She had changed out of the wedding dress and back into her clothes. It was like bringing a wounded soldier off of the battlefield.

Ben had just gotten his learner's permit and knew his mother could not drive. He buckled her in the passenger seat and carefully drove them home. After putting her to bed, Ben went to the kitchen to find something to eat. He stood with the refrigerator door open and started eating a two-day-old sandwich. He looked over to his right and saw a stack of mail untouched. Ben began picking at it. Beneath some advertisements were a bunch of letters with an "overdue" sign stamped on them.

Something occurred to Ben.

"Oh no!" he shouted as he dropped the sandwich. He ran to his room.

"Oh no, oh no, oh no, oh no," he muttered as he ran. He powered on his computer and went to the banking website. After logging in, he placed his hands on his forehead.

Their bank account had no money in it.

#

"Are you ok?" A young girl asks Ben, touching his arm. Ben looks down at her and wipes his eyes.

"Yeah," he says, forcing a smile. "Weddings always get me." He shrugs—the young girl giggles.

"You just seemed sad, crying here in the back. You should come and dance!" She attempts to pull him towards the dance floor. Ben gently shakes her off.

"What's your name, and how old are you?" he bends down and asks the girl.

"My name is Kayla, and I am twelve," the girl tells him proudly.

"Well, I won't dance now, Kayla, but maybe later." He winks.

The young girl smiles at him and runs towards the dance floor. Ben checks his internal clock. He has about thirty minutes left. He had proven his point, that he had shown up at Raj's wedding; it is best to walk away now and get on with it. But he feels uncomfortable and disingenuous. He feels like he is just using Raj as a means to an end. Maybe he had not shown up before, but it did not always have to be that way.

Ben walks towards the dance floor. He moves past the dancers and heads towards the center. Raj is in the middle with Indra, caught in a dancing embrace. Ben taps Raj on the shoulder.

"Excuse me, sir," Ben says with a smile. "Can I have this dance?"

#

As the light reappears, Ben is back in Raj's living room.

"Ok, ok, Ben, I get it," Raj says, shaking his head. "I know you were at my wedding, but you didn't have to guilt trip me by wearing your tux. I'll help you ... Damn!"

Ben grins.

After Ben's visit with Raj, he feels a sense of relief. Gone is the haunting guilt and sorrow. New memories popped into his head. He remembers things that he is not sure had never happened. Memories of dinner at Raj and Indra's place and nights out with them. He is flooded with memories that he had never really experienced, but they are pleasant.

Ben crawls into bed, feeling satisfied. Before closing his eyes, he recalls images of Raj's wedding. How he taps Raj on the shoulder, Raj's surprised look before a big embrace. Raj and Indra pulling Ben onto the dance floor. Indra whispering into Ben's ear, thanking him for coming. How Raj kept pointing at him and yelling, "I knew you would come!" every few minutes.

At the end of the song, Ben pulls Raj aside.

"Raj," Ben says as he fixes Raj's upturned collar. "I have to go."

Raj gives Ben one of his looks. "You just got here."

Ben chuckles. "I have been here for almost an hour. It took a lot for me to come." Ben looks Raj in the eye. "Remind me to tell you why I hate weddings. I think I am ready to talk about it."

Raj claps Ben on the shoulder. "C'mon, Ben, one last shot … please?" Raj pleads.

"I don't want you to get too drunk and forget I was here." Ben laughs.

"One last shot," With his hand still on Ben's shoulder, Raj squeezes it. Ben quickly checks the timer in his head. He has just enough time.

"Ok … Let's go!"

They both run to the bar and order two shots. Afterward, Ben hugs his friend goodbye. He makes his way towards the back of the crowd and can hear Raj screaming for everyone to take a shot.

Ben laughs as he fades away.

CHAPTER 19 - NSFW

The following day Ben wakes up early. He stretches awake. For the first time in a long while, he is feeling good. He checks his phone, answers emails, and replies to messages. He checks in with his team. His engineers are quiet and have nothing to say, as usual. He meets with Ulysses via Zoom later that day.

"Ben, how have you been … You look rested," Ulysses comments. Ben did feel rested. He felt great.

"I do feel good; thank you for asking—"

Ulysses cut him off. "Did you see the latest evaluation numbers from the street?" The "street" Ulysses is referring to is Wall Street.

"No … I haven't got a chance to—"

Ulysses cut him off again. "I just emailed them to you. This is huge, Ben, huge." Ulysses licks his lips. "They are going to get a ten billion dollar evaluation. Our cut is going to be worth one hundred million!" Ulysses leans back in his chair, throws his hands in the air, and spins around in his chair. "I knew all this would pay out one day," Ulysses continues. "I knew keeping this stupid god-forsaken company off the ground would someday pay out huge!" Ulysses emphasizes the word huge, drawing it out. Ben looks at him quizzically. "Don't give me that look of yours," Ulysses scolds him. "This is a business; businesses are to make a profit."

"It's not that," Ben replies defensively. "I've just never seen you like this."

"It's a new day, my boy." Ben hates it when Ulysses calls him "my boy." They only have an eight-year age gap. Ulysses' expression turns somber. "God, I wish we were back in the office. This would have been a champagne day." Ulysses sighs.

Ben bites his lower lip. He is happy that Ulysses is in a good mood, but he still has doubts about NikNak. Ben did not trust it because something strange was going on with their technology.

"Well," he begins while Ulysses is still contemplative. "We still need to finish our penetration test. We don't want another OnlyFans or Ashely Madison situation on our hands—"

Ulysses' eyes shoot up at Ben. "You're comparing NikNak to a porn site?" he asks as he grips his desk with both hands. "They are nothing alike. NikNak is the future of social media. OnlyFans is where all the strippers went after the strip clubs shut down. How dare you make that comparison!"

"First." Ben begins gearing up for an argument. "You don't call them strippers. They are called 'sex workers.' Second, I told you there is some shady shit going on in NikNak, but you refuse to believe me."

"You're going to bring up that allegedly underage girl again? What's her name, 'Catty Jane' or something?"

"Kitty Josephine," Ben corrects.

"Whatever." Ulysses waves his hand in dismissal. "News flash, Ben, she might be considered a legal adult in her country. She might be doing nothing wrong, and what is she making, like half a mil a month? Shit, I barely made ten dollars an hour when I started working."

"That's not the point," Ben fires back. "If she can get away with it, what stops others from—"

Ulysses raises his hands, cutting Ben off. "I don't give a shit. She might not be breaking any laws in her country. So what she might show her cooch, that is not a FrontSpark problem."

"And you have no issue with them only accepting crypto?" Ben shouts back. "I mean, don't you feel that they are being irresponsible?"

"Ben," Ulysses says calmly. "There are ten companies I can name off the top of my head who are publicly traded companies that only deal with crypto. Why should NikNak be any different? It's a new age; get with it or get out." Ulysses leaves the meeting.

Ben bangs his fists on the desk. He and Ulysses have worked together for a long time. Ben had started as a lowly software engineer in this company and worked his way up to a director. Each promotion got him more and more conversations with Ulysses. They have always had many back-and-forth conversations where things got heated, but this felt different. Ulysses had started FrontSpark almost twenty years ago. The company's modus operandi provided support, engineering, and legal counsel to companies wanting to go public. They did this for cash up front or a percentage of the stock being offered. The most they had made on any deal was a few million dollars. This is almost a hundred times that.

Ben recalls a time when they could work in the office when he and Ulysses had a long chat.

Ben was a lead software engineer at that time and had been with the company for around ten years. He was working late one night trying to get some code done when Ulysses appeared at his desk. Despite Ulysses interviewing and hiring him, they had few conversations until then.

"Working late?" Ulysses asked, leaning on Ben's cubicle wall.

Ben jumped, startled as he looked at the CEO of the company. Ben could smell the expensive whiskey on Ulysses' breath. He looked at the clock on his computer screen and realized it was 9:30 pm.

"Yeah," Ben replied. "Trying to get this work done for Azirion."

Ulysses scoffed.

"Those idiots," Ulysses said, waving his hands in dismissal. "Those guys think they can change the world with 'clean reusable energy.'" Ulysses snorts as he says those last words.

Ben shuffled uncomfortably in his chair. "I think what they are doing is admirable. They are creating solar farms in the desert and selling the energy they collect back to the energy companies. It seems like a pretty good idea to me."

Ulysses frowned. "Those guys will maybe make ten to fifteen million dollars a year doing that, and that excludes expenses. We already project their stock to debut at around $2.50." Ulysses ran his hand through his blonde hair. At that point, he had more of it and less gray in it. "Benjamin, wasn't it?" Ulysses asked.

"No," Ben corrected. "It's just Ben."

"Ben, forget that work. Join me in my office for a drink." Ulysses looked at him suspiciously. "You drink, right? You're not one of those vegan or religious wack jobs, are you?"

Ben laughed. "I am not, and I do drink."

Ulysses had never been one to hold his tongue. He had been sued twice in the time Ben had been involved in the company. One for sexual harassment, the other for a "hostile workplace environment." Ben had once tried to date the front desk receptionist. They went out for drinks once, and she spilled the beans to him on both lawsuits. They got so engrossed in talking about Ulysses that they forgot to hook up. Despite that, Ulysses never changed the way he spoke. The company's insurance covered all expenses.

Ben followed Ulysses to his office. He had only been in that office once, on the day of his job interview. It was a large corner office with large windows. His windows overlooked the fountain that sat in the middle of the courtyard. Ben walked towards the window to stare at the view. Ulysses got two glasses from the shelf and poured whiskey into them.

"Ben," Ulysses motioned for him to sit down. "Glad to see someone at this company wants to work. What are you working on again?"

"Just finishing up some code for Azirion and then some code reviews for Cleayn.com," Ben said as Ulysses sighed.

"God." He turned his chair and looked out the window. "The Cleayn.com was one shit deal we made. The company is looking more and more like a loser." Ulysses took a large swallow of his drink.

"You know what I hate about this world?" Ulysses asked while continuing to look out the window. "It's companies like

Cleayn.com. Gig work, my ass. 'We crowdsource cleaning your house or apartment.'" Ulysses repeated the company's slogan in a high sing-song voice. He then shook his head in disgust. He turned and faced Ben. "It's all this micro-economy crowdsourcing bullshit that has been going on for the last couple of years. I used to be able to rent a car at the airport, walk right up to the counter, and skip the line. You know why?"

Ben shook his head.

"'Cause I was a gold card member!"

Ben felt himself recoil.

Ulysses leaned back in his chair and downed the rest of his drink. He poured himself another. "Nowadays, it's all peer-to-peer. Instead of walking into a clean office with a cute receptionist, I got some balloon head dropping off his car for me at the airport with his wife following him. They always give me this stupid grin and say something silly." Ulysses took another sip of his drink. "Even porn, Ben, porn!"

Ben swirled the alcohol in his glass, staring at the circles it was making.

"Porn, for god's sake, used to be done by pros with good lighting. Now I have to pop on YouPorn or PornTube to see some poorly lit, user-generated, crowdsourced bullshit! Everyone is trying to make a few dollars instead of thinking big. This is what the world is coming to … What do you think of that?" Ulysses slammed his glass on the desk. He placed his hand behind his head and propped his feet on the desk. They sat in silence as Ben tried to come up with something to say.

"Well ... I mean ... it does spread the wealth around ... you know, like Uber—"

Ulysses cut him off. "That is exactly the problem!" He took his feet off the desk and swung his chair to face Ben. "The spreading of wealth, instead of some of us being rich, none of us are. People only want a peaceful life instead of working hard and making money. I am sure some of them can make their rent and some spending money, but it's such a short-term thing."

Ulysses paused to catch his breath and took another swig of his drink. He looked down at his feet.

"They don't even make good movies anymore," he said sadly.

"What about the new MCU movie that just came out? I think that was pretty—"

Ulysses cut him off again. "The MCU? The Em See fucking You? Those aren't movies. I am talking about real movies. Movies that starred Brad Pitt, Leonardo DiCaprio, and Robert De Niro. Those guys haven't made a movie in years, and do you know why?" Ben shook his head. "It's because some boob on YouTube makes a fake proposal to his girlfriend, and everyone wants to watch that! It's disgusting!"

Ulysses got silent for a moment, then continued his rant.

"No one thinks of the future anymore. How long can you create content on YouTube? How long can you show your tits on YouPorn? These things are all short-lived. Then what do you do? Nothing, that's what! We are all on the street asking for change like common fucking beggars. Everyone is looking for a handout, even me, for god's sake!" Ulysses grabbed his glass, and for a second, Ben thought he was going to throw it against the wall, but instead, he downed the content inside.

Ben decided that it was time to go. He quickly finished the rest of his drink and began to stand up. "Ulysses … thank you for the drink, but … I got to—"

Ulysses waved him away. "Ben," Ulysses called as he was at the door. Ben stopped and turned. "Thank you for all your hard work." Ben nodded and went back to his desk.

Ben later found out that Ulysses was in such a bad mood because Cleayn.com had refused to offer him shares. They wanted flat pricing for his company's services. Later that year, when the stock debuted at twenty dollars and fifty cents and soared to forty dollars, Ulysses was even more distraught. Yet another deal to set himself up financially had fallen through. NikNak was his latest chance. And he was not going to let this one go.

#

Ben finishes his work and starts pouring himself a drink. His phone buzzes, and he checks the caller ID to see who it is.

"Raj … hey," Ben says, holding the phone in the crane of his neck.

"Hey." They exchanged pleasantries and went silent for a bit.

"So," Raj starts. "I did some initial analysis on the problem you were having."

Ben smiles as he assumes that Indra is in the room with him, which makes Raj mask his words.

"Yes, and?" Ben asks.

"Well, we all know the dark web is a shi—um, a bad place. But I didn't realize really how bad it is."

Ben raises his eyebrows. "Get to the point, please."

Raj continues, "You know the company I work for has developed technology to scan the dark web for certain files, such as stolen credit card info. I took a copy of that program and modified it to look for something else."

Ben nods, urging Raj on.

"So after a few tries, I got the right parameters and set it loose. It took a couple of days, and it returned an interesting result."

"Yeah—What was it?" Ben asks.

"On the internet, especially on the dark web, there are over thirty-five million CSAM images and videos," Raj whispers.

"Wait ... what..." Ben nearly drops the phone; he feels dizzy. He grabs the counter to steady himself.

"Just on videos alone," Raj continues. "It counted over two million."

Ben shut his eyes tight. "How could there be that many?"

"I don't know."

"What do you mean you don't know?"

"Ben ... I don't ... I mean ... I didn't think it would be that much."

"How am I supposed to find one video in that haystack?"

"I don't know."

"Can I use your software to help me find what I am looking for?" Ben asks, hopefully.

"No, sorry, this is proprietary tech. Giving it to you could get me fired."

Ben feels defeated. "So you're saying I must watch two million videos to find the right one?"

"I don't know."

"Stop saying I don't know!" Ben shouts into the phone.

"Ben … maybe you should just let this one go," Raj says quietly. "I could have gotten in real trouble just doing this for you. What you are trying to do is highly illegal; people have gone to jail for downloading this material."

Ben rubs his eyes and tries to calm himself down. Raj is right. This is highly dangerous. There is no way some government agency is not watching. And what is he going to tell them if he is caught? "Sorry, officers, I was just trying to find this one video of my ex-girlfriend being abused by her uncle to superimpose myself to change the past, so maybe she wouldn't have killed herself." Ben knew that was not going to work. They would laugh and sentence him to many years in prison.

"Are you still there?" Raj asks.

"Yes."

"Then what are you going to do?"

"I don't know, I mean, I have to try at least—" Ben could hear Raj sigh.

"The good news is that I know a way to get you to access the dark web safely. The bad news is that you will have to go at this alone. I can't jeopardize my life and marriage for this. I am sure you understand."

Ben tells Raj that he did. They arranged for Raj to come over in a couple of days and set Ben up. They say their goodbyes, and Ben stares at his drink.

He downed it.

Raj texted Ben the next day with specific instructions:

Raj: *Buy a new computer, something cheap!*

Raj: *Pay cash!!!*

Raj: *Do not touch it until I get there!*

Ben: *Ok!*

Raj came over a few days later after Ben had confirmed that he had purchased a new desktop. Ben took it out of the box and laid it next to his desk.

"Jesus, you could have plugged it in," Raj says as he kneels and fiddles with the cables.

"I thought you said, 'Don't touch it!'" Ben shoots back.

"Oh shit!" Raj exclaims as he stops moving. He reaches into his back pocket and pulls out some disposable vinyl gloves.

"Raj, is that necessary—"

Raj cut him off. "Yes!" he shouts at Ben. "Better safe than sorry," Raj says quietly. Raj puts on the gloves and starts connecting cables to the back of the PC. Raj shouts various instructions at Ben, ordering him to get him multiple wires and equipment. After a while, Raj sits at Ben's desk, cracks his knuckles, and proceeds to power on the PC. After a few minutes of typing, he turns towards Ben.

"Ben," Raj says slowly and solemnly. "I don't want you to use this PC for anything. Don't look up your bank account. Don't use Google Maps… nothing." Raj stresses the last word.

Ben nods. Raj, satisfied, goes back to hammering on the keyboard. He nods at the screen and beckons Ben over.

"Ok, I set everything up." Raj cracks his knuckles again as Ben winces. "I encrypted your hard drive and set it to auto-erase if you fail to enter the correct password three times."

"What's the password?" Ben asks.

"'1234' but don't worry; you will be asked to enter a new password once I reboot the machine." Raj types on the keyboard some more. The screen goes dark. When the operating system login appears, Raj moves over so Ben can enter a password. Raj shields his eyes as Ben is typing. When Ben is done, he moves over and allows Raj to regain control. When the machine boots up, Raj begins giving Ben instructions.

"See this dot bat file." Raj points to the bottom of the screen. Ben nods. "Double-click on it whenever you want to connect to the dark web." Ben begins to ask a question, but Raj raises his hand, silencing him. "The first thing it will do is connect you to a VPN in Japan." Raj double-clicks on the .bat file. "You see this icon." Raj points at the bottom right of the screen. Ben nods. "Wait until this icon stops flashing." They wait in silence. After the icon stops blinking, Raj continues. "Now, see this onion icon." He points towards the middle of the screen. Ben nods again, this time with a sigh. "When the icon in the system tray stops flashing, double-click on this icon."

"Why Japan?" Ben asks.

"Huh?" Raj replies, looking up at Ben.

"Why a VPN in Japan?" Ben asks again.

"I don't know," Raj stammers. "It's the most populated VPN server; it makes you harder to track." Raj put his hand to his chin. "Maybe Japan has a lot of perverts," he says with a laugh. "Regardless, I set you up to be as protected as possible." Raj turns in his chair to look at Ben. "But you're still exposed here. So be careful."

Raj walks Ben through some more safety procedures. Ben nods in silence, half listening. His mind keeps telling him how absurd he is to do this. *Who am I kidding? This is a world I never knew existed, and I want even less to find out more. Maybe I should walk away.*

"Ben." Raj snaps his fingers in front of Ben's face. "Are you listening?" Ben nods again. "Ok, what did I say?"

"Something about an icon on the screen," Ben says.

"Not an icon, this icon," Raj exclaimed, pointing at the center of the screen. "This is your 'bug out bag,' your 'eject sequence,' your 'exit strategy.' If you ever suspect you have been exposed or compromised, double-click on this icon, and the program I installed will begin wiping everything on the machine. It's not reversible and will take a few minutes to run, but it will brick the machine and make it non-operable." Raj grows quiet. "Ben," Raj says in a low voice. "This is the only time I will do this for you. I am already an accomplice here, and I can't risk doing this again. So, click on this icon if you want to quit, stop, or get out."

Ben forces his eyes to focus on the screen. He reads the tiny words beneath the icon. It says:

"Hasta la vista, baby!"

They make some small talk, and Raj hugs Ben before he leaves. He wishes him good luck.

For the next few days, Ben walks back and forth between his new computer and his work laptop. He can not focus on work or proceed with his mission. He tried turning on the new computer and clicking on the "Start here" icon that Raj had set up, but that only took him to some generic homepage with links to other sites. Some were about hurt core; others were some guy ranting about the fall of the government. He had no idea even where to start. He texts Raj:

Ben: *So what do I do?*

Raj: *???*

Ben: *I mean, where do I go?*

Raj: *I don't know browse around and stop texting me about it!!*

He tries clicking on various links and waiting patiently for the page to appear. Everything is slow. After a few minutes, Ben powers down the machine in frustration. He walks over to his couch and picks up his smartphone.

"Where shall I go today?" he asks himself, browsing through videos of the top ten bars in the world. He finds a nice one in Paris, changes out of his work clothes, and combs his hair. He takes a look at himself in the mirror. The video is twenty minutes long, enough time to get a couple of drinks and get wasted.

He sits at a table by the end of the bar and orders five shots of vodka and some food. He finds it is best to order food with his drinks as they would usually wait to ask for payment until the food was eaten. It bought Ben enough time to down his shots without needing to pay for them. He looks around at the beautiful bar and stares out the window. He can see the Eiffel Tower lit up and looking beautiful. He thinks a scene like this would make him happy, but he only feels more lonely. He and Jinni always talked about a trip to Paris, but life seemed to have gotten in the way.

The server brings him his food. He did not even remember what he ordered, just pointing at the first thing on the menu. He pokes at it with his fork. He looks at his wrist at his imaginary watch and realizes he only has a few minutes left. Suddenly, the weight of the last couple of weeks hits Ben hard. He feels his chest tighten and a massive weight on his shoulders. Tears start to fill his eyes. As he wipes them away, his mind wanders to the day he first "superimposed" himself. When he first saw Jinni on the sidewalk. He vividly remembers the red blood pooling behind her head, the look in her eyes like glass had shattered within them. He gets up and starts to run out of the bar. The bartender shouts at him in French, but Ben ignores him. He runs out into the cool Paris night and starts running even faster. He runs as hard and fast as he can. When his mind tells him the time is up, he jumps. He jumps like an Olympic long jumper into the air, his arms splayed behind him. He closes his eyes and pushes his head back. He can see the light out of the corner of his closed eyes. He hears a crunch and then nothing.

Ben wakes up on the floor of his apartment. His head is ringing, and warm sticky liquid is all over his face. He reaches up and touches the wall next to his couch. His hand reaches out to his face and touches his nose; his head recoils in pain.

"Ow..." he complains. He pushes himself off the floor and looks at the pooled liquid. It is blood, his blood. Ben sighs loudly and walks into his bathroom. He turns on the light and looks at his face. His nose is bloodied. He grabs a towel off the rack, washes his nose, and inspects the damage. His nose did not appear to be broken, just bruised. He finishes cleaning himself and sits at his makeshift desk with his "special" computer. He turns it on and starts poking around.

CHAPTER 20 - ELI5

Ben is finishing his morning tea when the ringtone on his work laptop goes off. He looks at the notification tray and sees it is an incoming call from Ulysses. He clicks the accept button and sees an angry-looking Ulysses staring back at him.

"Hey, Ulysses—" Ben starts before being cut off.

"What the fuck did you do?" Ulysses asks angrily.

"Huh?" Ben responds.

"The S-1, why the fuck did you write that there could be an issue in the goddam S-1!" Ulysses is livid.

"What?" Ben is confused. A few months back, Ulysses had tasked him with a technical overview of NikNak and to complete that portion of the S-1. Ben completed the review on time and pointed out some issues he felt needed to be addressed.

"Ben!" Ulysses shouts, his voice rising with every syllable. "On the S-1, you wrote that NikNak had a potential security threat. Now the SEC is asking for clarification on this issue. The S-1 is on hold until we clear this up!"

"First of all," Ben replies calmly. "I never said NikNak had a security vulnerability; in fact, I said just the opposite. Their security is good, too good." Ulysses gives Ben a confused, angry look. Ben continues. "I said that since only the author of a private channel can supply subscribers with an encrypted key, a malicious actor could abuse that, and it would not be known to the administrators of NikNak."

"And? What of it?" Ulysses asks.

Ben adjusts himself in his seat.

"My concern, as stated in the S-1, is that since only the channel creator could generate encrypted keys, if someone were to post offensive content, NikNak would not be made aware of it and could not investigate since all private channels are encrypted. Even if they had been served a warrant, their hands would be tied since all key generation happens via a passphrase that is only known to the author. Which is a risk." Ben emphasizes the word risk. "Because NikNak would not be unable to comply with the order." Ben sits back in his chair. A moment of silence passes between them. Ben can see the red spreading all over Ulysses' face.

"That is the stupidest shit I have heard all year," Ulysses shouts. Ben begins to talk, but Ulysses speaks over him. "I use YouTube all the time, and once in a while, I am sent a private video that some of my friends have posted. Sometimes the video is a little raunchy, but YouTube doesn't strike them or take them down!"

"Ulysses," Ben is finding it harder and harder to remain calm. "YouTube and NikNak are entirely different platforms. YouTube provides mostly publicly consumable content that ad revenue supports. NikNak is short-form video content that is subscriber-supported. YouTube collects money from advertisers and doles it out to its content creators. NikNak channel creators can charge a flat, monthly, or per video cost in cryptocurrency to each of its private channels, and NikNak takes a cut because NikNak controls the crypto exchange. All transactions must go through its API. Then they 'improve—'" Ben makes air quotes with his fingers. "—the transaction privacy by breaking the on-chain link between the source and the destination address. They then proceed to withdraw via a new address. Whenever the withdrawal happens, there is no way to link the withdrawal to the deposit." Ben pauses.

"I don't understand what the hell you said, but what does this have to do with NikNak and people creating cute cat videos?" Ulysses asks impatiently. "Explain it to me like you would a five-year-old."

Ben rolls his eyes and begins explaining.

"When you create a video on YouTube, you can set it to public, private, or unlisted. If it is private or unlisted, you need a direct link because YouTube owns the search platform, and all private and unlisted videos will not be indexed for search." Ben pauses so Ulysses can take this in. "If you put the video as public, it can be monetized, which means ads can be played on it, and you will receive a cut of those ads based on how many people watched it."

"I know how YouTube works. Get to the point," Ulysses growls.

"On NikNak, you can post videos to the public feed or your private channel. Unlike YouTube, NikNak does not store any of its creator videos on its servers. Each video is compressed, broken down into smaller chunks, and saved to multiple devices like your phone." Ben picks up his phone and points at it. "I give Pavlov and Demetri credit. Their encryption and compression algorithm is top notch." Ulysses waves his hand at Ben, asking him to move it along. "On the public channel, there are no issues. No ads play there, but content creators can work with advertisers to hock their products if they want." Ben pauses, gathering his thoughts. "The problem lies in the private channels. NikNak does not control those encryption keys. The author or creator of the channel does. So any kind of content can be posted there, and NikNak would not know what that content is nor how to access it."

"Then why doesn't YouTube or other video-sharing platforms have this problem?" Ulysses asks, annoyed.

"That's a great question!" Ben says enthusiastically. "It's because regardless of whether your video is private or public, everything is stored on their servers where they can have a content filter scan each video for piracy or offensive content."

"Ok, what does this have to do with the other nonsense you were spewing about depositing and taking out cash?" Ulysses asks.

"Based on my review, they sever the link between the person depositing the crypto and NikNak withdrawing it. Then monthly, they redistribute it to the content creators, minus their cut, from another wallet, making the transaction from the consumer anonymous." Ben clarifies.

"What does that even mean?" Ulysses asks.

"I think back in the day; they used to call this money laundering."

Ulysses rubs the bridge of his nose and falls silent for a second.

"And you are saying this is illegal?" Ulysses asks.

"Well," Ben says. "Crypto is decentralized, so technically, it is not illegal; it's just—"

Ulysses raises his hand to cut Ben off.

"So what you are telling me is that you recommend NikNak, in the future, add a content filter to its application so bad actors cannot post 'offensive,'" Ulysses mocks Ben's air quotes, "content on their platform." Ben begins to speak, but Ulysses cuts him off again. "As for their financial transactions, based on the current regulation of cryptocurrencies, they conform to all current regulations and standards as they stand today. Is that correct?"

"That's not really what I was trying to—"

Ulysses gestures a stop with his hand and cuts him off again. "You are telling me that you recommend NikNak, in the future, add a content filter to its application so bad actors cannot post offensive content on their platform. Based on the current regulation of cryptocurrencies, they conform to all current regulations and standards as they stand today … Right?"

Ben looks down at his keyboard; he is ready to fight but knows he cannot win. "Ok, Ulysses, I'll amend the S-1 later today," Ben replies quietly.

"Thank you for all your hard work." Ulysses leaves the meeting.

#

Ben spends the next few days surfing the dark web. He is poking around, not finding anything that interesting. It's not like the dark web had a Google where he could type in "CSAM" and it would return results.

He finds the dark web a disorganized hodgepodge of websites alluring to the lowest common denominator of human nature. He views sites that claim (with extremely detailed written proof) that Hitler was right. Many sites condemned the communist leadership of China and are trying to unite its masses for revolution. Some sites are dedicated to death, and many are devoted to murder porn. He browses through a couple but finds them somewhat gross and scary. Ben is about to give up and go to bed when he notices something in the footer of the dark web page. It is a series of images advertising other sites. On the far left is a small picture of a young blonde girl. Ben clicks on the image.

He waits a few seconds for the page to load, and his eyes widen when it does. The header image is of a young blonde girl (maybe thirteen or fourteen years old) in a thong bikini with her back turned to the camera, her head turned, and she is smiling. Below additional movie clips are loading. Ben scrolls down. There are other images with a clickable link under each image combined with the movie title. As Ben scrolls down the page, he notices the movie titles getting more aggressive.

The first one says, "Watch Amber play in the sand." The next one says, "Watch Amber get all wet." The image is of the same girl being sprayed by a hose. The next "Amber goes topless!" with an image of the girl covering her chest with both hands. Ben also notices that the expression on the young girl's face is changing. She went from smiling and laughing in the first photo to an almost expressionless seriousness in the topless one. Ben's hand is starting to shake. He forces his fingers to scroll down even more. The following image is titled "Amber plays with herself." The young girl sits on the floor with her hand in her underwear. Ben notices dark rings around her eyes. It is as if she had not slept well in days.

Ben reaches down and shuts off the computer. He walks to the kitchen and makes himself a strong drink. When he is done with that, he makes himself another.

Sleep did not come easy for Ben that night. Every time he falls asleep, the image of the girl's face appears. Flashes of her face go from happy and playful to sad and hopeless, the images jar him awake. In his last dream, the girl looks at him and floats closer and closer. She grabs his hand and starts pulling, Ben tries to pull away, but the girl would not let go. Ben uses his other hand and grabs his wrist to pull his hand away before waking up startled in a cold sweat. He gets out of bed and goes to the kitchen for a glass of water. He leaves the lights off. He grabs some paper towels and wipes the sweat away from his face. He puts both hands on the kitchen counter and sighs.

"Maybe Raj is right," Ben says in the dark kitchen. "This is a stupid idea." He finishes his water and walks back to his bed. He grabs his phone and starts watching NikNak.

Over the next week, Ben does not touch his "special" computer. He fully engrosses himself in work. The IPO for NikNak would only be a few months after the S-1 got approved. He has many items to cross off his checklist before then. Ulysses is even more irritable and annoying than ever. Ben knew he could see the dollar signs and would not let this deal be screwed up. He constantly pestered Ben asking for nearly hourly updates. After a few days of this, Ben politely asks Ulysses to back the fuck off.

Still, things were progressing nicely with the IPO after the amended S-1 filing. Pavlov, for once, starts listening to Ben's suggestion and adds a content filter to the public NikNak feed. When Ben asks if he would do the same for the private channels, Pavlov dismisses him and tells him that what people do in private is their own damn business. NikNak is not going to suppress any freedom of expression.

Despite things going well with the NikNak project, Ben is falling apart. His drinking has progressed from a nuance (morning hangovers, pounding headaches) to problematic (throwing up mid-day, blurry vision, and overall dizziness). Ben still powers through. After work, Ben lies on the couch and watches NikNak videos. He hasn't "superimposed" himself in a couple of weeks. He did not have the energy nor the drive for it. He wants to work, drink, watch pretty girls dancing, and funny cat videos.

Subconsciously he knows that this is all coming to an end. During the day, his mind often drifts off to think of his favorite childhood hero, Spawn. Spawn was an armed forces soldier who had been murdered by his best friend. He then made a deal with the devil to be reborn as a hell-spawn so he could avenge his death and look after his wife. But Spawn's powers were limited. Once he used them all up, he would return to hell. So Spawn had to use his powers carefully to extend his stay on earth. Ben feels the same way. Maybe he only has a limited amount of "superimpositions" in him. Best to save them for when he needed them.

That night Ben gets blistering drunk. A couple of months ago, he consumed half a bottle of vodka daily. These days he is up to a bottle and a half. In terms of expenses, this does not put too much of a dent in his wallet. He is paid well. He is more concerned that purchasing that much alcohol will cause people to look at him funny. So he rotates his purchases. Sometimes he goes to Costco; other times, the supermarket; and occasionally, the liquor store down the street. Ben does not like confrontations, and if someone had asked him what he was doing buying so much alcohol, he would not know how to respond. So it is best to avoid those situations.

Ben sits in front of his "special" computer. He has finally mustered the courage to turn it on. He sits there looking at the login screen for over twenty minutes. His glass, filled with vodka, soda water, and ice, sits beside him, sweating on his desk. His fingers are lightly tapping on the keyboard keys without depressing them.

"Fuck it," Ben says aloud and logs in. He clicks on the file Raj had set up for him and waits for his browser to launch. He did not remember how he got to the "Amber" site he had found before. So he clicks around various sites trying to retrace his steps. He cannot find the site and slams his fist on the desk in frustration. Not having a history or search was making this difficult. This felt like the first days of the internet, where everything was haphazardly thrown together with zero organization. By chance, he finds a site advertising "young girls' videos," but when he clicks on it, he finds it's primarily videos of women in their thirties dressed up like teenagers. After a few frustrating hours, he gives up. He could not find anything, much less navigate the dark web. He shuts off his "special" computer and goes to bed (after a couple of nightcaps).

Lying in the dark, Ben can not sleep. A thought comes to him. He sits up in bed.

"Do you think he will do it?" Ben asks himself. He has nothing to lose by trying. He lies back down again. A few minutes later, he is sound asleep.

The next afternoon Ben sits nervously at his desk. His Zoom software is open on his screen, but no one is on the call except him. He looks at the clock; it is five minutes past the hour. Ben taps his finger on his desk.

Come on, you accepted the invite, join! Ben thinks. A few seconds later, a tired and annoyed face joins the call.

"Yes, what is it?" Pavlov asks.

Ben has replayed this conversation in his head all day. His initial approach is to make it seem like it's a work thing like he needs to check up on some stuff on the "dark web" to ensure NikNak security. Or he could lie and say he heard someone had put a copy of NikNak on the "dark web" and Ben needs to investigate. But he knows Pavlov will see right through that, or even worse, explore it himself and call Ben an idiot for wasting his time when he eventually found nothing. His second inclination is to come clean with Pavlov and tell him the truth.

Ben could say, "Pavlov, I can enter any video on the internet, including the dark web. I need your help finding some child sex abuse material to enter it and save my ex-girlfriend from years of abuse and eventually killing herself. Will you help me?"

Ben knew that Pavlov would laugh in his face and call him crazy. Then he would tell Ulysses that Ben is a liability to this project, and Ulysses would have no choice but to fire him. That is not the right option either. He needs to come up with something better.

"Pavlov, I hope you are doing well," Ben says. Pavlov nods. Ben continues, "As you know, my team and I have been tasked with doing an end-to-end security review of the NikNak app. Today the SEC contacted me and asked if I had conducted a 'dark web' malicious user search. As part of my duties, the final thing I need to do is make sure that user accounts and credentials are not being leaked to the dark web." This is a lie. The SEC had never contacted him.

"The dark web?" Pavlov interjects. "What the fuck you mean, the dark web?"

"Umm, well—" That is all Ben gets out before Pavlov cuts him off.

"I mean, which one, TOR, Freenet, or BitTorrent?" Pavlov clarifies.

"Primarily TOR," Ben replies. He has never heard of the other two.

"TOR, what a piece of shit software that turned out to be." Pavlov laughs. "So what about it."

"Well, my team and I need to create customized software to search through the TOR network and see if any sites are selling or distributing compromised NikNak accounts."

"We already have safeguards around that, two-factor authentication and such," Pavlov says as he waves his hand dismissively.

"True, but I ran some numbers, and not all of your revenue-generating accounts have turned that on," Ben lies. He has no clue who has it turned on or not.

"Ok … so again, what's the problem? Run your little program." Pavlov sounds annoyed.

"My team gave me an estimate this morning; they said it would take them six weeks to two months to create the software."

The call falls silent before Pavlov finally shouts.

"Six weeks to two months! Six weeks?" Pavlov screams into the chat; Ben has to lower the volume.

"Yes, that is our estimate, so, unfortunately, we may need to put the S-1 on hold until—" Ben stammers.

"Six weeks!" Pavlov yells again. "I could write something that could search the entire dark web in a day!" he shouts.

"Well," Ben tries to remain calm; his plan is working. "Unfortunately, we have no one on my staff that has your caliber of programming skills."

"Goddamnit, Ben!" Pavlov slams his desk. "I got enough shit to do, and now you drop this shit on my lap."

"We could always put the S-1 on hold—"

"Fuck you, Ben." Pavlov sighs and rubs his eyes. "I'll have it to you by the end of the day." Pavlov leaves the meeting.

Ben smiles.

Pavlov is a man of his word, and at 11:30 p.m., Ben hears the distinctive ding of an email arriving. He runs to his laptop and checks his email.

The email reads:

Here now stop bugging me.

-P

Attached to the email is a zip file. Ben downloads the software to a thumb drive (he did not dare open his work or personal email on his "special" computer) and copies the contents. He launches the executable, and the splash screen reads, "Ben stupid fucking program," which causes Ben to laugh and shake his head. *Never change, Pavlov, never change,* he thinks.

Pavlov created a pretty impressive piece of software reasonably quickly. It included options like Breadth First Search, Path-ascending crawling, checkboxes to search the header, footer, and body, or all three. It can use multiple keywords, Regex, and fuzzy search. On the bottom of the screen is a larger text box titled "Links," which Ben assumes would display the site's links when he got a keyword match. Ben claps his hands together. *It is time.* he thinks. *It is time to save Jinni.*

He scratches his head and types in:

"Jinni"

He waits a few minutes as his mouse cursor turns into an hourglass.

0 results found.

"Fuck!" Ben says aloud. *It was never going to be that easy.*

A thought entered Ben's mind. He recalls the weird short video on NikNak with the little girl and the red balloon. He types in "red balloon" into the search bar. After a few minutes, a couple of search results came back. Ben clicks on the first one. The page takes about thirty seconds to load. When it does, Ben's eyes widen. He reads the text:

So we all want access to the Red Balloon. The questions are challenging, and you will be locked out if you fail the entrance test three times. Since NikNak accounts are tied to your phone number, you must change your phone number and account name to get back in. As I said, the questions are TOUGH! Lol. Anyways here are some links that can help you prepare for the test.

So I am sure you are thinking, "Is the Red Ballon worth it?" I am here to tell you, oh yeah, it is. Imagine every video or image you ever wanted available to you at a click of a button. The best part is that there is nothing to download (unless you want to, hehe). So you bet your little girl's ass it's worth it.

OH! Before I forget, ensure you have $1200 in either BTC or ETH before taking the test. They require a one-year payment upfront. If you DON'T pay immediately after getting the test right, it will be a failed attempt. Just an FYI! After one year, it's $100 a month so have those crypto wallets ready!

Ben reads through the rest of the page. It contains TOR .onion links with some instructions on what to watch. Ben almost bookmarks the page but then stops himself. He grabs a pencil and paper and writes down the long URL. Paper is easier to hide and destroy if needed. He then logs off the "special" computer and goes to bed.

"Tomorrow," he says as he enters his bedroom door. "Tomorrow, I save Jinni."

CHAPTER 21 - IDGY

Ben begins to realize that the anonymity of the dark web is partially to do with its speed. It is slow as hell. As the bits and bytes slowly soar to his "special" PC, he realizes that the lack of bandwidth is crucial to protecting his anonymity. *Who would notice an infinitely small piece of data flowing in a sea of digital information?* It is like trying to find one specific plankton in the Pacific Ocean. Ben refreshes the browser, and the complete percentage number creeps up by 0.01%. He sighs and goes to the kitchen to make himself a drink. Three hours later, it has advanced past 40%. Six hours after that, it is at 75%. Like slow-drip water torture, Ben waits. Finally, after an additional three hours, the file download is complete.

Ben navigates to the download folder and sees the media file. He hovers his mouse over it but does not click it. He pauses and considers his thoughts. *Am I going to do this? Do I even want to do this?* Ben quickly shakes that thought off; he is on a mission. *One must break some eggs to create an omelet,* he thinks. His purpose here is to change things that should be changed. He decides to watch only as long as it takes to rule out that it is not Jinni in the video. Once he clarifies it is not her, he will move on to the next download.

Ben takes a deep breath and holds it. He double-clicks the file.

A grainy black-and-white video starts to play, and an out-of-focus image is blurred in the background. Ben squints his eyes to try and make out the figure. The movie's grainy quality and lack of color told Ben that this was shot probably in the late '70s or early '80s, long before Jinni was even born. Ben moves the mouse cursor to press the close icon when the blurred image comes into focus. Ben pauses. On his screen is a girl about twelve or thirteen years old. A set of ropes string her up on each wrist, and she has a burlap sack over her head. She is naked from the waist up with only her underwear on.

"Shit," Ben whispers. He begins to move his mouse again to close the video. A Man comes in from the side of the screen. He stops in front of the girl and squeezes one of her breasts. She flinches, and the Man laughs. Ben freezes. The Man walks towards the camera and picks it up. He walks towards the back of the room, where he has a table set up. On the table were various whips, switches, and canes. He picks up the object closest to him and shows it to the camera. It is like he is asking the viewer which is the right tool. Ben grips the sides of his chair. The Man moves over to the next object and does the same thing.

Ben's hands start to shake. The Man moves to what looks like a bamboo switch. He picks it up and swings it. Ben can make out the sound of it cutting the air. Satisfied, the Man puts the camera back to face the girl. He says something in Russian (Ukrainian?) to the girl. She shakes her head, and the Man laughs again. Ben is gripping the armrest of his chair tightly. His nails dig into the rubber on the underside. Ben is leaning forward, breathing heavily. The Man enters the frame with the switch in hand.

"No!" Ben shouts. The Man swishes the switch through the air again. The girl's head flicks back. "No!" Ben shouts louder.

His hands tightly grip the armrest. He is gripping them so hard that he is shaking all over. The Man walks up to the girl, switch in hand. He grabs her hard. The girl cries out. The Man steps back and brings his hand back, ready to swing.

"No!" Ben screams as he kicks the chair away from under him. He looks around his desk and finds a purple five-pound weight he had bought at the start of the pandemic. He told himself at the time that he would use it every day to get into shape while working from home. He used it once and never touched it again. He picks it up with his left hand and moves towards the monitor. He touches the screen and closes his eyes.

The smell engulfs him. It smells dusty, dirty, and sweaty, with the distinct odor of vodka and sperm. He opens his eyes and covers his mouth to suppress a cough. He stands behind the Man. The girl's head moves in his direction as if she could sense his presence (maybe she could see through the bag on her head, Ben wonders later). The Man pauses mid-swing as if he feels something in the room too. He begins to turn his head around slowly. Knowing this is his chance, Ben attempts to move the 5-pound weight into his dominant right hand. Except he feels nothing. He looks down and realizes the five-pound weight is not there.

Shit! Ben thinks.

The Man starts turning his body. Ben has to act; it is now or never. He quickly moves towards the Man and unleashes an overhand right with all his strength.

Ben had heard from his friends (when he still had some) that the camera always lies. They talked about how it added ten pounds, could make a short person look tall, and vice versus. When Ben is again in the hospital recovering, he looks back at this incident and wonders how he got his perception wrong. He didn't realize at the time that the girl was much taller than he thought. She looked small in the video, but when Ben saw her now, she stood around 5'4. The Man stands about a foot taller than her. When Ben swings at the Man, he is aiming for his face. When the punch connects, it lands on the Man's chest. Ben has a flashback to his fight with Sean O'Connell. For a moment, no one moves.

Ben looks up as the Man looks down at him. The Man is in his mid-forties, with short graying hair. He has a complex nose and an even harder face. Behind that are cold blue eyes. He is tall, around 6'3 or 6'4, and weighs about 270 pounds. He looks down at Ben and then looks down at Ben's fist still logged in his chest. He moves quickly for a person his size, and with the switch still in his right hand, he shoves Ben back hard. Ben slams into the wall behind him. The Man starts shouting at him. Ben pushes against the wall and charges at the Man. The Man reaches back and strikes Ben hard in the face.

Ben lies on the floor with dust clouds swirling around him. The Man is standing with his foot on top of his ribs, screaming at him in Russian (or Ukrainian, Ben did not know the difference). Ben puts his hands on the Man's foot and tries to lift it off him. The Man swiftly kicks him in the face. Ben hears a "crack" as his nose breaks. He curls up into a ball while grabbing his gushing nose. The Man stands over him, screaming some more. He then turns around and walks out of the room.

Get the fuck up! his mind screams at him. *Get up and get out of here, or you're dead!* Ben pushes himself off the ground and stumbles to his feet. He looks up at the girl. Her head is turned in his direction. He puts his bloodied hand on the wall for balance and walks out of the room.

He emerges into a small apartment. Directly in front of him is a sizable two-glass pane window. Underneath the window is a dirty pale yellow couch. On the couch is a woman (The Man's wife? His girlfriend? The girl's mother?). She is sleeping peacefully despite all the ruckus. Curled up in her hands like a baby is a bottle of vodka. Ben looks to the right and sees the Man emerging from a doorway. Their eyes lock for a second. The Man has a gun in his right hand.

"Kakogo khrena ty zdes' delayesh'?" The Man shouts at Ben.

Ben looks at the Man and back at the window. The Man raises his gun. Ben runs for the window. A large "bang" goes off—Ben vaults off the couch and crashes through the window. The woman doesn't wake up.

As Ben flies through the window, he realizes a couple of things. He has no idea how long the video is, so he does not know how long he will be stuck here. He also does not know what floor the apartment is on. As he crashes through the window, he squeezes his eyes shut. He tightens his muscles and prepares for a long fall. A quarter of a second later, he lets out the air in his body as he lands on the outside walkway. He opens his eyes and jumps to his feet. Ben looks around and realizes he is in what appears to be a Russian block-style apartment complex. He is about six stories up, and it is in the late afternoon or early morning. He turns and looks back through the window. He sees the Man pointing the gun at him again. Ben ducks away from the apartment.

A mosquito-like sound buzzes past his ear. He is lucky that the apartment is the last one on the floor, so he has only one way to go. Ben sees some stairs before him. He beelines for them. He can hear an apartment door opening, followed by another loud bang. A buzzing sound passes his ear, this time closer. Ben grabs the railing, ignoring the pain in his shoulder, and starts descending.

Ben flies down the stairs. He can hear the Man still shouting at him. The Man fires a few more shots at Ben as he descends the stairs. One came dangerously close to hitting his hand. Sparks fly from the metal railing. Ben emerges on the ground floor; he quickly looks around. All he can see is a bunch of apartment buildings around him. He takes a chance and heads right. He runs through a courtyard that has a rusty makeshift playground where some kids are playing. The kids stop playing and look up at him. Ben keeps running. As he comes up to the street, he heels over and grabs his knees to catch his breath. He looks back the way he came and sees the kids still looking in his direction but no one else. Ben walks briskly onto the sidewalk and takes a left. He looks at the cars parked on the street. Most are old, dirty, and from the '60s or '70s. Ben realizes that he is an American stuck behind the Iron Curtain at the height of the Cold War. He curses himself for not checking the length of the video.

Ben is halfway up the block when he hears shouting behind him. He turns and where he had initially emerged is the Man standing with two men. They are pointing and yelling angrily at him. Ben turns and runs. He ducks into an alley and realizes he has no idea where he is going. The path could lead to a dead end, but he does not have a choice. Ben is halfway down the alley when he sees an old dumpster sitting against the wall. He lifts the lid and, with some effort, climbs in. He is lucky his nose is broken because he can feel the smell of the garbage around him. Something moves in the container, but Ben stays still.

A few minutes later, he hears men running past him, shouting. Ben holds his breath and stays still. He hears voices shouting, and then footsteps coming towards him. The footsteps come closer and closer. They fall silent. Ben tenses up.

Light begins peeking through the lid of the dumpster as it opens. Ben sees three angry faces staring down at him. The Man raises his gun. A light flashes in front of Ben's eyes. When he finally opens them, he is sitting on the floor of his apartment. His hands are up, defending his face.

He blinks a few times and stands up. He goes to his bathroom. His shirt is covered in blood and trash. Ben attempts to take his shirt off, but his shoulder screams in pain. He touches the back of his shoulder and whimpers. He turns his back to the mirror and realizes his shirt has a hole in it. He gently pushes his finger through it and jumps in pain. He looks at the side of his shirt and realizes blood is streaming down onto the bathroom floor. Ben feels dizzy. He returns to the living room, picks up his smartphone, and dials 911.

#

When Ben wakes up, someone is sitting next to him.

"Jinni?" he calls out.

265

"No, Ben," the voice says.

Ben closes one of his eyes to help him focus and gently turns his head to look at the person in the chair.

"How are you feeling?" Detective Susan Gonzales asks.

"Susan?" Ben replies.

"Yes," she answers.

Ben slumps back in his bed. Once again, he finds himself in a hospital with a cop by his side. Ben lies there in silence.

"Why are you here?" he asks.

"Just ... you know, checking up on a good citizen," Susan responds coldly.

"Am I in trouble?" Ben asks.

"You must have said that a lot as a kid," Susan replies.

"Excuse me?"

"Am I in trouble? Am I in trouble?" Susan says, mocking Ben's voice. "I bet you used to ask your mom or dad that all the time." Susan crosses her arms.

"Then why are you here?" Ben asks.

"When the paramedics found you in your apartment, you had passed out due to blood loss. Their protocol is to notify the department of any active shootings. When the officer ran your name, she noticed you had a pending case with Homicide. She called us, and here I am."

"Where is Detective Bateson?" Ben asks.

"Karl and I are taking shifts. Homicide doesn't usually get involved in non-fatal shootings, but there was no guarantee that you would make it through. Plus, we already have a repartee." Susan smiles.

"I see," is all Ben can reply.

"Oh indeed," Susan replies sarcastically as she stands up. "How's the shoulder?"

"It hurts."

"Getting shot with a 9mm full metal jacket bullet will do that to you," Susan says calmly. "And the nose?"

"It also hurts."

"Well, the break was pretty clean, according to the doctor. And one of your ribs was partially cracked, but there isn't much you can do about that other than wrap it."

Ben lies in silence.

Susan starts, "So ... do you want to tell me what happened?"

Ben shrugs and immediately regrets it. His eyes water in pain.

"Yeah, I wouldn't do that if I was you. Bullet wounds can take some time to heal." Susan sits back down. "Do you want to tell me what happened?" she repeats.

"I don't know." Ben thinks quickly. "I was walking home and heard a loud bang, and now I am here."

"You mean you were shot by a 9x18 millimeter full metal jacket bullet from a Makarov pistol circa the '70s, you end up with a broken nose, a cracked rib, and you don't know what happened?" Susan raises her eyebrows at Ben. "I find that very, very hard to believe." She starts tapping her foot on the floor. No one speaks.

Finally, Ben breaks the silence. "I don't know. Maybe I fell after I got shot. I heard a loud bang, and then I woke up—"

"Stop lying to me, Ben!" Susan stands to her feet. "I cased your apartment. There was no blood out on the sidewalk or a blood trail that led to your apartment. The only blood we found was in the apartment."

Ben starts to panic. "You were in my apartment?" he tries to reply loudly, but the bandage around his nose muffles his voice. His heart is racing. He wonders if she has seen his "special" computer.

"Yes, your super let me in. Blood was everywhere, from the living room to the bathroom. I talked to the paramedic, and he said he didn't notice any blood in the hall or by the front door. I spoke with your neighbors, who confirmed that they didn't hear any loud shots inside or outside your complex. So," Susan says as she sits down again. "Do you want to tell me what happened?"

Ben grew angry. *Ok, Susan, here is what happened.* Ben ran the scenario in his head. *I downloaded an illegal video from the dark web. Why, do you ask? Here, let me explain it to you. I can superimpose myself into any video on the internet. I don't know how I do it; I just can. I am looking for a specific video of my ex-girlfriend that I know is out there. This time I found a video of a large Man about to beat a young girl with a stick. I got angry and jumped in. I didn't know he was twice my size, and he kicked my ass. He also had a gun and shot me. I ran away until the video ended. Yes, Susan, I can only stay in the video for its length and not a second longer.* Ben sighs and shakes his head. He realizes how crazy he would sound. Detective Gonzales would probably lock him up in the psych ward for his safety.

"I don't know what happened," Ben hears himself repeating. "As I said, I was walking up to my apartment, and here I am." A tear runs down his eye. He wipes it away with his good hand.

Susan crosses her arms and stares at him. "If you are in trouble, now is the time to tell me. I can't help if I don't know what the problem is." Ben shakes his head. "I don't get you," she says as she stands up. "You seem to be finding yourself in a lot of shit lately. One day you're going to wish you asked for help." She starts putting on her jacket. She shoots Ben one more look and pulls out her phone from her pocket as she walks towards the door. "Karl ... Yeah, you were right. He had nothing to say ... I owe you ten...." She walks out of the room.

Ben breathes a sigh of relief and goes back to sleep.

They release Ben the next day, citing that he has already used all his insurance-covered days. They explained that it would have to come out of his pocket if he wanted to stay longer. Ben declines, and they begin processing him. Dr. Kamal visits and gives him instructions on keeping the wound clean.

"Wash the wound with water two times a day," Dr. Kamal explains. "Do not use hydrogen peroxide or alcohol. You can cover the wound with Vaseline or any petroleum jelly. Only use non-stick bandages."

Ben nods through the explanation, but his mind is elsewhere.

He takes an Uber home and takes down the police tape that covers the door to his apartment. Again his key does not work. He goes to his super for a new key and a new bill for another lock change. Ben goes back to his apartment. He goes in, looks around, and spots the blood trail on the floor. He goes to the kitchen, gets a mop, and cleans as much blood as possible from the floor with one hand. He then grabs his phone and calls Ulysses. He lies to Ulysses about what happened and tells him some gangbangers had shot and robbed him. Ulysses asks him if he is ok to work or needs more time off. Ben says he is fine and might type a little slower than usual. Ulysses commends him on his work ethic and hangs up the phone. After Ben is done cleaning, he sits at his "special" computer and logs in.

"I am going to heal up, and I am coming for you, you sick fuck," Ben whispers as he waits for the "special" computer to boot up. Ben navigates to his downloads folder and suddenly pushes back from his desk.

The file is not there.

Ben starts to panic. *Did Susan find it?* he wonders. He quickly pulls himself (with one hand) back towards the desk and minimizes all windows. He navigates to the desktop and almost clicks the panic icon that Raj had set up for him. As his mouse cursor hovers over the icon, Ben stops and realizes what has happened.

It had happened before with Jinni's suicide Nak. His intervention has changed the timeline. Perhaps the Man was now too scared to record his videos, considering what had happened. Maybe the Man decided to stop recording and chose to keep his abuse private. Ben no longer has a window of entry. The girl is lost in time. *Did she get away? Is she even alive?* Ben has a multitude of thoughts going through his head. Ben will never know. He gets up from the desk and goes to the kitchen to make himself a drink.

CHAPTER 22 - KYS

It takes Ben only three weeks to regain the use of his shoulder and arm. (Ben is a fast healer). He meets with Dr. Kamal for a follow-up. Dr. Kamal assures him that the wound has healed quite well, and Ben is lucky that no bones were broken and no significant arteries were damaged. Ben complains about the pain, and Dr. Kamal prescribes him some Oxy.

Ben soon realizes that mixing the Oxy and alcohol has become his new favorite thing. He would use his drinking glass to crush the pills into powder and mix them with his drink. It calms him considerably and makes him feel happy.

One night he grabs his prescription bottle, opens it, and shakes out a pill. He then looks into the bottle and realizes this is the last one. Panic overcomes him, and he grabs his phone to book another appointment with Dr. Kamal. The first available appointment is over three weeks away. Ben makes a mental note to call the doctor in the morning.

Ben had begun drinking earlier in the day. Usually, he would start late in the evening, but now he starts right after work. He justifies this by telling himself that getting drunk earlier would mean passing out earlier, giving him more time to sleep and not miss work. But tonight, he has trouble sleeping. Most nights, he would start with a "pill and soda," as he likes to call it, and then have a few drinks in between; he would end his night with another "pill and soda." He does not have another pill and is tossing and turning in bed. Ben gives up trying to sleep and grabs his phone. He opens the NikNak app and starts scrolling through the feed.

Ben finds himself spending more and more time on NikNak. Regardless of his issues with it, he still finds it entertaining. It is a mix of tutorials, unlicensed mental health advice (one Nak gave you five reasons not to kill yourself), questionable financial advice (mostly about crypto), and funny skits. The problem is that someone like Kitty Josephine or one of her imitators would bombard his feed and ask him to join their private channel. They are usually scantily dressed, seductively dancing, and talking in a low sexy voice. Ben clicks on the Kitty Josephine subscribe button, which asks him to join the "pussy army" for $15 a month or $150 for a year, all in crypto. He checks her subscriber count and sees it is now over thirty thousand. Ben whistles softly. Kitty Josephine is now making over $450,000 a month! Ben shakes his head in disbelief.

Ben attempts to sleep that night, but the Oxy withdrawal and the shoulder pain see him tossing and turning for most of the night. He keeps having quick dreams, flashes of something or another. At one moment, his mom is crying in her wedding dress. In another, Jinni is shoving him away from the door. Each time he would jump awake, move to the other side of the bed, and attempt to sleep again. Finally, as the first light of dawn breaks, he falls asleep.

Ben wakes to his phone alarm buzzing by his head. He reaches out for it and checks on the time. It is 11:30 a.m.; Ben tries to jump up from his bed but does not even make it halfway. The pain in his shoulder is too strong.

Ulysses had sent him ten messages. As he calls, Ben explains that he has overslept because his shoulder is hurting him. Ulysses is disappointed but apprehensive and begrudgingly accepts his excuse. Ben promises to make the next meeting in thirty minutes. He changes, brushes his teeth, and puts eyedrops in his red eyes. He logs in and gets to work.

That night, he finds himself drunk in his living room shadowboxing (with one hand, his shoulder still hurts), screaming at the Russian (or Ukrainian) Man, telling him he would have killed him if given another chance. He repeatedly replays that day in his head and wonders what he should have done differently.

"I should have head-butted him," Ben tells himself as he sips his drink. "I should have broken his fuckin' nose and kicked him in the balls." He takes another sip. "I should have run at him when he had his gun, taken it away, and then shot him in the face." He is lying face down on the couch, his drool covering the cushion below him. Ben is waking up more and more on the sofa with the lights on these days.

When he manages to drag himself to his bed, nightmares soon follow. A constant dream is being back in the Man's room. He is on the floor, and the Man is on top of him, hitting him. Ben has his arms up and is attempting to protect his face. The Man keeps hitting him and hitting him and hitting him. He can see the girl in the corner of the room through the blows. She is curled into a ball, crying, her arm covering her face. Ben tries to call out to her, but the Man keeps striking him. Ben wants to tell her that it will be ok, but as he tries to speak, the Man hits him in the chest. Ben takes a deep

274

breath and tells the girl not to cry. As the final fist comes crashing into Ben's face, he takes one last look at the girl, only this time, it is Jinni he is staring at.

Ben decides that sleep is not his thing right now. He stays up most of the night watching NikNak. When the sun starts to rise, he takes a nap and repeats the process daily.

NikNak is starting to fascinate him; there is so much content! Since every Nak is short, it is impressive how its content creators could convey so much in a short length of time.

One night (at 4 a.m.), Ben is tapping through his NikNak feed. On his screen are two men facing each other. One is standing on the left, and one is on the right. "Boring!" Ben mutters aloud and is about to tap the video away when the voice-over starts.

"It always starts with a shove," a guy with a slight Israeli accent says. "A push is needed to get worked up and confident before a fight. It's about dominance." As the man is talking, the man on the right, in slow motion, reaches his hands back and brings them forward in a shoving motion.

Ben raises the volume.

"The push is a linear attack; it is used to psyche up the attacker for the fight," the man's voice says over the Nak. "The first move is to get out of his line." In the Nak, the man who is about to be pushed slides his right foot behind him. "The second thing is to control." The man on the left brings his hands down onto the man on the right, slapping them down and placing his left hand over them. "And the last step is incapacitating." The man on the left quickly brings his right hand under the bridge of the nose of the man on the right, causing his head to spring backward. The man on the left loops around his opponent and grabs the man on the right's head with both hands. He then brings him down to the ground and simulates punches to his head.

The man on the left then turns towards the camera. "And that is how you win a fight in three seconds. If you like my content, leave a Nik, and please subscribe for more Naks like this. KM-Asher out!" The video loops and plays again. Ben watches it again.

After a horrid night of little sleep and lots of alcohol, Ben goes to the coffee shop to get a double espresso. He grabs a seat and scrolls through his social media feeds. While sipping his espresso and rubbing his eyes, Ben sees Jeremy walk into the store. Jeremy walks up to the counter and orders a coffee. Jeremy, leaning on the counter, scans the shop and sees Ben.

"Fuck," Ben says quietly as Jeremy walks towards him.

"Ben, what's up, man?" Jeremy extends his fist towards Ben. Ben sighs and politely taps it. Jeremy sits across from Ben. "You look tired," Jeremy says casually as he drinks his coffee. Ben stares at him and looks back at his phone. Jeremy starts drumming his fingers against the table.

"Can you stop doing that, please?" Ben asks.

"Doing what?"

"Can you stop tapping your fingers on the table?" Ben asks.

Jeremy nods and stops, and Ben resumes going through his phone.

"I heard from Raj that you are working with NikNak?" Jeremy questions. Ben keeps staring at his phone and doesn't look up. "You don't need any help, do you?" Jeremy asks apprehensively. Ben shakes his head. "'Cause I would love to meet the founders and see if I can get them to give me the secrets of their algorithm!" Jeremy starts laughing hard and slaps the table.

"What do you mean?" Ben asks.

"Well," Jeremy says, stirring his iced coffee. "You know I am trying to get my NikNak channel up and running. I have been doing these tricks, stunts, and advice videos for months, and not much is coming from it. I barely have five hundred subs, and to create a private channel, you need at least a thousand." Jeremy continues to stir his coffee. Ben pulls up the NikNak app on his phone and searches his following list for @JerBear69. He has three hundred ninety-six subscribers.

"Oh." Ben doesn't know what to say.

"I was hoping to run into you today." Ben watches Jeremy take off the stupid beanie he is always wearing and run his hands through his hair.

"Why is that?" Ben asks.

"I wanted to see if you could help me," Jeremy says quietly.

"Jeremy, what do you want? I got a splitting headache and —"

"All right, I am sorry," Jeremy says, putting his hands up and showing his palms to Ben.

Ben is perplexed. He has never seen Jeremy apologize, much less not antagonize him.

"I was texting Raj the other day," Jeremy starts. "He says you have been working with NikNak, and the company you work for is helping them go public."

Ben shakes his head. "I can't talk about that," Ben says gruffly.

Jeremy drops his head into his hands. He continues. "I got to stop doing this stupid fucking gig shit, man. Lyft, Uber, fucking Postmates." He lifts his head. His eyes are red and watery. "I used to be the man, Ben, and you know, you were there." Ben stares at Jeremy. "I was making anywhere from $2k to $5k a weekend, hustling, promoting, grinding, getting mad bitches." Jeremy sips his coffee. "Now I am a nobody. The women I pick up in my car don't even look at me. Whenever I pick up a hot girl, I think, 'Back in the day, you would have been begging to fuck me.' Now they don't even look in my direction. I got to be somebody again." Jeremy continues to stir and stare at his coffee.

Ben sits back and stares at the man he used to know. A man he gave quite a bit of money to. Money to help get him into clubs and parties that they would have never gotten into without Jeremy's help. He is right. He did get a lot of "bitches" back in the day. Jeremy always had a smoking hot lady (or two) by his side. Ben felt a twinge of sorrow for him.

"What do you want me to do?" Ben asks.

Jeremy goes silent for a moment and then speaks, "Help me, talk to the founders, show them my account, help me promote my Naks. Or at least tell me the secret to their algorithm."

Ben leans back in his chair. "I can't do that, sorry. The founders barely like me, and even so, if I propose something like this to them, they will laugh me out of the building, plus my boss will fire me or, at the very least, rip me a new one. I'm sorry, Jeremy, I truly am; I know times are tough."

"Fuck this virus," Jeremy says under his breath. He gets up from the table. "I thought I would give it a shot. I have nothing left to lose. See ya, Ben." Jeremy walks away. Ben watches him walk away and notices a few things. Jeremy had always dressed very fashionably (minus the stupid beanie he always wore) and kept himself in excellent shape. But as he walks out the door, Ben notices the holes in his clothes and the protruding gut around his waist. Ben thinks about how the last few years have been tough on everyone. Well, tough on almost everyone. Ben has made more money in the previous three years than ever before. Ben jumps as Jeremy peels out of his parking spot.

Times are tough, he thinks.

#

Ben picks up his phone on the third ring. Ulysses is on the other line.

"Ben!" Ulysses screams so loud that Ben has to move the phone from his ear.

"Yes."

"I have wonderful news. The S-1 has been approved!" Ulysses shouts with delight.

"Oh ... ok," is all Ben can muster. He has an uneasy feeling in his stomach.

"'Oh'? 'Oh,' is that all you can say?" Ulysses asks incredulously. "This is what we have been working so hard for! Do you know what they priced the IPO at?"

Ben says that he did not know.

"Twenty mother-fucking dollars! And they are issuing one billion shares. Do you know what their market cap will be?"

"Uh … twenty billion?"

"Bingo! Twenty mother-fucking billion!" Ben keeps the phone an inch or two away from his ear. "And do you know what our one percent is worth?" Ulysses asks excitedly.

Ben sighs. "Two hundred million," he says nonchalantly.

"Two mother-fucking hundred million!" Ben is growing tired of Ulysses's screaming. "That is not even the best part. We got those shares at the IPO price. I spoke to some analysts this morning, and they told me that the stock could be priced at around sixty dollars by the end of the year. Sixty mother-fucking dollars! You know what that could potentially make our stake worth?"

"A lot, Ulysses," Ben says quietly.

"Goddamn right, a mother-fucking—"

Ben hangs up the phone. He texts Ulysses and explains that he had a bad connection. Ulysses messages him back that it is not a problem. *Nothing is going to bring down Ulysses*, thinks Ben.

Later that night, Ben sits in front of his "special" computer. He takes large sips of his alcoholic beverage while his other hand hovers over the power button. It had been a few days since he had powered it on.

The news of NikNak going public upset him, and he did not know why. Maybe deep down, subconsciously, he knew their business model would perpetuate more videos like the one with the Russian (or Ukrainian) Man. He shudders. The second thought in his head is the pointlessness of this whole exercise. The first time he "superimposed" himself, he broke his arms. The last time he "superimposed" himself, he ended up with a bullet in his shoulder.

Ben has only seen a single picture of Jinni's uncle. One time Jinni had been showing him old photos of herself on her phone. In one of the pictures, Ben noticed a large hand draped across her shoulder. The man next to her was cut off at his chest. When Ben queried about the figure standing next to her, Jinni replied it was "No one important." Replaying that memory in his head, Ben, at the time, did not notice Jinni's body language when he had asked. Before that, they were laughing, poking fun at her clothes and hair, but her mood changed when Ben asked about the figure next to her. It was subtle, and he had not noticed it at the time. He remembered her body stiffening and her smile fading. She got off the bed, kissed him, and then went to the bathroom, where she did not emerge until an hour later.

Ben did not remember much about that picture, but he did remember the size of the man's hand. He was a big fellow. He was towering a few feet over little Jinni. His large hand draped around her shoulders. His wide gut was three times the body width of hers. *What could I reasonably do if I came face to face with him?* Ben wonders. He needs to test something.

He runs into the kitchen and grabs a knife. He picks up his phone and opens YouTube. He looks for any video from around the time of the late '90s to the early 2000s. He finds one of the news channels reporting on reopening a park in some midwest state. Not many people are around, and the video is only two minutes long. Ben puts the small knife in his hand and heads to the middle of the room. He touches his screen in the upper right corner and closes his eyes. A moment later, he could feel an intense cold breeze on his face. He blinks his eyes open against the bright sun. He looks around and stands far behind the reporter and her camera crew. He is standing on wet grass (he had forgotten to put on shoes). He opens his hands. It is empty. He gets down on his knees and feels around the grass. The knife is not there. A few minutes later, he is back in his living room. His pants are stained with grass residue. The blade is on the floor. He picks it up and puts it in his pants pocket. He restarts the video and "superimposed" himself again, pressing on the upper left corner of the video; Ben closes his eyes. He is west of his "other" position when he opens them. He looks across the park to see the silhouette of himself. The other "Ben" gets on his knees and feels around the grass. Ben reaches into his pocket. The knife is not there.

Sitting on his couch, holding his bleeding arm, Ben is puzzled. He has tried everything to bring the knife with him. He tried holding it against his body, underneath his armpit. He had even stabbed himself (with the knife in his arm enough so that it would not fall when he let go) to no avail. The blade would not journey with him. If he were to do anything, he would only have to rely on himself. His hands and his mind, nothing else. He walks over to the refrigerator and makes himself a drink.

Later that week, Ben is on the couch scrolling through NikNak. He came across a skit about the follies of a relationship. A young man and his girlfriend cover the emotions of a relationship from inception to break up. The first part was of them happy and laughing, and they could not keep their hands off each other. Then a cut. The second scene has them sitting on the couch, bored. Both are looking at their phones instead of each other. The next scene has them fighting. They were shouting at each other and appearing angry. The final scene is the breakup. The girl has packed a bag and is with the young man at the door. They hug each other goodbye, but when they end the embrace, she pulls away, and the young man keeps holding onto her hand. He asks her to stay, to give the relationship another chance. She shakes her head no. She leaves the house and goes outside, and the young man slumps to the floor. As she goes to the curb, an even better-looking man in a flashy car is waiting for her. They smile at each other, and the video ends.

Nak by:
@RelationsMeme
7,435,636 Views
2,212,234 Niks
NikNak©

Tears start streaming down Ben's face. He wipes his eyes and laughs. He has been feeling very sensitive lately. He even shouts at Ulysses when Ulysses asks how his work is coming.

"It will be done when it's done," Ben tells him.

"Understandable, but things are time-sensitive these days —"

"When are things not time-sensitive?" Ben shouts back. "Every day for the last eight months, things have been time-sensitive. You dump something on me at the last second and expect it the next day. It. Will. Be. Done. When. It's. Done"

"Ok, Jesus, I just wanted to check up on your—"

Ben cut him off again, "When have I not delivered for you, Ulysses? Every goddamn day I deliver. And what do I get for doing good work? Even more time-sensitive work. So back the fuck off and let me do my thing."

"Jesus Christ, Ben, what has got into you—"

Ben kills the video chat. He is breathing hard, and his heart is beating fast. He looks at his phone, and the time is 2 p.m.

"It's six o'clock somewhere—" Ben gets up from his desk and pours a stiff drink. He can hear his computer ringing and the chimes of messages coming through. He ignores it. He stays in the kitchen for a long time, mostly staring at and drinking his drink. When it is empty, he pours himself another. He looks around the counter for his pills. He has ten left. Dr. Kamal had told him no more refills, but after pleading with him and explaining how the pain affected his work, Dr. Kamal relented. He pours one out on the counter. He grabs a thick glass from the cabinet and crushes the pill into a fine powder. He takes an envelope from his desk and expertly pushes the powder into his drink. He stirs it, takes a large gulp, and sighs loudly. He could feel the Oxy coursing through his veins. Ben makes another drink and crushes another...

Ben wakes up; it is pitch black. His neck and head are hurting. Against his face is a hard, smooth substance, cool and sleek. He is on the kitchen floor. There is liquid pooled around his legs. He tries to push himself off the floor, but a small sharp object cuts into his hand.

"Ouch!" he screeches. He looks around and tries to assess his situation. *Why am I on the kitchen floor? Why does my head hurt?* he asks himself. Slowly and carefully, he works his way up to a sitting position. He gingerly touches the side of his head and quickly pulls his hand back as he feels the sore spot. He slowly manages to get to his feet. He walks away from the pool of water towards the kitchen door to turn on the light. The light blinds him as his eyes adjust. He looks back to where he had laid. There is a small pool of blood where his head was, and broken glass with its contents pooled on the floor next to it.

After cleaning up the mess and checking on his head (small cut on the side), Ben gets the courage to look at his phone. It is 1 a.m. He somehow had lost eleven hours. He tries to recall what had happened, but it hurts to think. As he finishes mopping the kitchen, Ben notices something under his kitchen table. It is his prescription bottle. He bends down and retrieves it.

It is empty.

Ben works and drinks for the next few days. At night, he watches NikNak and YouTube. He ignores all calls, texts, and DMs from his co-workers, mother, and Raj. He does not talk much in meetings; he agrees with everyone in the room and does not have the energy or fortitude to challenge anything. One night, drunk, Ben is browsing YouTube. He watches a few minutes of the video before moving on to the next one. In his recommendation section is a video from a creator called "TheDigitizer" titled: "My Grandfather the Psychiatrist —Old video from the '80s." Ben, curious and bored, plays the video.

The content creator starts by talking about his now-deceased grandfather and how he was a pioneer in his field. The creator has recently found some old VHS tapes, which he digitized and is excited to show his audience. Ben watches as an older, heavy-set man with a nice trim white beard and balding hairline begins talking.

"Depression," the older man starts, "is probably one of the most misunderstood conditions in the world. Even today, with our modern medicine, we struggle to diagnose this condition properly." Ben sits up on the couch. "While some of my colleagues may disagree with me, depression is a devastating illness that can't be cured by telling someone to 'keep their chin up.'"

The older man grooms his beard with his hands.

"This illness will rob you of your sleep, energy, and enjoyment of life and may cause you to consider suicide. Being depressed for most is torment, agony, and even can feel like torture."

Ben raises the volume.

"So what is depression, and what causes depression?" the older man asks. "My name is Dr. Herbert Hollum, and today we will talk about depression." The screen goes black. A title screen labeled "Depression: A in-depth study" appears.

"What is depression, and what causes it?" Dr. Hollum continues. "In my many years of studying psychiatry, it usually comes down to a single trigger. A trigger that sets everything off. A catalyst like getting left at the altar or even something as simple as failing a test. Throughout our lives, we all experience some form of depression, but most commonly, we mistake depression for sadness.

"Now, what can you do to combat depression?" Dr. Herbert asks. He looks intensely into the camera. "I want to do a thought experiment with you. I want you to think of depression as a bullet. A bullet that is being fired directly at you. If you stand there, the bullet will likely hit you. The shot could be fatal." Dr. Herbert makes a gun symbol with his hand and fingers and points it at the camera, mocking a shot. "Or it might wing you, and you might need to go to the hospital to get patched up." Ben stares intently at his phone screen. "What else can you do?" Dr. Herbert asks again. "Well, you can duck and cower in fear. Hide behind some cover and hope whatever is shooting at you will eventually give up."

Dr. Herbert continues, "Or you can fire back and hopefully get it to stop." He points his finger pistols at the camera and mocks a few shots. "You may miss the first few times, but eventually, with a little focus and grit, you will stop the bullets from being fired at you." Dr. Herbert gives the camera a slight nod.

He continues talking about depression, and when the video is over, Ben replays it.

He stands up in his living room (he is only wobbling a little) and looks down at himself. It is Sunday, and he has not showered, shaved, or changed his clothes in three days.

"Fuck it." Ben brings up his phone and touches the lower part of the screen.

"So what is depression and what—Jesus fucking Christ!" Dr. Herbert screams. Ben stands in front of Dr. Herbert's desk. Ben looks around. It is a medium-sized room in what appears to be an old Victorian-style house. A perplexed and scared Dr.

Herbert is sitting behind a large wooden desk. He has a large camera in front of him, and Ben stands directly beside it. The camera whirls softly as Ben and Dr. Herbert look at each other. Dr. Herbert pushes his chair back from his desk and stands up.

"Son, I don't know why you are here, but I have about $100 on me, and I keep all my drugs locked in my office. Take the money." Dr. Herbert reaches into his pocket. "And leave my house." They both stand in silence, Dr. Herbert watching Ben closely with his hand in his pocket.

"I don't want your money," Ben says.

"Then what do you want?" Dr. Herbert asks.

"I just want to talk."

"Ok … Sure … Just please don't hurt me. Now let me shut this thing off." Dr. Herbert reaches over to shut off the camera.

"No!" Ben screams. Dr. Herbert flinches. "Please don't!" Ben asks, lowering his voice. "I need your help." Ben's legs begin to give out as he slumps to the ground. "I need help." He cries out as he falls to the floor. He slumps down to a seated position with his back to the office's wall. Dr. Herbert rushes over to Ben.

"It's ok, son, just relax." Dr. Herbert feels Ben's pulse. "I am going to call you an ambulance."

"No." Ben reaches out and grabs Dr. Herbert's arm. "I need to talk to someone." Dr. Herbert sniffs the air in front of Ben.

"Son," he asks. "Have you been drinking?"

Ben nods.

"Dr. Herbert," Ben starts. "Please sit down. I am ok, I am sorry I scared you and showed up here unannounced, but I have a problem, and I don't know what do to. Could you please sit down and talk to me for a few moments? I can explain everything."

"Are you sure you don't need a doctor?" Dr. Herbert asks, concerned.

"My name is Ben, and no, I don't need a doctor; I just need to talk to you, and then I promise I will be on my way."

"Ok, Ben," Dr. Herbert says; he stands up and walks back to his desk. "Talk, but when we are done, I am calling you an ambulance, deal?"

"Deal. And Dr. Herbert, can you do me one more favor?" Ben asks.

"Yes, what is it?"

"Can you please leave the camera running?" Ben pleads. Dr. Herbert looks at him quizzically and then nods.

"Why?" he asks.

"Just don't stop recording."

"Ok." Dr. Herbert sits back in his seat.

Ben talks and tells Dr. Herbert about how he went to his ex-girlfriend's funeral and his ability to "superimpose" himself into videos on his phone and his computer. Dr. Herbert has a perplexed look on his face, but Ben continues. He talks about how he enjoyed it at first, but now it is a burden. Ben explains what happened to Jinni when she was a pre-teen, how her uncle recorded her abuse, and how the videos are somewhere on the internet. He also tells him about the Russian (or Ukrainian) Man and what happened when he tried to intervene. The whole time Dr. Herbert looks at Ben with a puzzled look.

"The inter...net?" Dr. Herbert asks, confused.

"It doesn't matter," Ben replies. "The real question here is should I do it? Should I find the video and change the trajectory of her life? Or should I let it be? She is dead now, so maybe I am doing this just for my conscience. The only thing I can do is either try and forget or make a change. "

"First off, I don't know what drugs you have been taking, but I think you are suffering from a delusion of grandeur. I think you should seek professional help immediately." Dr. Herbert looks at Ben.

"Humor me, Doctor, let's say that what I am saying is completely true. What is the correct thing to do here?"

"What you are asking me is life fate or free will, and if either of those is true, then do you have the right to change that?" Ben nods. Dr. Herbert leans back in his chair. "I mean, that's a heady question." Dr. Herbert begins stroking his beard. "Last time you quote-unquote superimposed yourself —" Dr. Herbert makes air quotes with his fingers, causing Ben to smile. "On this 'video' on your 'smart phone' on the 'internet,' you felt that you did not affect the outcome. You just intervened briefly. The situation where you thought you could have had the most impact was with this Russian or Ukrainian man, but you felt you did nothing. Is that correct?"

Ben nods.

"So to have a true cause to a different outcome, you have to do something, shall we say ... more drastic?"

Ben nods again.

"And you are asking me whether that is the correct decision. Should we change someone's fate, someone close to us, if we could? Or should we just let what has already happened to be the end all of be all?" Dr. Herbert takes a sip of his water. "I don't know the correct answer, Ben." Dr. Herbert places his hands behind his head. "What do you think you should do?"

"I don't know either. I am scared that if I fail, then things may change for the worse, but if I do nothing, then I am resigning her to years of abuse."

"Whatever you decide, remember that this is a decision you will have to live with. Is that something you can do?"

"I am not sure."

"Before you rudely interrupted me, I was going to make a video about depression."

"I know, you were going to compare depression to someone shooting bullets at you," Ben says quickly.

"How ... how ... did you know that?" Dr. Herbert asks as he leans forward.

"As I said, Doctor Herbert, I have seen where this thing here goes," Ben says as he points at the camera. "But I merely interrupted you; you could still record your message and get your thoughts out later."

"It's not thoughts, Ben. This is medical science." Dr. Herbert crosses his arms.

"Sorry, sure, but you have done nothing wrong, and as far as I know, will do nothing wrong. If the problem I am trying to solve is stopping someone like Hitler, then you would have no problem with what I am about to do. Also, I think your diagnosis of depression is ahead of its time; trust me on that one."

"Well, thank you, Ben—wait, are you planning on killing Hitler?"

Ben has to laugh at that one. "No, Dr. Herbert—"

"Just Herbert, please."

"No, Herbert, I thought about killing Hitler, but I know it would never work. As I said, I cannot bring anything besides the clothes on my back. And even if I could surprise Hitler and start choking him, his bodyguards would kill me in a few seconds. And I assume that if I die in one of these videos, I die in real life."

"But why not, Ben?" Dr. Herbert asks. "From your story, you told me you tried to overdose with this 'Ox-zy,' why not go out trying to right a wrong? If you have nothing to live for? Did you not tell me about the incident in your kitchen where you tried to end it?"

Ben sits silently. He looks at Dr. Herbert and tries to speak, but nothing comes out of his mouth.

"Ben," Dr. Herbert says gently. "If you truly had watched this video that I was attempting to make, then you would know I describe certain scenarios in dealing with the depression bullet." Ben listens. "One of my scenarios is cowering in fear; another is fighting back. What will you do, cower or fight?" Ben's eyes begin to water. "You have much more control of your life than you think. Make a decision, but whatever choice you make, live with it and move on. Sometimes there are no correct choices in life, but stop tormenting yourself and make a decision. Do you understand?"

Ben nods as tears stream down his face.

"Now, I did my part and listened." Dr. Herbert reaches over and stops the camera from recording; he then turns around and grabs his landline. "Now it's time to get you some help. Ok?"

"Ben ... Ben ... Ben?"

#

Ben sits at his "special" computer, waiting for the following downloads to complete. By this time, he has viewed over a hundred different videos. He has a newfound focus, and he defined some rules:

Rule 1: Only watch the video long enough to identify if it is Jinni.

Rule 2: Catalog the file, so he doesn't mistakenly download it again and then permanently delete it.

Rule 3: No "superimposing" unless it's Jinni.

He has these rules taped on the wall above his monitor. They are good rules. They protected him from seeing things that would destroy his fragile mind. And it keeps his emotions in check. It allows him to focus on the task at hand.

While Ben is waiting for the items to download, he starts exploring the "dark web." He hates that name and quickly realizes there isn't much dark about it. It is just software called TOR. TOR stands for The Onion Routing Project. Ben did a little research (in between the long download times). The United States Navy developed it to protect American intelligence communication. Since it offers strong anonymity, it is used by hackers, drug dealers, credit card frauds, and people who distribute illegal videos. It operates like the regular web, just slower and harder to navigate.

Pavlov's program was a godsend here. Ben could use key terms he found through other videos and bring up a new set of links. When a file is fully downloaded, Ben watches as little as possible. Once he confirms that the video was not of Jinni, he documents the file in his notebook, and then he immediately deletes the file. The going is slow and difficult. While he never watches a video in its entirety, the images he does see stick in his head.

After a couple of weeks of repeating the process, he comes across a dark web site called: "Korean School Girl Lessons." Interested, he opens the page. On the page were images of a young Korean girl and pictures of a girl who looked like a young Jinni.

Ben kicks out the chair from under him and stands up.

"No fuckin' way!" he exclaims out loud. The preview images show a young Asian girl in various stages of undress. The pictures looked like they were taken in a dark basement. One of the images has a man, only his torso, standing naked next to her. He has his arm wrapped around her shoulder. The young Asian girl is smiling a small crooked smile. Ben has flashbacks of the only image that Jinni had shown him of her uncle. He towers over her, and his belly button comes up to her shoulders. The rest of his body is cut off, but Ben can see that he is a large man.

Ben immediately starts downloading all of the videos on the page. There are ten in total. Each has a "part" and a date associated with the file. From the first one to the last one, there is almost a two-year difference. The next twelve hours are the longest of Ben's life, and he does not sleep, eat, or drink. All he does is sit at the edge of his chair, constantly refreshing the downloads page, waiting impatiently for the videos to download. Ben navigates to the folder and double-clicks on the file when the first one is completed. It's called "Korean School Girl Lessons - Part 2."

The video starts with a black screen. An image comes into focus. The room is dark, with some natural light coming through an unseen window. As the video focuses, Ben could see a young Asian girl sitting with her back against the wall. She is fully clothed, with her knees curled up to her chest. She had her chin resting on her knees. A man, off-screen, speaks to her in Korean, and she answers. The man talks again, and the young girl responds.

Ben watched intensely. The girl stands up, and Ben looks at her face. He squints at the video, and the girl pushes the hair back from her face. Ben's eyes open wider.

"Holy shit, I think that's Jinni!" he shouts. The girl in the video starts undressing—the man crosses in front of the camera. Ben's hands tighten up into fists. The man begins shouting instructions to the girl in Korean. She nods and continues to take off her clothes. The man walks up to her when she is topless and grabs her by the shoulders. He spins her around for the camera. Then he reaches down and takes off the shorts she is wearing. Ben closes his hands tighter. His nails dig into his palm, and he can feel warm liquid start to cover his hand.

The man in the video spins the half-naked Jinni again for the camera. He reaches down and takes off her socks. Her uncle weighs about two hundred and thirty pounds and is about 6'1 or 6'2. He has broad shoulders, a blacksmith's gut, and large, muscular arms. Ben's hands start to shake, he opens his palm, and his right hand starts moving towards the screen, his finger sticking out. As his right hand moves towards the screen, his left hand strikes and grabs it. Ben sits at his desk with both hands fighting each other. Even though Ben is right-handed, his left hand wins the battle. His hand drops to his lap. Ben closes the video and leans back in his chair. He runs his hand through his hair.

Ben considers the situation. The last time he acted impulsively, things did not go well. The Russian (or Ukrainian) Man had taken him by surprise. Ben recognizes that if he is ill-equipped for that situation, he will fare no better in this situation. Ben stands at 5'9 and does not know the first thing about defending himself. The last time he acted impulsively, it resulted in the disappearance of the video. *If my "superimposing" changes the future,* he thinks. *What happens if I go back and fail, and her uncle gets scared and never records again? What would happen to Jinni?*

Ben stands up from his chair, walks into the kitchen, opens his freezer, and starts chugging the bottle of vodka he has in there. He does not know what to do.

#

"This is KM-Asher," the video starts. "What do you do when someone bigger and stronger than you starts choking you on the ground?"

"Uh huh?" Ben slurs. He is lying down face-first on the couch. His phone is on the floor, his head lying over the edge, drool running down his mouth. He closes one eye to better focus on his phone. The video continues.

Ben watches as KM-Asher exits the chokehold by holding the attacker's hand, pushing him back with his free hand, and sticking his knee between himself and the attacker's torso. He brings his free leg over the attacker's arm and mocks kicking him. He then pushes him back with his other leg until the attacker falls over. He then jumps to his feet and mock-strikes the attacker with a hard punch.

"And that," KM-Asher says, turning to the camera, "is how you escape a chokehold. Nik, comment, and subscribe for more Naks just like this. KM-Asher out!" He flashes the camera a thumbs-up symbol, and the Nak ends.

Nak by:
@KM-Asher
22,137 Views
2,875 Niks
NikNak©

Ben subscribes to his channel and spends the rest of the night watching KM-Asher's Naks.

CHAPTER 23 - DIY

"So," KM-Asher asks. "What brings you out here, and why the urgency."

Ben shrugs. He is still hungover from the night before. He is dressed in athletic shorts and a white t-shirt. After he had watched all of KM-Asher's Naks, he had private messaged him and asked him where he was located and if he did private lessons. KM-Asher responded the next day; he luckily lived somewhat close and said he offers private lessons at $100 a session. Ben agrees and asks if he can start the next day. KM-Asher sends him an address.

KM-Asher's home studio was about an hour away. They had set the meeting time for after Ben was done with work. As soon as Ben finishes his day, he runs into his room, changes, and begins driving. When Ben arrives at KM-Asher's house, KM-Asher is already outside and waves. Ben parks, exits his car, and walks towards him.

"Hello, Ben," he says, extending his hand in greeting. Ben hesitates. KM-Asher laughs. "Sorry, I forget." He closes his open hand into a fist. Ben fist-bumps him. "You can also take that thing off if you want," KM-Asher says, pointing towards Ben's mask as they walk towards his house. Ben shakes his head. "As you like," KM-Asher says. Ben did not care about catching COVID. He did not want KM-Asher to get a good look at him.

"So KM-Asher, where do you want me?" Ben asks nervously.

"Right where you are is fine. Let's do a couple of laps around the gym and get warmed up. Follow me."

After a few minutes, Ben kneels, hands on his knees, trying to suck in air through his mask. KM-Asher comes over to check up on him.

"It's ok … Just take your time."

"Sorry, it's been a while since I did any physical activity, KM-Asher," Ben says between gasps for air.

"Just call me Asher," Asher smiles.

#

"So," Asher asks again. "What brings you out here, and why the urgency?"

Ben sits against the wall at the back of Asher's home gym. His muscles are screaming for oxygen, his shirt is drenched, and his head is pounding.

"Just … you know … just trying to lose these COVID-19 pounds," Ben says with a nervous laugh between breaths.

Asher smiles and says, "Well, you trained like a madman today; most people just come to learn a little self-defense and don't take the class so seriously. You trained today as if your life depended on it."

Ben remains silent.

"It was a good session, and I think you got some of the basics down," Asher continues. "Next week, we will get into more self-defense techniques—"

"Are you free at the same time tomorrow?" Ben asks, cutting Asher off.

Asher raises an eyebrow.

"Sure," he tells Ben. "Business has been a little slow lately. Are you sure you don't want to take a few days—".

Ben shakes his head, cutting him off again. He looks over at Asher's side wall. A rack of fake weapons consisting of rubber knives, wooden sticks, plastic handguns, fake hammers, and a BB rifle catches Ben's eye.

"When can we start training with those?" Ben asks, nodding towards the weapon rack.

"Oh," Asher says as he turns around and confirms what Ben is looking at. "Usually, we go through a few sessions before we get to weapon training," Asher explains. "But seeing how motivated you are, maybe we can incorporate a few of those in the next session."

Over the next month, Asher puts Ben through the gauntlet. Every day when Ben finishes work, he changes and drives to Asher's house. Night after night, they train. Asher kicks things off with a warm-up and then moves into various scenarios. They practice each method repeatedly (what to do when someone comes at you with a knife, a stick, or a gun; choke-holds from the front, back, and on the ground) until Ben gets it right. They train hard, Asher praising Ben when he does well, correcting him when he does wrong—pushing, pulling, grabbing.

After over a month of almost nightly training, Asher calls an end to the session and invites Ben for a beer. Ben declines; he has been trying to cut back on his drinking.

"C'mon," Asher says, laughing and clasping him on the back. "I got this great Israeli beer that one of my clients bought for me. Come out to the porch and have a single beer with me."

Ben relents and follows Asher outside.

They sit silently, watching as the sun goes down and the night emerges. Ben takes uncomfortable sips of his beer, lifting his sweaty mask each time.

"You're doing well," Asher says, breaking the silence. "Most people do this for a couple of sessions and then move on to something else. Very few people these days have the resiliency to continue." Asher takes a sip of his beer. "You have been like a man possessed. It makes me wonder...."

"Wonder what?" Ben asks.

"Makes me wonder if everything is ok with you. I saw the gunshot wound on your shoulder." Ben instinctively grabs his shoulder. "It's ok. I got a couple myself," Asher says as he lifts his shirt to reveal two bullet-sized scars on the lower part of his abdomen. Ben stares at the wounds.

"Happened over ten years ago when I was doing my conscription for the IDF." Asher takes another sip of his beer. "I was doing a routine patrol when some Palestinian kid jumped out with an AK and started spraying my squad." Ben turns his body towards Asher. "I didn't even see the kid. All of a sudden, it was like *Pop! Pop! Pop!* and I am on the ground, clutching my stomach." Asher swirls his beer. "Then I look around and see my squad members are down and bleeding out. I pull out my sidearm and look back down the street. The Palestinian kid is standing there frozen, surprised that his attack succeeded. I empty my clip and put four in his chest and two in his neck."

"Jesus," Ben whispers.

"Later that night, the doctors informed me that both bullets missed vital organs by this much." Asher held his thumb and forefinger so close together that they were almost touching. "After that, I was honorably discharged from the IDF, and I decided that I had enough with my country, and I moved to the U.S." Asher sets his beer down and grabs another one from the pack. He pops it open with his thumb.

"I always remember that look on the kid's face. It wasn't hatred but pure determination, as if he had been training for months for this moment, knowing full well that he probably wouldn't survive. The weird thing was that after he was successful, he froze. It's like he didn't know what to do next. Success surprised him, and instead of completing the job, he stood there frozen on the street, not knowing his next move."

"Why are you telling me this?" Ben asks.

Asher pauses for a moment. He takes a deep breath. "I see the same look on you as I did that Palestinian kid. It is determined but uncertain. You are determined when you start, but you hesitate for a split second after you win and take me down. I don't know what's going on in your life. That bullet wound tells me that you have a hard road ahead. It's not my business to ask, but the only suggestion I have for you is: don't hesitate, complete your task. Don't get gunned down like that Palestinian kid."

The air around them grew silent and uncomfortable.

Asher laughs. "This is the first beer I've had in over ten years. I quit alcohol when I got shot. Beer always makes me talk too much."

He stands up. He extends his hand for a shake; this time, Ben takes it.

"Until tomorrow?" Asher asks.

"Tomorrow," Ben replies.

As Ben walks towards his car, he calls back to Asher. "What happened to your squad mates?"

"What?" Asher shouts back.

"Your squad mates," Ben shouts louder. "What happened to them."

"Well, one lost his spleen, and the other has to shit through a colostomy bag for the rest of his life, but they survived."

"Oh," Ben shouts back.

"Remember, Ben," Asher shouts as he enters his house. "Always complete the job!"

Their relationship changes after that night. Ben initially felt that he and Asher were moving towards friendship, but now Asher is more serious and direct towards Ben. He scolds him more and pushes him harder.

"No, Ben, grab me here!" Asher shouts through gritted teeth.

"Faster, Ben, move faster!" Asher shouts.

"Goddamnit, Ben, left hand, left hand!" Asher screams in frustration.

After a particularly grueling session, Ben, out of breath, asks Asher for a break.

"No break! No break!" Asher says, pushing Ben. "You think they will give you a break!" Asher says as he shoves Ben with both hands. "They will keep coming for you!" Asher grabs Ben by his t-shirt and flings him to the ground. "Do you think they will stop!" Asher raises his foot and is about to bring it down on Ben's head. Instinctively Ben brings up both hands and catches Asher's foot. He then pushes up, twisting it, and takes Asher to the ground. He jumps on top of Asher and raises his fist to strike.

"Good, Ben, good," Asher says, smiling. Ben keeps his fist raised. "It's ok, Ben, the fight is over," Asher says calmly. Ben puts his fist down. Immediately Asher's leg wraps around Ben's neck. He brings Ben down to the mat and grabs his arm. Asher's leg is choking Ben while both his hands hold Ben's arm for leverage.

"Never stop!" Asher hisses. "Finish it, or don't start it at all!"

Ben tries to reply, but he can't. The back of Asher's leg is crushing his trachea. Ben tries to yell at Asher to stop, but no sound comes out of his throat. Ben taps the mat twice with his free hand in submission.

"You think that is going to help you?" Asher says, growling at Ben. "You want to give up?"

Ben could see Asher's eyes tearing up. He looks back up towards the ceiling. Specks of black started to surround his eyes. The black tunnel grew larger until it began to engulf his eyes. In the blackness, a pair of eyes look back at him. They blink and stare at him. Ben can recognize those eyes anywhere. Ben uses his left hand to push Asher's leg away from his throat, allowing some airflow in.

"Good!" Asher yells.

Ben slides his leg towards Asher, kicking him hard.

"Yes!" Asher shouts.

With Asher stunned, Ben could maneuver his head out from under Asher's leg. With Asher still holding his arm, Ben manages to rise to his knees, and with his free hand, he strikes Asher hard in the face.

"Keep going!" Asher shouts, his teeth bloodied.

Ben gets his feet under him and lifts the lower part of Asher's body off the mat. He reverses the hold, places his foot on Asher's throat, and pushes down hard.

After a few seconds, Asher lets go of his arm and taps the mat hard. Ben relents and moves far away, rubbing his throat. Asher comes up and clasps him on the shoulder. Ben flinches, clenching his hand into a fist, and swings it at Asher. Asher calmly catches his hand.

"It's ok, Ben, it's over," Asher says, bringing Ben's arm down to his side. "You are ready, my friend; you are ready."

After that session, Asher would not return Ben's calls, DMs, or texts. Ben tries to schedule a few more sessions with him, but there is no response. After a few days of getting ghosted, Ben drives to Asher's house. He knocks on his door and rings the doorbell a few times. Ben could see the lights on in Asher's place, but no one came to the door. After a few minutes of trying, Ben gives up and goes home.

#

Ben wakes to the sound of his phone ringing. He looks at the caller ID; it is Ulysses.

"We did it!" Ulysses screams as soon as Ben answers.

"Did what?" Ben asks, muting the phone so he can yawn.

"We got an IPO date. It's next week. Jason and Demetri invited me to join them to ring the bell at the Nasdaq MarketSite in New York. We leave this Saturday and will ring the bell on Monday morning."

Ben opens his calendar app. It is Tuesday, and he is running out of time.

"Isn't this exciting!"

"Yeah, totally," Ben replies. "Ulysses, I am not feeling that well. Do you mind if I take the rest of the day off?"

"You already had many days off this year," Ulysses reminds him.

"I know, but I need another. I completed the job."

"Ok … Fine, but I need you up and working tomorrow. We still have much to do."

"Ok."

"Oh, before I let you go, I got even more good news."

"What is it?" Ben could feel his heart start to race.

"After additional financial due diligence, NikNak decided to up the initial public offering to thirty dollars a share. Do you know what that means?"

"It means they get another ten billion, and FrontSpark gets an additional hundred million," Ben replies.

"Goddamn right!" Ulysses laughs.

#

Ben sits at his desk with his arms folded in his lap. He had just finished watching "Korean School Girl Lessons - Part 1" for the third time. His eyes try to avoid what is happening on screen and focus on what little information he can gather about the room. Occasionally he would look towards the center of the screen and immediately regret it.

He decided his "superimposing" point would be at 0:13. The video is nine minutes and thirty-four seconds long, giving him very little margin for error. What scares him the most is that he has one shot at this. If he doesn't stop Jinni's uncle, there might not be a second chance. Like the Russian (or Ukrainian) Man, if Ben spooks him, the filming might stop, but the abuse would continue.

Ben psyches himself up and presses play. He then pauses the video. Ben realizes he does not know Jinni's uncle's name. Not that it mattered but if he learned anything from Asher, it was to try and take every advantage possible. Ben theorizes that a strange man showing up in your house and calling you out by your name would most definitely cause you to pause, giving Ben a chance to take advantage. He needs every advantage he can get. He calls Yumi.

"What?" Yumi sounds annoyed.

"Hello, Yumi … How have you been?"

"What do you want?" she asks in a hostile voice.

Ben sighs. He knew this conversation would be difficult. "Yumi, I am sorry I did not make Jinni's funeral, and I was just where she died by luck. I had no idea what Jinni was about to do," Ben lies. "I just could not deal with it. I am sorry I let you down. I tried to save her; you know that I loved her."

Silence cuts between them. Ben fears that Yumi has hung up. He is about to ask her if she is still there, but then she speaks.

"You really let my mom and me down, Ben." He can hear Yumi cry.

"I know; I am sorry. I wish I could go back and change things." Ben closes his eyes tightly. "Yumi, I have a favor to ask you."

"What is it?" she asks apprehensively.

"This is going to sound weird … But can you tell me about your uncle?"

"What?" Yumi sounds confused.

"The one Jinni stayed with when she first moved here," Ben says softly.

"Oh … but he's dead," Yumi replies.

"I know. I just wanted to know if you knew anything about him."

"But … But why?" Yumi's voice starts to get hostile.

Ben softens his voice, "Yumi … I know this seems odd, but I am trying to find something. I wish I could tell you, but please … please, trust me. At the very least, give me his name."

Yumi hesitates for a moment and says, "I never really knew him, I met him only once, and I only know him by his American name, Billy. We used to call him Uncle Billy." Ben could hear the confusion in her voice. "Why would you want to know about my dead uncle?"

"Thank you, that's all I wanted to know. I am sorry I bothered you." Ben starts to remove the phone from his ear to end the call.

"You know he is buried not far from here," Yumi says as Ben is about to hang up.

"Huh … What did you say?" Ben grips the phone tightly.

"I said he is buried not far from here. About an hour away."

"Jinni once told me he died in L.A.," Ben says, confused.

"He did, but he had purchased a burial site long before his death. I remember my parents and I had just lived out here for about a year when my dad dragged me to his grave. I hated it, but we went. I remember my dad cursing at his grave."

"Do you remember where it is?" Ben asks. He didn't know why he asked that question; the words just came out of his mouth.

"I don't remember … Hold on, let me ask my mom." Ben hears her shout in Korean and hears her mother call back. They go back and forth for a while before Yumi comes back on the line.

"Ben … are you still there?"

"Yes."

"I have the address. I will text it to you."

#

Ben stands in the mud, looking at the grave. It is raining, and he has forgotten his umbrella. He shivers and wraps his jacket tightly around his body.

All he can think is how this was like the movies—the good guy (him) visiting the grave of his nemesis (Uncle Billy). Ben has been standing at the grave for about ten minutes now. He did not know why it was necessary to come here. He just felt compelled to do so.

Ben looks down at the grave. It has Korean writing on it with some English text. Uncle Billy's real name was Beom-Seok Yoon. He was thirty-eight when he died.

Ben stares down at the grave for a while. Lighting cinematically flashes around him. After a few more stares, Ben speaks.

"I am coming for you, you son of a bitch." Ben spits on the grave and walks back to his car.

CHAPTER 24 - SADGE

Ben presses play, and the seconds ascend on the bottom of the screen. Thirteen seconds is his entry point.

At 0:01, a dark, grainy black screen appears.

At 0:02, a blurry, out-of-focus image appears.

It is Wednesday evening. He had been on a call with Ulysses all morning. Ulysses had asked him what he should do for the employees once NikNak went public. Ben suggested a bonus. Ulysses just laughed.

At 0:03, the screen shakes and moves as someone adjusts the camera.

At 0:04, the camera goes into focus and goes out of focus as a figure emerges in front of it.

Ben is wearing athletic pants, sneakers, and a tight shirt. Ben knows he looks foolish in his tight shirt, but it will make it harder to grab him.

At 0:05, the screen goes black again as the figure in front blocks the lens.

At 0:06, the figure moves away from the camera, and the image goes blurry as the camera tries to refocus.

Ben had called his mother this morning. She immediately picked up on the tone of his voice and asked what was wrong. He told her nothing was, but he had a favor to ask her. He told her he had transferred most of the money in his bank account to hers. When she asked why he told her that he was changing banks and that he would get a check from her when it was done.

At 0:07, a small blurry figure can be seen in the background. The camera makes a faint buzzing sound as it tries to focus.

At 0:08, a young Jinni emerges into focus. She sits on the floor with her knees held tightly to her chest.

Ben cleaned his apartment last night and wrote a letter. In the letter, he explained that he would never come back and to not look for him. Ben glances at the letter next to his hand.

At 0:09, Jinni is entirely in focus now, and a large, half-naked man walks away from the camera towards her.

At 0:10, Jinni's uncle stops and talks to her in Korean. Jinni doesn't reply

At 0:11, Jinni's uncle speaks again, this time louder. A young Jinni nods.

Ben did some light stretches before sitting down at his desk. He decided to wait until it just got dark before booting up his "special" computer. Asher had taught him that warming up is necessary.

At 0:12, Jinni's uncle positions himself before Jinni and commands some more instructions.

At 0:13, Jinni rises from the ground and starts towards her uncle's waist.

Ben shuts his eyes and presses on the screen.

Ben had "superimposed" himself a lot over the last nine months. When he arrives, there are two things that he notices. One is the change in the air around him. A few months ago, when he "superimposed" himself into a video about the Carnaval in Brazil, he immediately could feel Rio's sticky, humid air. The second thing is the change in smell.

That usually hit Ben the hardest. When he "went" to Octoberfest in Germany, the smell of beer, piss, and sweat almost made him throw up.

Right now, he could feel the heat and dust of the cellar. The smell bothered him the most. This place smelled like mold, sweat, and fear. Ben opens his eyes.

He positions himself to land next to the camera. He blinks a few times to get used to the low light. He looks ahead. Standing about ten feet in front of him are Jinni and her uncle. So far, neither of them has noticed him. Ben quietly turns the camera to face the wall. Her uncle is talking to Jinni in Korean, and she is directly in front of him, on her knees. Her hands are on the waistband of his underwear.

"Billy!" Ben shouts.

Both of them jump, and Jinni falls back on her bottom and immediately covers her breast. Uncle Billy turns to look at Ben. The confusion on his face quickly turns to anger.

"Billy!" Ben shouts again, moving towards the predator. Ben quickly scans the room for anything that could be used as a weapon. Uncle Billy starts shouting at Ben in Korean but promptly switches to English.

"What are you doing here? Get the fuck out of my house!" Uncle Billy shouts. Ben keeps walking towards him. Jinni quickly scrambles back into the corner and covers herself with a dirty blanket that is on the ground.

Ben takes a look at Uncle Billy as he walks closer. Ben is right in his initial assessment; Uncle Billy is not a tiny man. Ben estimates that he stands over six feet tall and weighs around two hundred and thirty pounds. The video is just under nine minutes long, and Ben has to end this quickly.

Ben can see the surprise and confusion on Uncle Billy's face. He can see that Uncle Billy is looking around for his clothes. Ben spots a small wooden chair. As he walks towards Uncle Billy, he grabs it, and while Uncle Billy is distracted, he swings it at his chest. Uncle Billy yells out as the chair crumbles against his body. Uncle Billy quickly grabs his chest and takes a few stumbling steps back. Ben can hear Jinni scream.

Ben looks around for another object to strike Uncle Billy with. As he surveys the room, he makes a mistake; he takes his eyes off his target. Ben flies off his feet as Uncle Billy recovers from the chair bash and rushes Ben like a linebacker trying to sack a quarterback. Ben hits the floor hard, knocking the wind out of him. He can hear Jinni scream again.

Ben lies on the floor, trying to catch his breath; immediately, Jinni's uncle is on top of him. Uncle Billy sits on Ben's chest and starts raining down blows on his head and body. Ben, who still hasn't caught his breath, does his best to block him.

"Who the fuck are you?" Uncle Billy screams in between blows. Ben can smell the soju and cigarettes on his breath. One of his punches connects with Ben's chin, causing him to see stars. Ben shakes his head, trying to regain his senses.

"Tell me, who the fuck are you? How did you get into my house!" Uncle Billy screams in Ben's face.

"Fuck you!" Ben screams back in between dodging blows.

"How do you know my name? Tell me!" Uncle Billy now has him by the shirt and is shaking him. Uncle Billy looks towards Jinni and talks to her in Korean. His head points towards the back wall where a dirty, rusty hammer lays. Jinni gets up tentatively and starts moving towards the hammer when Ben shouts at her.

"Jinni, no!" Ben screams.

Jinni jumps and looks towards both of them. Ben could see the fear and tears streaming down her face. Uncle Billy softens his voice and speaks to Jinni again, urging her towards the hammer. Jinni shakes her head. Ben uses the break to hit Uncle Billy as hard as possible in the solar plexus. Uncle Billy grunts but seems largely unaffected. He turns his attention back to Ben.

"Fuck you, you piece of shit!" Uncle Billy says as he puts his massive hands around Ben's neck. Ben starts to panic. Blood is getting into his eyes, and he wipes them before trying to stop Uncle Billy from choking him. His hands are slippery from the blood.

"Who are you? How did you get in here?" Uncle Billy continues to scream questions. Ben finds it increasingly harder to breathe as Uncle Billy's stronger hands choke him. Ben can see black clouds surrounding his vision as his air is cut off. He turns his eyes towards Jinni. She has crumbled on the floor, weeping.

"Jinni," Ben calls out in a low rasping voice.

She looks up at him.

"Jinni … it's ok," Ben says with his last breath. Jinni looks at him and blinks. Ben turned towards an angry and screaming Uncle Billy. The dark cloud around his eyes is starting to block his vision. Ben can hear Asher's voice.

"Never give up, Ben!" Asher shouts at him. "Finish it or never start it!"

Ben's instincts kick in. He reaches his right hand back and strikes Uncle Billy hard in the chest. This causes Uncle Billy to recoil enough for Ben to pull his knee up in between their bodies.

"It's not about strength, Ben; it's about leverage!" Asher screams at Ben again.

Ben uses his left hand to grab Uncle Billy's right hand. He then used his knee to start pushing into Uncle Billy's chest.

"Don't stop, Ben!" Asher shouts at him. "Finish it!"

Ben brings his left leg over their hands and uses his left leg to strike Uncle Billy in the throat. Uncle Billy lets go of Ben's neck and grabs his own throat. Ben uses this opening to slide his right foot from under Uncle Billy's body and plants it squarely on his chest. Ben kicks Uncle Billy away. Ben springs to his feet but immediately keels over as he tries to put oxygen back in his body. He looks towards Jinni, who has stopped crying and is now watching.

Ben points towards the hammer and looks Jinni in the eyes. Their relationship flashes in front of him. He sees the crooked smile she flashed him the first time they met. He sees the time she sat him down and planted a kiss. He sees them laughing on the bed together. He sees her holding his arm, resting her head on his shoulder.

Jinni nods and scrambles over to the hammer, clumsily throwing it at Ben. Out of the corner of Ben's eyes, he can see Uncle Billy starting to rise to his feet. Ben catches the hammer just as Uncle Billy begins to pounce at him. Ben brings the hammer down on his face.

Uncle Billy screams and grabs his eye. Ben does not have time to adjust the hammer as he catches it, so the claw part goes directly into Uncle Billy's eye. Uncle Billy lies on the floor screaming. He begins cursing at Ben, telling him to leave. Ben looks at Jinni and points at the door. Jinni gets up and runs out. Ben turns back towards Uncle Billy.

"Why ... Why?" Uncle Billy asks as the blood spews from his face.

"You know why, you sick fuck!" Ben says as he reaches down and pulls the hammer out of Uncle Billy's eye. Uncle Billy screams again. Ben brings the hammer down on Uncle Billy's head. Ben brings it down again. And again. And again.

Ben sits with his back to the wall breathing hard. By his internal clock estimate, it has been almost nine minutes since he "superimposed" himself. Soon he will be back. He looks towards the door. Jinni stares at him with wide, dark eyes behind a barely opened door.

"You're going to be ok, Jinni..." Ben calls out to her. She opens the door and sits by it. "You're going to be ok." Ben can hear the sirens outside the house. He assumes that all the ruckus has caused the neighbors to call the cops. Jinni looks out towards the basement window as black boots run by. They both sit there for a moment, not speaking. Someone upstairs is banging at the door. Jinni looks up towards the stairs. When she looks back, Ben is gone.

When Ben returns to his apartment, he collapses on the floor, exhausted. An immense pain hits Ben in the heart. He clutches his chest and thinks he is having a heart attack. Ben bends over, grabbing his chest as he falls to his knees. He contemplates calling 911, but after a few moments, it subsides. Ben picks himself off the floor and heads to his bathroom. He washes his face and looks at his neck in the mirror. His neck has dark red marks all over it. Ben applies some cream to it. He gingerly walks over to his bed. The king-sized bed that Jinni had suggested they purchase is gone. A smaller twin replaces it. Ben shuts off the light and falls into a deep sleep.

When Ben wakes up the next day, he realizes that his apartment is different. When he looks around his apartment, he sees a lot has changed. The furniture and paintings that he and Jinni bought were gone. His couch is missing, replaced with his old couch that Jinni made him get rid of when she first moved in.

"Oh," Ben says out loud.

He pulls out his phone and looks through his photos. The pictures of him and Jinni are gone. He goes to his Instagram and tries to find the images he had posted there; they are gone. Ben begins to panic.

He goes through his contacts and tries to find Yumi's number, but it is not there. He jumps back onto Instagram and tries to direct message Yumi, but they are not connected, and her account is private. Ben does not understand what is going on. In his mind, two conflicting lives play in his head, one with Jinni and one without. He starts feeling claustrophobic and needs some fresh air. He goes down to the coffee shop and runs into Jeremy.

"Jeremy!" Ben shouts at him; surely he would know what happened to Jinni.

"Ben-German, how's it hanging?" Jeremy says as he pays for his coffee.

"Jinni," Ben frantically asks. "Jeremy, do you know what happened to Jinni?"

Jeremy had a confused look on his face. "Jinni? Hmm ... who's that?"

Ben grabs him by his jacket.

"Jinni, do you know what happened to her? She committed suicide. You're the one who told me. Don't you remember?" Ben asks frantically.

"First of all, get your hands off my fucking jacket, and second, I don't know any Jinni. What the fuck are you on?" Jeremy pushes Ben's hands away.

Ben runs out of the shop and pulls out his phone to call Kairo. "Kairo, it's Ben. Do you remember the party you took me to?"

"A hello would be nice," Kairo says, annoyed.

"Do you remember the party we went to at Bobby's place?"

"Barely. Why, what about it?"

"Do you remember I was talking with that one girl Jinni?" Ben asks hopefully.

Kairo laughs. "No, but I remember you striking out badly and leaving the party alone. In fact, I remember you acting like a bitch and bailing early. You told me something was missing or some bullshit like that. Ben, what the fuck is this about?"

Ben hangs up the phone.

Jinni is gone.

#

The next day after work, Ben needs some fresh air, so he starts walking. He walks around his neighborhood and into the downtown area. It is Friday night, so the bars are as full as the lockdown allows, and people are inside trying to enjoy themselves. Most places have long lines for safety rules. They could only allow so many people inside.

Ben recalls the happenings of the last couple of months as he walks. It all feels like a dream to him. He would not have believed it if he did not have the red marks on his neck. As he continues walking, he contemplates his actions. *Did I do any good?* he asks himself. *Why do I feel so empty?* Regardless he had to face the facts; even if Jinni was alive, she had never been a part of his life. He had never met her, and their time together did not happen. Ben is not satisfied with that trade-off, but there is not much he can do about it.

The night turns cold and nippy. Ben sees a restaurant that he and Jinni used to frequent, and he goes in to grab a bite. The hostess tells him the only openings they have are at the bar. Ben agrees, removes his mask, and sits down. The bartender asks if he wants a drink, but Ben says no, and asks for water and a menu. He orders a burger and fries and sips his water as he looks around the place.

In the corner of the restaurant are a few well-dressed people who look like they just got off work. They are laughing, drinking, and celebrating. Ben watches the crowd. His food comes, and he begins eating. Someone laughs. Ben's head pops up. He stops chewing and starts listening to the group.

"Everyone," an older gentleman in a slick suit shouts at the crowd. He starts banging his champagne glass with a fork. "Everyone, settle down now ... Yes, even you, Berkstein." The crowd laughs. "Today, I want to officially welcome Jinni Yoon to the law offices of Berglman and Perk.

She has completed her first week here, so congrats on your first week at the firm!"

The small crowd cheers.

Ben freezes in place and slowly turns around on his stool to face the crowd.

"Jinni, any last words?" the well-dressed older gentleman asks.

The crowd laughs again. A girl stands up, and Ben watches as Jinni starts speaking.

"Thank you, Ronald," she says enthusiastically. "Thank you all for coming, and it's been a wonderful yet hard week. I am so happy to be part of this firm—"

Ben sits at the bar with his mouth open. It is his Jinni, but she also isn't. She looks very different than he remembers. Her hair is shorter, with bangs. Gone were the colored streaks she so adored. She is also about thirty pounds heavier than when they were together. Jinni always watched her weight, sometimes going days without eating. She still looks beautiful to Ben. He sits there watching her, impressed with her vocal cadence. The way the crowd admired her made Ben's heart hurt. He realizes that she is no longer his Jinni. She grew up in a different life with fewer burdens, less childhood trauma, and more control.

Ben can not take it anymore. He gets up and starts walking out of the restaurant.

"Hey! You didn't pay for that!" the bartender shouts at him as he gets to the door. Ben meekly walks back in, apologizes, and offers up his credit card. As Ben waits for the bill to be settled, he glances back at the crowd, at Jinni. This time she looks up and meets his eyes. Her face scrunches up in faint recognition. She bites her lower lip as if trying to recall something. Ben quickly returns his gaze to the bar. Ben signs, puts on his mask, and promptly exits the restaurant when the bartender brings his bill.

"Excuse me, do I know you?" Jinni asks. She had followed him out to the sidewalk. They stand outside in the cold air, looking at each other. Jinni stares at Ben intensely.

"I don't think so," Ben says quietly.

"You look so familiar," she says as she moves closer to him. "I swear I know you from somewhere." She moves her hand to his face touching his cheek. "I know I have seen those eyes before, and I just don't know where." Jinni gently pulls down his mask. She removes her hand from his face. Jinni stares at him intently. "Won't you come inside and join us for a drink?" she asks.

"I don't think that would be a good idea," Ben replies. Tears began to flow from his eyes.

"Why are you crying?" she asks.

"It's nothing," Ben says, blinking away the tears. "I am really happy right now."

Ben smiles at her and turns into the night.

#

The following day, Ulysses calls him. Ulysses is driving to the airport and asks if Ben is as happy as he is.

"Sure," Ben says.

After his call with Ulysses, Ben goes to his desk. He notices that his "special" computer is no longer sitting under his desk. *It makes sense, I guess,* Ben thinks. He did not need it now. He thinks about Ulysses, Demetri, and Pavlov. How by

322

the end of the day Monday, they would all be extremely wealthy.

That night Ben browses NikNak. He sees the same Naks as before. Kitty Josephine, KM-Asher, and many more. The girl with the red balloon pops up on his feed. Ben sits up in his chair. Ben presses the "Subscribe" button after the Nak plays. Earlier that day, he had filled his crypto wallet with $1200 of ETH. When the assessment appears, Ben answers each of the questions quickly. His time looking for Jinni's video taught him much about this world. After the final question, he gets a page congratulating him on passing. He transfers the $1200 in ETH to the wallet displayed on the screen. Once the transaction goes through, he is in.

Ben picks up his phone and calls the SFPD. He asks for Detective Susan Gonzales and leaves her a message. When she calls back an hour later, Ben knows she will not know who he is. But that did not matter. He tells her he needs to meet her as soon as possible. They set up a meeting for the next day at her office.

Ben sits quietly in her office, waiting for Detective Gonzales to finish her call. When she is done, she turns to Ben and says, "So, Mr. White, what do you have for me?"

Ben begins telling her a story. The story is full of lies and embellishments. He tells her he works for FrontSpark, and they have NikNak as a client. He tells her that he has discovered something sinister and illegal on their app. When she asks what it is, Ben pulls out his phone and shows her. Her eyes widen.

#

"Good morning, everybody," the news anchor chirps. "It is 8 a.m. Monday and this is your news. Today there was a huge scandal on Wall St. NikNak, the new internet darling, has delayed its IPO indefinitely. There have been rumors that the FBI got a tip about the site's housing illegal underage content. Both Apple and Google have removed the app from their marketplaces. We reached out to NikNak for comments, but they have not gotten back to us. We will keep you informed as more details come out. Melina—"

Ben sits alone in the coffee shop and watches the news on his phone.

#

Ben sits with Raj in his living room. He has just finished telling Raj everything. They both sit still.

"Did that really happen?" Raj asks, perplexed. Ben nods, not looking at Raj. "And … you killed him?"

"He was already dead; the way I see it, I just accelerated the timeline." Ben stares up at Raj; he is looking at Ben in horror. "Don't give me that look, Raj."

"You just told me some strange dark shit—how do you want me to look?" Raj asks.

Ben sighs and says, "Maybe I have been drinking too much lately. It's starting to fuck with my brain."

"Can you still do it?" Raj asks. "Quote-unquote superimpose yourself?"

"I haven't tried since then; not sure if I ever will again."

Raj stares at his friend. He stands up. "C'mon, let's get out of this apartment and go and get something to eat. And tomorrow," he grabs Ben by the shoulder. "we are going to AA, ok?"

Ben nods.

As they leave Ben's apartment, Ben stands by the door and looks back at his desk. He has a new "special" computer sitting beneath it. It took him a few weeks of Googling to set it up properly. He still didn't know what he was doing and did not have Pavlov's program to help him this time, but he was confident he would figure it out. He no longer has a job to worry about. He looks down at his new "special" computer and leaves his apartment.

AFTERWORD

As I finish writing this book, I find myself watching a lot of repair videos. Mostly vintage watches and iPhone repairs. We don't repair anything anymore. When something breaks, we throw it away and buy another. What do we do when we break?

How do we handle years of abuse? How can we cope? Do we turn to drugs and alcohol to mask the pain? How do we repair ourselves?

In this book, I take a look at two people who are broken: Ben and Jinni. Jinni takes her life because she cannot repair herself. Ben turns to alcohol to mask the pain that he has. One thing the pandemic did for me was force me to spend time with myself and understand what I was about. You cannot hide from yourself when you're locked into an apartment for over two years. You cannot be distracted by going to work or going to happy hour after (luckily, I had my future wife with me in lockdown.)

When I was much younger, I remember watching "America's Most Wanted" with my mom. There was a story about a manhunt and how they had finally caught the perpetrator in Hong Kong. On the show, they said that his daughter, whom he had been videotaping their abuse and putting it out on the internet, and had been downloaded over two million times. I sat there wondering what her life had been like being the most infamous for a horrible crime (She is doing just fine, by the way. Google "Kylie Freeman" if you want to know more).

As I dated more and more in life, a few of my girlfriends told me horrible stories of the abuse they had endured and how it affected them daily. How it ruined their relationships. It always made me angry that I could never do anything about it.

At its heart, *Superimposed* is a story about repair. Ben is trying to fix himself, his past, and his ex-girlfriend. He is blessed with an amazing superpower, and as the saying goes: "With great power comes great responsibility."

ACKNOWLEDGMENTS

Writing this book was the hardest thing I have ever done. I have always loved reading. I read my first book when I was seven years old. My favorite authors are Stephen King, Neil Gaiman, Richard Price, George Pelecanos, and Neal Stephenson. I always wished I could one day write a book as well as they could.

With *Superimposed*, I hope I accomplished that dream. I want to thank my wife, first and foremost, for encouraging me to write this book. My editor Jessica Powers for giving me positive feedback and helping me shape this book. To Victor Swastik, an author, for giving me valuable advice and encouraging me to write. My parents for buying me all the books I wanted to read. And finally, my wife for encouraging me to write this story.

This book is for you all...

A READER'S GUIDE

1. Why does Ben have this power? Why him?

2. What do you think are the rules for Ben's time travel? Earlier, he watched a content creator talk about Time Travel on NikNak and said he felt like he missed something. What do you think that is? (Hint: Read *The Dark Tower* by Stephen King.)

3. Do you think this ability is permanent? If so, does Ben have a moral responsibility to use or not use it? Could he not right the wrongs of many, but should he?

4. Do you think Ben tried to knowingly kill himself when he woke up on the kitchen floor after taking ten Oxy pills? Or was he too drunk and distracted to keep track?

5. Why do you think Ben didn't try and stop Jinni from leaving his apartment when she surprises him at his doorstep?

6. What do you think Jinni meant when she said: "I always thought you would be the one to save me"?

7. What do you think of Ben's and Ulysses' relationship? Does Ulysses care about Ben at all?

8. What do you think of the business model of a company like NikNak?

9. What do you think will happen to NikNak? Will they get shut down, or will they just add more moderation and still go public?

10. If you had Ben's power, what would you do?

ABOUT THE AUTHOR

Omar Albadri lives in San Francisco, CA, with his wife. He is a tech enthusiast and can be found at most bars in San Francisco. This is his first novel.

If you would like to contact him, you can go to his website at:

www.omaralbadri.com

or

Twitter: @oalbad